Jove titles by Janet Chapman

HIGHLANDER FOR THE HOLIDAYS
SPELLBOUND FALLS
CHARMED BY HIS LOVE
COURTING CAROLINA
THE HEART OF A HERO
FOR THE LOVE OF MAGIC

"When combining magic, passion, and w
no one does it better than Chapman

Praise for the novels of Janet Chapman

"Janet Chapman is a keeper."
—Linda Howard, *New York Times* bestselling author

"Chapman continues to maintain a great blend of magic, romance, and realism in a small-town setting; tales in the style of Barbara Bretton's popular books." —*Booklist*

"Heartwarming . . . Readers will enjoy the enchanting town and characters." —*Publishers Weekly*

"Chapman is unmatched and unforgettable."
—**RT Book Reviews*

"A captivating, heartwarming paranormal romance that will capture your attention from the very beginning . . . The combination of wit, clever dialogue, charismatic characters, magic, and love makes this story absolutely enchanting."
—*Romance Junkies*

"One can't beat a love story that combines magic and a man willing to move mountains for the woman he loves! Great elements of humor, magic, and romance."
—*Night Owl Reviews*

"A spectacular and brilliant novel for those who love the juxtaposition of the paranormal and the real world . . . A PERFECT 10 is a fitting rating for . . . a novel which is both tender and joyful, but also has beasts looking for peace and a new way of life after centuries of struggle."
—*Romance Reviews Today*

For the Love of Magic

Janet Chapman

JOVE BOOKS, NEW YORK

THE BERKLEY PUBLISHING GROUP
Published by the Penguin Group
Penguin Group (USA)
375 Hudson Street, New York, New York 10014, USA

USA | Canada | UK | Ireland | Australia | New Zealand | India | South Africa | China

Penguin Books Ltd., Registered Offices: 80 Strand, London WC2R 0RL, England
For more information about the Penguin Group, visit penguin.com.

FOR THE LOVE OF MAGIC

A Jove Book / published by arrangement with the author

For information, address: The Berkley Publishing Group,
a division of Penguin Group (USA).
375 Hudson Street, New York, New York 10014.

ISBN: 978-0-515-15321-7

PUBLISHING HISTORY
Jove mass-market edition / September 2013

PRINTED IN THE UNITED STATES OF AMERICA

10 9 8 7 6 5 4 3 2 1

Cover art by Jim Griffin.
Cover design by George Long.

For the Love of Magic

Chapter One

Rana slid her gaze away from the uncertain brown eyes of the woman in the mirror and focused instead on the reflection of the cramped bedroom behind her as she wondered—not for the first time in recent weeks—if she would even be alive this time next year. Or worse, assuming she did survive the two distinctly separate battles she was facing, if she would still be married to the love of her life.

The first battle, of which *she* had fired the first salvo, was actually proceeding better than she'd anticipated. Though considerably more rustic than she was used to, the small house she'd moved into four days ago was so far proving to be a wise purchase. It sat on a generous lot directly on the shore of the Bottomless Sea, was within walking distance of Spellbound Falls' town center, and the eccentricity of its previous owner spoke to her heart.

It also was close enough to Nova Mare, her son and daughter-in-law's five-star resort on the summit of Whisper Mountain, to allow her to continue seeing her grandchildren on a regular basis. In fact, Henry—who was ten going on a hundred and ten years old—could paddle over in his kayak, since her new home sat only a mile down the shoreline from Inglenook, a family-oriented resort that Maximilian and Olivia also owned.

Rana slid her gaze back to the woman in the mirror as she took a deep breath to square her shoulders and beamed herself an over-bright smile. For better or worse, she'd done the unthinkable and there was no turning back. But having been married to Titus for forty years—give or take several thousand—she not only had a pretty good idea of what to expect from him, she'd also learned a thing or two about fighting dirty.

Although in truth she wasn't actually trying to win their little domestic war. Rather, she was using it to prepare for her second battle, which she desperately needed to survive if she wanted her big powerful husband to also be alive this time next year.

Sweet Athena, she loved the maddening man.

Dropping her gaze with a frown, Rana tugged on the underwires of her blue lace bra to settle her breasts deeper into the *C* cups, only to sigh when the now obviously size *D*s continued spilling over the top. Somewhat mollified that some of the eight pounds she'd gained had settled in her bosom, she turned and looked over her shoulder at the mirror to discover the rest of her weight gain making itself at home on her backside.

"Well, it would appear I left just in time," she murmured

as she walked to the bed and picked up her slacks, "before *someone* said something he would certainly regret."

Hearing a now-familiar diesel engine rattle to a stop at her garage that sat across the road from her driveway, Rana quickly pulled on her pants and fastened the snug waistband. She rushed to the window at the sound of two truck doors closing and peered through the lace curtain to see Gene Latimer and his son entering the large garage—the teenager's shoulders hunched as he glanced toward the house before disappearing inside.

Rana grabbed her heavy chambray shirt off the bed as she rushed past, slipping it on and buttoning it up as she hurried down the stairs and through the great room to the kitchen. "Aw, Zack, I'll have you smiling in no time," she said as she wiggled her feet into her sneakers. "And your father, too, when he leaves here with another big fat check," she added, stepping onto the porch and sprinting out her short driveway.

Not bothering to look for traffic as she crossed the narrow dirt road that dissected her property in half, Rana slowed long enough to put her serene smile in place before walking into the garage. "Good morning, Gene. Zack," she said warmly.

A flash went off as both men turned to her, the elder Latimer lowering his hand in surprise and Zack sighing in relief. "Mrs. Oceanus," Gene said, his close-cropped beard bristling with his grin. "I'm sorry if we disturbed you, but I wanted to take some pictures of the equipment so I can post it on Craigslist this morning. With any luck, I'll have everything out of your way by next weekend."

"Actually, I was watching for you." She gestured at the machines coated in rust-colored soot. "I've decided to purchase the equipment."

Gene went back to being surprised. "What in tarnation for?" He flushed slightly. "I'm sorry, Mrs. . . . Rana," he quickly amended when she started to correct him. "But what do you want with a bunch of old metal-working machinery?"

"I'm going to use it. My father was a blacksmith, and I have many fond memories of helping out in his forge, so I thought to revisit my childhood by re-creating it here."

"But this place isn't set up for ironwork. It's a welding shop. Pops worked mostly on logging trucks and skidders, cutting and welding their steel frames."

Rana arched a brow. "But did you not tell me that he made all the door hinges and handles in the house, as well as that beautiful balcony rail and stairway?"

"Do you even know how to run a MIG welder?" Gene asked, pointing at a trunk-sized box with a long set of hoses snaking out of it. "Or a cutting torch?"

"Not yet. But Zack is confident he can have me welding like a professional by the end of the summer."

"I'm sorry," Gene said, shaking his head, "but the boy had no business offering to teach you to weld, because he'll be too busy working full time once school lets out. Because," he added with a scowl at Zack, "he needs to earn enough spending money to last him through his first two semesters of college."

Rana looked down to hide her smile. "Then I guess it's fortuitous that I've offered Zack full-time employment mowing my lawn and doing some painting and sprucing up around here." She lifted her gaze and imbued her smile with as much serenity as she could muster, considering Gene was now scowling at *her.* "And that I also agreed to let him use the equipment on his off-hours to work on trucks like he did with his grandfather, as Zack assures me he can easily triple the four hundred dollars a week I'll be paying him. That should be enough spending money to see him through his freshman year, shouldn't it?"

The elder Latimer looked down at the camera in his hand, his brows pinched together in a frown, and Rana finally got Zack to smile by shooting him a wink.

"Please don't take offense, Gene," she said softly, "but your father's creative genius defeats me. There are still cupboards I can't open, and I've yet to gain entrance to the shed down at the beach. Without Zack's help, there's a very real chance I'll spend all this spring and summer breaking into various parts of my new home instead of enjoying it. And I much prefer to be out on Bottomless in the beautiful daysailer you kindly let go with the house, rather than mowing lawns and painting trim."

"Shawn Pike asked if I couldn't straighten out the frame of a '69 Roadrunner he's rebuilding," Zack interjected. "And Chester Beal still can't find anyone to fix the mess he made of the logging chains he tried welding himself. Those two jobs alone should pay at least a thousand dollars."

Gene gave his son a hard look, then slowly took in the cluttered shop before looking back at Rana. "No offense taken," he said with a sheepish grin, "since I'm still trying to open the puzzle box Pops gave me last Christmas." He folded his arms over his chest, his gaze turning direct. "I'd planned to ask six thousand for the equipment and another thousand for the stockpile of metal out back, but if you're serious about getting into metalwork and hiring Zack, it's all yours for an even five."

Suspecting a good part of this morning's check was going toward Zack's college tuition, Rana didn't even try to haggle him down. "Deal," she said, extending her hand—but not shaking Gene's when he took it. "Assuming the pickup is considered equipment."

She once again caught the man by surprise. "You actually want that old rust-bucket?" He gently pumped her hand up and down. "Heck, I thought I was going to have to pay someone to haul it off for scrap." He stopped pumping. "Hey, you don't intend to drive it, do you?" He glanced out the bay-door windows at her empty driveway across the road. "Gosh, Mrs. Oceanus, I don't even know if that truck will pass inspection."

"Zack assures me that everything works and the frame is solid."

Gene narrowed his eyes at his son. "Seems to me the boy's been giving you a lot of assurances he didn't discuss with me first."

"Then let *me* assure you, Mr. Latimer," Rana said, drawing his attention again, "that everything we've discussed this morning has been my idea. Knowing how much time he spent here with his grandfather, I approached Zack in town yesterday with an offer of employment. I also asked if he could teach me to use this equipment. Because, truthfully?" She gestured in the direction of Bottomless. "I want to learn from the artist who created that beautiful metal whale down on my beachfront."

"That'll be kind of hard," Gene said quietly, "since he died two months ago."

Rana glanced toward Zack to see him looking down at his feet as he scuffed a grease spot on the floor. "I'll settle for the artist's apprentice, then," she said, heading for the door. "Let me go get you a check."

Zack followed her outside. "How did you know?" he whispered as he fell into step beside her.

Rana stopped in the road. "Last time I checked, an *A* didn't look anything like a *Z*."

It was Zack's turn to be surprised. "You actually found the signature?"

She started walking again. "Once you get to know me better, you'll realize that I don't give up very easily when I consider something is important."

"Well, thanks for not ratting me out to Dad," he said as he rushed to catch up again. "He'd have a cow if he knew I'm the one who made that whale."

Rana turned to him when she reached the porch. "I believe you'll also discover that I'm very good at keeping secrets, Zack, which makes me a very good confidant." She opened the door and waved him in ahead of her, then touched his arm when he hesitated. "I know you said it wouldn't be a problem, but are you certain working here won't bother you? It can't be easy to see me living in your grandfather's house and using his tools."

The boy threw back his shoulders on a deep breath. "Pops would be okay with it," he said as he stepped inside, "since you claim all his weird metalwork is one of the reasons you bought the house. And I like the idea of continuing to look after the place for him. I mean you." Two flags of red appeared on his cheeks. "I know you asked me to, but my mom would skin me alive if she ever caught me using your first name. So I thought about it last night and . . . um, would you mind if I call you *boss*?"

Rana walked into the kitchen and started rummaging through her purse on the counter. "That will be fine, Zack," she said, pulling out her checkbook. "When I suggested you use my first name yesterday, it was because I couldn't see us working together with you calling me Mrs. Oceanus every five minutes." She pointed at the peninsula separating the kitchen from the great room. "So as your boss, my first assignment for you is to get me in that cupboard."

"This cupboard?" Zack drawled, walking over and rattling the intricate steel clasp. He straightened with a grin. "Sorry, boss, but that's one of only a few locks I've never been able to figure out. This is where Pops kept his booze, so he got even more diabolical with the design to keep me honest." He chuckled, nudging the door with his knee. "The kicker is that every so often he couldn't remember his own secret and would have to drive into town and buy another bottle."

"I'm not going to be able to use that cupboard?" Rana clutched the checkbook to her chest as she glanced around the small kitchen. "But there are so few as it— Wait, what are the other clasps you can't open?"

"The small shed down by the beach. Pops didn't want me taking the kayak or daysailer out alone after the earthquake turned Bottomless into a sea with tides and whales and *sharks* four years ago, so he locked up the sails and paddles." He frowned, then gestured behind her at the bathroom just off the kitchen. "And I just remembered that the back panel of the towel closet is really a door that leads to a small chamber under the stairs. I have no idea if there's anything in there, because I haven't seen inside it since we replaced the camp's underpinning with steel beams several years ago."

Still clutching the checkbook to her bosom, Rana frowned down at the cupboard's intricate clasp, undecided if she was confounded or even more intrigued with her new home. Averill Latimer had apparently spent the last ten years of his life *creatively* remodeling the eighty-year-old camp into a cozy and definitely one-of-a-kind house, which she'd purchased last week when she had finally worked up the nerve to run away from home.

Not that she'd gone very far.

"If you want," Zack said, nudging the cupboard again, "I can come by after church tomorrow and cut off the clasp and replace it with an ordinary handle."

"Absolutely not," Rana rushed out in response to the sadness in his voice. "Where's the fun in that? And besides, I love a good challenge almost as much as I love keeping secrets. Don't worry, I'll—"

Footsteps sounded on the porch. "Zack, Chester Beal just drove in," Gene said as he stepped through the open door and shot his son a grin. "And by the looks of that mess in his truck bed, those tire chains are a five-hundred-dollar job." He sobered. "If he gives you any grief about trying to get a man's wage out of him, you politely remind Beal that *he* came looking for *you*." Gene went back to grinning. "And then you ask whose welds he wants holding those chains together when he's dragging a six-ton load of trees through the woods: a certified welder's or his bubblegum job."

As Zack headed out the door, his father stopped him with a hand on his shoulder. "Which is something you also need to keep in mind, son," he said gently. "Men are staking their lives on your work."

"Wasn't a day went by that Pops didn't tell me the same thing," Zack said, staring level into eyes the mirror image of his as he gave his father a nod. "And not only do my welds hold, they're pretty, too," he added with a wave over his shoulder as he strode onto the porch.

Gene closed the door against the crisp March air and stared out the window.

"You must be very proud of Zachary," Rana said into the silence, "as I can't remember ever dealing with such a well-grounded and personable young man. I often have to remind myself that he's barely eighteen."

"Thank you, but I'm reserving my pride for the day Zack comes to me holding a college degree for any profession that doesn't require scrubbing half a pound of dirt off his hands every night." He shoved his own hands in his pockets and turned to her. "I appreciate your hiring the boy for a fair wage, and you have my personal guarantee that he'll keep this place in tip-top shape. But," he continued, his tone growing as direct as his gaze, "I'm going to have to insist he pay you for the use of your equipment."

"That really isn't necessary, Gene."

"Yes, it is. I don't want Zack getting the notion he's entitled to anything he doesn't earn." His hazel eyes lit up with his grin. "And I certainly don't want him getting in the habit of taking advantage of soft-hearted women holding checkbooks."

Rana arched a brow. "Have you considered that maybe I'm the one taking advantage of Zack?"

Gene gave a soft snort and shook his head. "The boy

will pay you twenty-five percent of whatever he earns in *your* shop using *your* equipment."

"Fifteen percent," she countered, even as she realized negotiating against herself only confirmed her soft heart. "And I'll make him pay for any material he uses from the stockpile."

"Twenty-five percent," he said with another shake of his head. "And you promise that you won't accidentally start forgetting to collect your share as summer wears on."

Rana turned to the counter and opened her checkbook. "I would have thought I learned my lesson negotiating with you last week, when you included a sailboat in the price of the house but failed to mention the sails were locked in a shed I can't access."

Gene walked over to stand beside her. "You won't get lax about collecting?"

She looked up from signing the check and nodded. "I respect your desire to raise a self-reliant young man, and I—"

Rana froze at the sound of a smooth but obviously powerful engine pulling in her driveway, and went to the sink to look out the window at the same time Gene headed to the door. Stifling a muttered curse, she ripped out the check and rushed over to hand it to him. "Thank you for the fair price on the equipment," she said, opening the door to usher Gene outside—only to bump into him when he didn't move.

"That's your husband, isn't it?" he said, frowning at the tall, leather-clad man getting off the shiny red motorcycle and pulling off a matching helmet to expose a head of wavy white hair. Gene looked at her. "Titus, isn't it?"

She nodded, then once again bumped into him when,

instead of moving, Gene Latimer folded his arms over his barrel chest and subtly widened his stance. "I've got no place I need to be," he said quietly, "if you'd like me to hang around for a while."

Rana stilled in surprise, then gave a small laugh. "Thank you, but I assure you that isn't necessary," she said, finally just walking around him. Her amusement was short-lived, however, when she found herself having to brace a hand on her husband's chest to stop his advance up her porch steps.

Not that Titus was paying any attention to her, since he was busy glaring at Gene, who still hadn't moved. "Behave," she whispered tightly just as another valiant rescuer came running in her driveway, the previously clean knight now covered in rust and carrying a hammer.

Sweet Athena, would she ever be free of overprotective males? She understood Titus's posturing, since few husbands would be pleased to find a strange man standing in their wives' kitchen door posturing back at them, but the Latimers shouldn't be putting themselves in harm's way for a woman they barely knew.

"Gentlemen," she said brightly when Zack halted beside the motorcycle, "I'd like you to meet my husband, Titus. Honey, this is Gene Latimer," she said as Gene moved up beside her. "And his son, Zack," she added, nodding behind Titus, who gave only a cursory glance over his shoulder before returning his piercing gaze to the elder Latimer. "I purchased this beautiful home from Gene, and we were just going over some final details of the sale."

Titus moved away from her hand still pressed to his chest by simply backing down the bottom two steps. "I will wait at the shoreline then, while you conclude your business," he said, giving Gene a nod and Rana a slight bow before striding away with his helmet tucked under his arm.

Rana echoed Gene's barely perceptible sigh as her husband disappeared around the side of the house, even as she motioned for Zack to come closer. "Thank you both for your obvious concern." She turned to Gene. "But before you worry that Zack might rush into the middle of a domestic dispute as he did just now, I can assure you that despite his size and somewhat formidable demeanor, Titus would never hurt me." She turned to Zack as she lifted her arms and let them fall back to her sides. "And please don't assume my lack of male physical strength means I'm helpless, or we'll be in for a long summer if you drop what you're doing and come running every time someone pulls in the driveway."

The boy looked down at the hammer in his hand, but not quickly enough to hide his scowl, then gave a silent nod and turned away.

"Are you certain you're not proud of him *right now*?" Rana asked softly, watching Zack walk out the driveway.

"Yeah," Gene said on another sigh. "I guess I am."

"You have my word that your son will be safe in my employ. Titus and I are—"

"What the heck?" Gene yelped when his truck parked across the road suddenly roared to life before idling back to a rattling rumble. "I don't have a remote starter," he said as he rushed down the steps, his words trailing behind him as he broke into a run. "It must be an electrical short or something."

"More likely some*one*," Rana muttered, aiming a glare at the motorcycle she knew for a fact had been purchased the day she'd moved into her new home. The sleek red machine appeared to be nothing more than two wheels attached to a large chrome engine, and she couldn't help but wonder what Titus thought he was doing racing around on the twenty-first-century equivalent of a powerful stallion. He no longer was a young warrior who needed to intimidate foes or impress women; the man was older than the mountains surrounding Bottomless!

Chapter Two

Rana went in the house, softly closing the door behind her. "Yes, well, he better not think he can roar in here unannounced whenever the mood strikes him," she said, walking through the living room crammed full of furniture as eccentric as its previous owner. Stopping at the door, which led onto an even larger porch facing the water, she watched the love of her life casually stroll from her shed to the beach, where he then stood with his hands clasped behind his back as he stared out at the inland sea their son had created four years ago in an epic attempt to impress the love of *his* life.

Rana stepped onto the porch, wondering how many times her daughter-in-law had wanted to run away from home over the last four years. She was sure the notion had crossed Olivia's mind a time or two, she decided with a smile as she headed down the expansive lawn studded with patches of melting snow.

Titus turned to her, his hands still clasped behind his back and one regal white eyebrow lifting with his gaze as he looked past her at the house. "You're living in a hovel," he said as she approached. "And a crooked one, at that."

"Really?" She halted and turned around. "And here I thought I'd purchased a quaint seaside cottage." She canted her head to study her new home as he moved up beside her. "And I believe its being crooked is a deliberate illusion, as I've recently discovered that Averill Latimer, the deceased owner of my beautiful cottage, had a diabolical streak. I wouldn't be surprised if he was attempting to keep the taxes low, which is probably why he also never got around to painting the trim."

"Is that also why he installed a diabolical lock on the boathouse?" Titus walked back to the small shed tucked into the trees at the northern edge of the lawn and jiggled the clasp. "To keep out the tax collector?"

"No, that was to keep his grandson from taking out the daysailer," she explained, gesturing at the sailboat sitting on its side just above the low tide mark, its mast more tilted than her house, "after *someone* filled Bottomless with whales and sharks."

"Those magnificent beasts pose no threat, but are in fact protective."

"Tell that to the good people of Spellbound Falls and Turtleback Station when they spot a pod of orcas swimming offshore of the town beaches. What are you doing here, Titus?"

He bent to study the intricate lock on the shed door.

"A man doesn't have the right to see where his wife *prefers* to live?"

"What I prefer is that you not drop in unannounced, as it more or less defeats the purpose of my leaving in the first place."

He turned to her. "And what again is the purpose of your leaving—other than the misguided notion that you *need a breath of fresh air*?"

She shot him a serene—albeit tight—smile. "We're not having this conversation again, husband. If you weren't listening the first five times, why would I think you're interested in what I have to say this time?"

He started toward her, his entire countenance darkening. "Because this time we're having the conversation in front of a hovel you now *live* in. Do you hope to make me prove—" He halted in midstep. "By the gods, woman, you didn't have to go to such lengths. You merely had to *say* you were feeling unappreciated."

Rana dropped her head and stared down at her size *D* bosom. "I suggest you go home now, Titus."

When he didn't respond, she looked up to see him brushing at his jacket. "My home is wherever you are," he said thickly.

"Not right now it isn't."

He snapped his head up. "Need I remind you that our vows were for *forever*?"

"Forever being relative," she growled right back at him, only to immediately regret her words when he paled. She took a calming breath. "I'm still your wife, Titus, now and forever." She went to the old wooden lawn chair and picked up his helmet, then walked over and handed it to him. "We're simply not living together at the moment."

"I can't completely protect you off the mountain."

"I remember how to protect myself. Or have you forgotten the day we met?" she quickly added, deciding to redirect yet another conversation that was going nowhere.

His glare only intensified. "I practically had to go down that beast's throat to get you away from it while you were punching its nose and screaming bloody murder."

"I was screaming at its owner for training the beast to sneak up on tournament goers and steal their purses." She narrowed her eyes at the sudden amusement in his. "That dog had snatched my friend's coin bag just the day before, which is why I had lashed mine to my waist."

"Which is why that spawn of Cerberus was dragging you off."

"Every drachma I'd pinched and saved for an entire year was in that bag, and I wasn't about to let some thieving mutt abscond with it." She rested a hand on his broad chest, the memory of that long ago day making her smile. "But then this tall, handsome young warrior broke through the crowd of onlookers and valiantly pulled me *and* my coins from the jaws of the beast, then sent it running away with its tail between its legs."

He touched her cheek. "At which time the beautiful young maiden I had saved disappeared into the crowd," he said gruffly, "leaving me with nothing to show for my valiant efforts but a torn shirt. I didn't even get the requisite kiss."

"I was aware of the custom," she said, staring at the zipper on his jacket in hopes he wouldn't notice her blush, even as she wondered how he'd manage to turn the tables on her *again*. "I was also worldly enough to know who you were, and that a lowly blacksmith's daughter had no business kissing a . . . man of your stature."

She heard his helmet thud to the ground just as he pulled her into his embrace. "It wasn't a blacksmith's daughter I wanted my reward from, but my future queen." He threaded his fingers through her loose hair and tipped her head back, his chuckle completely ruining his scowl. "Even though she made me spend two full days scouring the tournament grounds to get it."

"Yet it took my father a mere two minutes to know you were trouble when you swaggered up to our booth and purchased *all* our ironware."

"It was the only thing I could think of to get you away from your accursed duties long enough to come watch me compete." He touched his forehead to hers. "Such a stubborn maiden you were, Stasia," he said softly, using her birth name that he'd imperially changed to *Rana*—which was Sanskrit for queen—upon marrying her.

But then, who would dare question a divine agent of human affairs—better known in that long ago time as a theurgist—who was determined no one ever mistook his wife for a lowly blacksmith's daughter? Certainly not his fifteen-year-old bride. And definitely not the bride's parents, who had still been reeling from the speed of Titus's courtship, which had ended with their only child's vow of forever not two months after their magical son-in-law had saved her from the coin-stealing beast.

"Come home with me," he whispered, his breath on her cheek making her shiver all the way to her toes.

Holy Hades, where was that hammer-carrying young knight when she needed him? Because despite her best intentions, she was sorely tempted to climb onto that powerful motorcycle, wrap her arms around her big powerful husband, and go home. That is until one of his hands slipped down to her backside—where it stilled, then softly squeezed, then stilled again—and she remembered *why* she'd run off in the first place.

"Have you gain—"

She leaned back and pressed her hand to his mouth. "I had hopes you might grow *wiser* with age. Go away, my love, before you say something you truly will regret." She met his sudden glare with a threatening glare of her own. "Besides my purchasing a hovel and having gained a few pounds, not to mention my *misguided* need to breathe fresh air."

He took her hand from his mouth and tucked it between them, effectively trapping it there by tightening his embrace. "How in Hades can you use *my love* and *go away* in the same sentence?" he asked, apparently not regretting anything. His deep green eyes darkened with his complexion. "I can force you to come home."

"But you won't." She dropped her forehead to his chest. "Because you love me."

"Tell me how to fix this," he whispered against her hair, making her shiver again.

"Even your powerful magic can't fix this, husband." She tilted her head back. "Only *time* can."

"How much time? A week? A month?" He looked at the house. "A *century*?"

She stepped free of his embrace with a soft laugh. "Longer than a month but definitely less than a century." She turned serious. "*How* it passes is the true question, Titus, and the only thing you have any real control over.

You can choose to spend our time apart being angry and resentful and eventually alienating everyone who loves you, or you can take this opportunity to reacquaint yourself with the small, everyday wonders of this beautiful world."

"Poseidon's teeth, *I'm* not the one going through a midlife crisis." He gestured at Whisper Mountain looming to the north. "I knew something like this would happen if we spent too much time here. It's this accursed century, with all its postulating about getting in touch with our *true natures*." He snorted. "In my time, all a man need worry about was surviving to fight another day."

Rana turned to face the sea. "It was merely a suggestion," she said, shrugging to disguise the fact that her shoulders were shaking with laughter. Sweet Athena, the man was clueless. "Because personally, I intend to spend this time cutting and welding metal into what I hope will be beautiful works of art like that one," she said, gesturing at the large metal statue of a whale breaching just above the low tide mark. She turned back to face Titus and smiled at his obvious shock. "Do you have any idea how often I've wondered who I would be today if my life had taken a different path?"

"You would be thousands of years dead," he snapped.

"Would I have died happy, do you think?"

The breeze blowing off the water ruffled his crown of wavy white hair as he bent to pick up his helmet, forcing her to lean forward to hear when he muttered, "You likely would have died in a crooked hovel giving birth to some toothless bastard's child."

Rana straightened with a gasp. "Well, fine," she said as she spun away. "Angry and resentful it will be, then."

He gave a deep-bellied laugh and caught her before she'd taken two steps. "Ah, little one, but you love firing my blood." He suddenly sobered, his eyes searching hers for several heartbeats before he looked toward Bottomless and blew out a heavy sigh. "At least you had the good sense to live within reach of the sea creatures."

"Contrary to popular belief, I haven't taken leave of all my senses."

"Am I permitted to call on you?" He held up his hand. "If I phone first?"

She hesitated and then nodded. "Of course. In fact, you may even invite me to go for a ride on your motorcycle." She brushed at the front of his jacket. "Say . . . down to Turtleback Station some evening for dinner and maybe dancing?"

She looked up when he didn't respond to see his jaw had slackened—that is until his eyes narrowed. "Do you mean for us to have a modern *date*?"

"If that's what you wish to call it." She canted her head. "When was the last time you did anything for the sheer fun of it?"

His eyes closed on another heavy sigh.

Her sigh was one of relief when he suddenly strode off—that is, until she realized he was heading for the porch. "Wait," she said, running after him. "Where do you think you're going?"

"To see the inside of your hovel," he said without breaking stride.

"No!" She pulled him to a halt. "I mean, not today," she said calmly. "Some other time. Soon. After I— Once I've settled in."

He looked at her home and slowly tilted his head to

match the lopsided roofline. "Would your reluctance to let me inside mean the exterior is its . . . best quality?"

"I told you that's an illusion." She slipped her arm through his and guided him toward the side of the house. "The interior walls and floors are perfectly plumb and the structure is sound, which you will see when I invite you to dinner. Once I've settled in."

She managed to get him all the way to his motorcycle before he made one last attempt to talk some sense into her. How he went about it, however, was so typically *Titus* that it might have been comical if it weren't so sad.

He set his helmet on the seat, then turned and palmed her face to hold her looking at him—apparently not wanting her to miss the tender concern in his vivid green eyes. "I have a worry you're not looking after yourself properly. Please don't feel that you can't come to Nova Mare, as I know how much you enjoy swimming in the outdoor heated pool and horseback riding on the trails."

The blackguard; she couldn't decide if he was concerned about her expanding posterior or wanted to remind her of all that she'd walked away from.

He slid a thumb to her lips when she tried to speak. "Just because you're no longer living at the resort doesn't mean we can't continue our morning swims together." He shrugged one shoulder. "Or by yourself, if you prefer."

Well, she did miss that heated pool. Titus and their two children, Maximilian and Carolina, had no problem swimming in the Bottomless Sea—or any of the world's oceans, for that matter—but since she was a mere mortal and didn't have command of the magic, she'd never been able to handle frigid water.

"Are you eating well? *Healthy* foods?" he clarified when he leaned away just enough to look down at her, his eyes stopping on her bosom before snapping back to her eyes in surprise. "Or a steady diet of cinnamon buns?"

Well, the man did know her body rather intimately.

Rana stepped free of his hands on her cheeks before he felt her blush. "I've only dined at the Drunken Moose once this past week." She walked up the porch steps, deciding it was time to end this conversation before *she* said something she'd regret. "Good-bye, my love. Remember to breathe the fresh air as you ride your motorcycle."

"Wife," he said, his intimate tone making her hand still on the doorknob. "Your added pounds please me."

Not exactly sure how to take the compliment, considering it had been those very pounds that had sent her running from him in the first place, Rana turned and inclined her head. "Then I shall endeavor to hold on to them." She shot him a cheeky smile. "And maybe even add a few more." But then she frowned when he picked up his helmet. "You have a care, husband, when you're riding that speed demon."

His eyes widened in surprise. "You're worried I'm going to kill or maim myself?"

Not wanting him to leave here believing he'd won this round, she gave a loud, exasperated sigh. "Not you, but the unsuspecting drivers you're *sharing* the road with."

He pulled the helmet down over his sudden scowl, then flipped up the visor to expose deep green eyes crinkled with his equally sudden grin. "So long as you remember to share Bottomless when you're racing through the waves in that monstrous sailboat you—" He froze in the middle of fastening the chin strap. "Please tell me that old scow came with the house and not that you purchased it on purpose."

Rana silently turned and went inside, then softly closed the door on his quiet laughter. The maddening man knew of her obsession for fast sailing vessels, since she already owned *several*—all of which were back home on Atlantis.

Chapter Three

Titus stopped at the end of the camp road and waited for one of Nova Mare's limousines heading toward the resort to pass, then pulled onto the main road behind it. For the love of Zeus, his wife was living in a house half the size of their palace bedroom. And yet the confounding woman not only managed to appear every bit the queen of her crooked, unpainted castle, the morning sun sparkling in her big brown eyes had added a glowing vitality to her intrinsic beauty.

Yes, her small weight gain did indeed please him—the downside being that it also turned him on. But he hadn't dared act on his urge to carry her inside and explore those luscious curves more intimately, as he hadn't wanted to risk sending their already precarious relationship off in an even more disastrous direction. Not that he knew *why* their marriage had strayed so badly off course.

Having left the town proper, Titus glanced over his shoulder, then twisted the throttle and leaned into the oncoming lane. The responsive bike shot past the limo as he shifted through the gears until the engine's throaty pitch smoothed to its optimum power range, the burst of speed doing nothing to lift his mood as he remembered the silent war Rana had waged against him four months ago.

Nicholas had been two weeks overdue returning from what should have been an easy mission to pull a child out of harm's way before history had to be rewritten when Rana had started insisting someone go find him. And although the mythical warrior was more like family than his personal peacemaker, Titus hadn't started worrying until the third week had passed with no word from the man. But when Nicholas finally had returned, badly wounded and carrying the remains of one of his elite soldiers, Rana had been so relieved he was alive that she'd suddenly forgotten all about her anger.

In fact, the ensuing months had been nothing short of a honeymoon—although Nicholas's wedding nine days after his return may have had something to do with Rana's amorous mood. Then again, the fact that their daughter and daughter-in-law, as well as Nicholas's and Duncan's wives, were expecting babies also might have contributed to her acting like a young bride herself.

Titus flipped up his visor to dissipate the heat of his escalating frustration as he shot past the road to Inglenook, remembering how the honeymoon had come to an abrupt end two weeks ago—although for the life of him he still didn't know *why*. There had been no inciting incident or warning signs, as one day they'd been galloping the resort trails like flirtatious young lovers—which had led to a passionate interlude on the sun-bathed sands of a hidden grotto at the north end of the fiord—and not two days after that the woman had suddenly announced she was leaving him. Something about feeling suffocated and needing a breath of fresh air, he recalled her saying.

The one thing he *did* know was that once Rana made up her mind on a matter, the combined power of the gods couldn't alter her course. Within a week she'd purchased a house, and three days later he'd found himself sleeping in an empty bed.

Realizing he was about to overshoot his destination, Titus quickly decelerated and somehow managed to enter the marina without killing or maiming himself. He pulled up next to his son's SUV, set the kickstand and shut off the engine, then took off his helmet and scanned the docks for Duncan MacKeage's pontoon boat.

"Nice of you to finally show up," Maximilian said as he walked from the direction of the office. He stopped beside the motorcycle and peered down at the instrument panel. "The Japanese didn't think to put a clock on this model?"

Titus got off the bike and pulled the key from the ignition. "I can't be late, since MacKeage isn't even here yet."

"We've all been here for nearly an hour."

He looked at where Mac was gesturing to see Nicholas step off a large boat and start untying lines just as its motor started. "Is there a reason we're taking a tour boat?" Titus asked, following his son down the ramp to the floating dock.

"We're on a covert mission," Mac drawled, stepping to the side to let him board.

"Both Duncan's pontoon boat and cruiser are easily recognized," Nicholas added as he also stepped onboard, his Nordic blue eyes suddenly narrowed and direct. "Why am I seeing *camp road* dust on your new toy?"

Titus walked over and sat down on the first row of benches directly behind the wheelhouse. "Because nine miles wasn't far enough to blow it off."

Nicholas sat down beside him. "I thought we agreed you'd give her all the time *and space* she needed to come back on her own."

"You agreed," Titus said as he slid his helmet under his seat. He straightened with a threatening scowl. "And I suggest you mind your own marriage before your new wife discovers your cats are more civilized than you are."

"Well?" Mac asked with a chuckle, sitting on the other side of him. "Are you satisfied *your* wife hasn't run off to live with another man?"

"She's living in a hovel. I've seen outhouses that looked better."

Nicholas released a heavy sigh. "Please tell me you didn't say that to her face."

Titus stood and walked to the wheelhouse as Duncan guided the large vessel through the narrow channel protecting the marina, which had been nothing more than a gravel pit before Maximilian's little epic stunt had flooded it with seawater. "Remind me again who we're disguising ourselves from?" he asked Duncan.

The highlander glanced over at him, his eyes widening with his grin. "I hope the dealership threw that suit in with the bike."

"You've had command of the magic for almost four years," Titus said, arching an equally impudent brow, "and you still require two wizards and a mythical warrior to back you up at the first hint of trouble?"

That got rid of the cocky bastard's grin. "I wouldn't," Duncan muttered as he sent the tour boat surging into the swells of the fiord, "if I'd been given a mountain that could stay awake." He shot a glare over his shoulder at Maximilian. "Ye could have warned me there was such a thing as contrary magic."

"It usually takes on the disposition of its master." Mac turned serious. "Which brings us back to Dad's question of why you've asked the three of us for help, when it's *your* calling to protect Bottomless and the surrounding wilderness."

"Dad?" Titus repeated before Duncan could answer, only to close his eyes on a silent groan. "Henry finally got to you."

"No," Mac said with a chuckle. "Ella did, although likely at Henry's urging." He shook his head. "You try arguing with a three-year-old cherub. Or have you forgotten that Carolina had you wrapped around her princess pinky finger at three *months*?"

Only because it had taken him that long to stop blaming his daughter for nearly killing his wife, Titus remembered as he turned to stare out the windshield. And it had been Nicholas—a mere child himself and Carolina's self-appointed protector—who had finally brought him to his senses. Not that he knew how a boy who'd been spewed from a whale onto a local beach and raised by the island midwife had had the gonads to call his king—much less the man who had built Atlantis—an idiot.

"You don't deserve the miracle your wife nearly died giving you," Titus recalled the seven-year-old saying when the boy had caught him standing over Carolina's crib the day they'd learned Rana would live. "Her highness isn't still weak from childbirth; she's heartsick that you want nothing to do with Lina." Nicholas had crowded Titus out of the way to pick up Carolina, protectively holding the week-old infant to his chest as he'd glared up at his towering king. "So why don't you just walk into the sea and never come back, and save me the trouble of killing you the moment I'm big enough."

Which would have been only a few years, at the rate the boy had been growing.

Despite moving Nicholas's adoptive mother and father into the palace as their family healer and gardener, and installing Nicholas in the bedroom next to Carolina's as her bodyguard, the boy had kept up the verbal attacks until the morning Titus had nearly walked past a whispered conversation taking place in the garden. He'd stood frozen behind a tree and listened to Nicholas pleading with Rana to let him help her run off with Maximilian and Carolina, the boy promising he would find someplace beautiful to raise her children where everyone truly loved one another.

But it had been Rana's response that had nearly brought Titus to his knees. *Unconditional love*, she'd told Nicholas, *sometimes required an awful lot of patience*. She'd then patted the boy's scowling cheek, saying she had faith that *time* and a few baby belly laughs would soften Titus's heart. And it so happened, she'd gone on to assure Nicholas, that her big powerful husband had an infinite amount of time to remember that small, everyday miracles were all that really mattered.

Somewhat similar to what she'd said this morning.

Except what in Hades had happened to the *unconditional* part? Because to his thinking, living in separate houses while he was supposed to explore the everyday wonders of the world was damned conditional and not the least bit patient.

"That's why dealing with Lina for thirty-one years," Nicholas said as Titus merely continued staring out the windshield, "made me decide I'm only having sons."

Mac snorted. "Assuming Providence even wants your soul in exchange."

Want it, Titus thought with his own silent snort. Providence already owned all six foot seven inches, two hundred and twenty pounds of the warrior. And that was why to this day Nicholas continued being his voice of reason—more often than not as direct and insolent as he'd been as a child. Which had Titus wondering why he hadn't listened when, just days before he'd left on his mission last November, Nicholas had reminded him that even gods needed to take time out of their busy schedules to play with their wives.

Poseidon's teeth; he'd apparently been suffocating Rana with his attention.

"Hey," Duncan said over his shoulder, "try having *twin* daughters." He turned to face the two other expectant fathers. "It was bad enough they found two babes at the ultrasound last week, but I had to physically restrain Peg when they couldn't find any extra appendages." The highlander shook his head with a chuckle. "She still managed to grab the device out of the technician's hand and run it over her belly, all while yelling at me to watch the monitor for signs of exterior plumbing." Duncan checked to make sure they weren't about to run over any boats or navigational buoys, then shot Nicholas a grin. "I don't suppose ye could put in a word for me and see if Providence couldn't put some stones on those babes? Big ones," he clarified, holding his fingers in a large circle, "so they'll be the first thing Peg sees at our next ultrasound."

Nicholas sat up straighter. "I thought Peg was going to let Mom start caring for her. My Julia is looking forward to having a home birth with a midwife." Nicholas glanced at Mac. "Olivia's using my mother, isn't she?" He looked at Duncan again when Mac nodded. "That was the whole point of my parents moving here. Rana asked Mom to stay on after Lina gives birth and open a women's clinic. And midwives can usually tell the sex of a child just by how a woman is carrying."

"Carrying *twins*?" Duncan thought to clarify as he turned back to the wheel.

"Their gender matters not," Titus said. "Peg will love them unconditionally."

"Aye," Duncan said with a sigh. He slowed the engine back to an idle as they neared the uninhabited eastern shoreline halfway down the forty-mile-long inland sea. "Grab the binoculars out of the holders on the benches and try to look like tourists in awe of this ninth *unnatural* wonder of the world," he instructed. "Oh, Mac, I promised Ray Byram a weekend stay in one of your hotel suites for letting us use his new boat."

Mac stopped the binoculars halfway to his eyes. "Didn't Olivia's secretary marry Ray Byram last summer? But as an executive employee," he continued when Duncan nodded, "Lucy is entitled to a free weekend at Nova Mare each year."

Duncan grinned. "I guess she forgot to tell Ray about that little perk."

"We're back to my original question," Titus said, taking the binoculars Nicholas handed him. "Who exactly are we disguising ourselves from?"

"And more importantly, why?" Mac added.

"Ye know the small colony that set up camp near the Turtleback town line shortly after the earthquake? Well," Duncan said when Mac nodded, "this past winter they started acting weirder than usual." He pointed at the island they were passing as the boat idled between it and the eastern shoreline. "And from what I've been able to learn, they've started holding secret ceremonies out here."

"People gathering in ceremony is now a crime?" Mac asked as he scanned the densely forested island with the binoculars.

"Well, no," Duncan admitted.

"Are they performing human or animal sacrifices?" Titus asked.

"I guess they feel whoever they're worshipping is also a vegetarian," Duncan said with a chuckle, only to just as quickly sober. "I did find what looked like an altar when I checked out the island a few nights ago, but no signs of blood. Just some clay pots filled with grain and a pile of rotting vegetables."

"Then what is your concern? Why are we spying on a bunch of hippies?"

"Hippies?" Duncan said in surprise. "I'm afraid you've got the wrong decade. No, the wrong *century*. The only hippies left are wrinkled and bald and have traded in their Birkenstocks for orthopedic shoes." He gestured at the smoke rising from several chimneys across Bottomless, now that the western shoreline was no longer blocked by the island. "Near as I can tell, this is a good old-fashioned cult, complete with a new charismatic and probably psychotic leader."

"Have any members of this cult committed any crimes against the good people of Spellbound or Turtleback," Titus asked, "or against humanity in general?"

Duncan rubbed the back of his neck. "Well, no, not that I've heard. And when any of them come to town, they've been peaceful and gracious and buy most of their supplies from Ezra at the Trading Post. But rumor has it they've started practicing some sort of magic." He grinned. "And I thought ye might want to check out your competition."

"We don't have a monopoly on the magic," Mac said, lowering his binoculars. "And a practicing cult in the area might serve to keep suspicion off *us*."

"But that's exactly why I'm worried," Duncan said. "If anything that can't be explained by science happens around here again, it could be the last straw for the townspeople. And panicked people start looking for something or some*one* to blame, and I'm afraid they'll decide these people are responsible and go after them. A group of protestors has already started gathering at the road leading down to the colony."

"I don't recall anyone panicking four years ago," Titus said. "In fact, it was almost unanimously decided that Maximilian's little stunt was a blessing."

"Because it immediately started putting money in everyone's pockets," Duncan countered. "But what if the magic these people are practicing," he said, waving at the western shore, "*isn't* benevolent? What if they're worshipping some badass demon?"

"A vegetarian demon?" Mac drawled.

"Titus and Mac can't stop these people, Duncan, if that's why you brought us out here today," Nicholas said. "They *protect* man's free will—without judgment."

"And we will not interfere," Titus added, "even if that will is deemed evil."

"Even if it wreaks havoc on innocent people?" Duncan growled.

"Theurgists have no control over mankind," Nicholas explained. "They're divine agents of human affairs—the operative word being *agents*. They can only broker solutions, not step in and arbitrarily solve the problems men create. That's why they have us." He grinned at the highlander's surprise. "You and I are not bound by such constraints. If we see something that needs fixing, we're free to fix it."

"I signed on to protect the *wilderness*," Duncan said, glaring at Mac, "not people's right to call up some ancient, obsolete god. For all we know, it could suddenly show up and start rearranging these mountains—*again*."

Mac merely smiled.

Titus gestured at the island on their starboard side. "This isn't an ancient deity, Duncan. Though still weak, the energy these people appear to be calling forth is unlike any I've felt before."

"A new god? Can they do that?"

"If one is needed to serve their purpose."

"Just by making him up?"

"Or her," Titus said on a chuckle. "How do you suppose I came to exist? Do you think all the deities of the world simply appeared for no reason? Each of us was *imagined* into being, Duncan, by developing cultures wishing to answer the uniquely human question of life's purpose. Since the dawn of man, people have wondered where they came from, why they are here, and where they are going."

"We're *myths*, Duncan," Mac added.

"Because," Titus continued at the highlander's scowl, "long before modern science could explain the seemingly random events that played such defining roles in their lives, mankind decided an unseen entity must be at work. It was the only way they could make sense of fierce storms, the earth shaking and mountains spewing lava, or entire crops dying for no discernable reason. And so mythologies were born, and grew to be as varied and complex as the societies that created them."

"But why imagine a new god into existence? What's wrong with the hundreds of old gods already kicking around? Hell, some of them must be begging for a shot at the limelight again."

"Because for all of its advancements, science still hasn't answered the question of *purpose*," Mac interjected. "Man is beginning to grasp how he came to be, but still searches for *why* he exists."

"Especially," Titus added, "since you haven't found any signs of life anywhere else in your universe yet. And none of us *old gods kicking around* appear to be who these people are searching for."

Duncan gave a muttered curse.

"If a new deity is being called forth," Mac continued quietly, nodding toward the colony's campsite several miles away on the western shoreline, "then we have no choice but to accept the will of the people who are creating it."

"Even if whatever they're creating is evil?" Duncan repeated through gritted teeth.

"One man's demon is another man's god," Mac said softly, "and the very reason Dad built Atlantis on which to cultivate his Trees of Life. We protect free will by ensuring mankind's *knowledge* is protected, and will only act if the Trees themselves are threatened—by god or demon *or* mortal."

Apparently deciding he wasn't getting anywhere with the two wizards he'd brought out here today, Duncan folded his arms over his chest and looked at Nicholas. "But you and I can do something about this new demon?"

Nicholas sat down on the bench. "We've decided it's a demon?"

Duncan turned back to the steering wheel with a snort. "They sure as hell aren't reinventing the tooth fairy." He sent the boat surging through the swells, but suddenly turned to Nicholas again. "Wait," he said over the loud hum of the engine. "I thought your father was *Odin*."

Nicholas dropped his head—to hide his grin, Titus suspected—and shrugged.

"Then if you're the son of one of these mythical deities like Mac is," Duncan continued, "how come *you* can help me?"

"I never vowed to protect man's free will," Nicholas said as he looked up—indeed grinning. "In fact, I've made a career of bending many a man's will to mine."

Duncan stared at him for several heartbeats before glancing at Titus and then Mac, then made sure he wasn't running over any boats or navigational buoys before looking at Nicholas again. "What about your man, Rowan? Did he make any vows?"

Nicholas stiffened. "Why?"

"Because I've finally talked the councilmen of both Turtleback and Spellbound into pooling our resources and hiring a chief of police and a couple of officers."

"Why?" Mac echoed as he also sat back down.

"Because the population of both towns has almost doubled in four years, and it can take over an hour for a sheriff's deputy to arrive from the other side of the county."

"Installing your own police force sounds sensible," Titus said, stepping to the wheel to angle the boat past a distant group of kayakers.

"That's what we did in Pine Creek several years ago," Duncan continued as he walked over and sat on the bench. "The townships of Frog Cove and Lost Gore joined up with us. In fact, Greylen MacKeage's daughter, Megan, is married to the chief of police, Jack Stone." Duncan leaned forward and rested his elbows on his knees to see Nicholas. "So what about Rowan? Do ye think he'd be interested in being our chief of police? We'll give him a truck instead of a resort cart, and I talked the councilmen into adding an apartment over the storefront we intend to remodel into a police station."

Nicholas was already shaking his head. "You're not getting my man. Rowan is content being second in command of Nova Mare's security force."

"What about Dante then? Or Micah?"

"They're overseeing Inglenook's security," Nicholas growled.

"Why not hire a local?" Mac asked.

"Because I want an Atlantean warrior," Duncan said. "I need someone I can trust not to shoot first and *then* ask questions when one of your time-traveling guests gets drunk and starts busting up one of the towns' bars."

Nicholas leaned back and folded his arms over his chest. “No.”

“Would this chief of police not be required to have graduated from your state’s law enforcement academy?” Titus asked.

Duncan snorted. “Even I can conjure up a diploma.”

“No,” Nicholas repeated, this time directing his dissent at Titus. “I’m not giving up one of my men.” He leaned forward to glare at Duncan. “Offer the position to Alec or another one of your MacKeage or MacBain cousins. All the men in your clans have served in the military and they’re familiar with the magic.”

“Jane’s not going to let Alec strap on a gun,” Duncan countered, using his nephew’s pet name for Carolina. “Assuming I could even talk him into it,” he added with a shake of his head. “I’m not sure what happened, but Alec came home from his last tour of duty a friggin’ pacifist.”

“He must have forgotten that a year ago last September,” Mac drawled as he rubbed his jaw, referring to his heated little encounter with the man who was about to become his brother-in-law—hopefully *before* he became a father.

Apparently deciding he wasn’t getting anywhere with Nicholas this time, Duncan looked up at Titus. “Give me one of your Atlantean warriors.”

Knowing Nicholas wasn’t budging, Titus offered an alternative. “What about your ancestor, Niall MacKeage? He’s had a year and a half to acclimate to this century.”

Duncan stilled in surprise, then suddenly shook his head. “The guy’s wrecked two trucks, a snowmobile, *and* a jet boat, and last fall he somehow managed to bury one of my excavators under ten feet of dirt *while* he was in it." His eyes turned pained. "Niall also has a love-hate relationship with firearms, and his solution to most problems is bludgeoning them to death."

"He sounds perfect," Nicholas snapped.

Duncan shot to his feet. "He's a loose cannon," the highlander snapped back. "Jack's already hauled Niall into jail twice; once for tossing some guy out of Pete's Bar and Grill *without* opening the door first, then another time for asking a young girl on a date."

"Dating is a crime?" Mac said in surprise.

"She was *sixteen*."

"Then why hasn't de Gairn sent Niall back to his original time?" Mac asked, referring to Matt Gregor—who was married to Greylen MacKeage's youngest daughter—by his drùidh name.

Duncan dropped his head with a sigh. "Because Niall is old Uncle Ian's eldest son, and apparently after Ian returned home, he secretly told Niall all about living in this time and that his dying wish was for his son to live in this century."

"How accommodating of us to invite him here to court Carolina," Mac muttered.

"Has no one considered that Niall might simply be bored?" Titus asked. "The man was laird of the clan MacKeage back in the twelfth century, after all, and is likely having trouble adjusting to a society where his skills are outdated. Perhaps he merely needs something on which to focus his passion and energy."

"I agree," Nicholas interjected, leaning back again and folding his arms with a smug smile. "Niall MacKeage would make a perfect chief of police."

"Not as perfect as an Atlantean warrior," Duncan returned tightly. "This place is crawling with foreign tourists, and Niall doesn't speak all the languages like your men."

"Neither do you, Duncan," Titus quietly pointed out.

"God dammit, the guy's likely to shoot somebody his first day on the job!"

"Clans don't elect stupid men as their lairds," Maximilian calmly interjected. "Could you not at least think about offering the position to Niall?"

Duncan narrowed his eyes at him. "You want *another* MacKeage moving to Spellbound Falls?"

Mac grinned. "I have no more sisters to protect from your clansmen."

Not that he'd succeeded in protecting Carolina from falling in love with Alec, Titus thought with a silent chuckle as he handed the wheel back over to Duncan. But then, being very much her mother's daughter, once Carolina made up her mind on a matter, the gods themselves couldn't alter her course.

"What in hell is that?" Duncan asked, leaning out of the wheelhouse. "When are people going to realize that a sea with strong currents and friggin' whales is no place for bathtubs posing as boats," he muttered, changing course to avoid the small sailboat entering the choppy swells in front of the point of land separating the fiord from the main body of Bottomless.

Yes, Maximilian's little epic stunt four years ago, when he'd sent an underground river surging inland from the Gulf of Maine and moved mountains to create a fiord that extended Bottomless another twelve miles northward, had turned Spellbound Falls and Turtleback Station from forgotten dots on a wilderness road into tourist boomtowns.

"Maybe what the idiot needs is a good scare," Duncan continued, adjusting their course again to cut across the sailboat's bow. He blew out a heavy sigh. "I'm thinking we probably need a marine patrol more than we need a police force."

"That's well and good, Duncan," Titus said with a chuckle, realizing Rana had discovered he'd unlocked her boathouse. "But I prefer you not teach this particular idiot a lesson, as I do believe that's my wife."

"Mother?" Mac said, shooting to his feet as Duncan immediately brought the boat back to an idle.

"What in Hades is she doing in that barnacle-infested old scow?" Nicholas asked, also standing to lean against the rail. He looked at Titus. "You can't mean to let her on Bottomless in that tub. The water is barely above freezing and that boat's not safe in anything over a breeze."

Titus brushed at nothing on his jacket. "I apparently no longer have any say over what Rana does." He met Nicholas's glare with one of his own. "You think you can fare any better, then by all means you try talking some sense into her."

Mac stepped between them and gestured at the fiord. "Well, gentlemen, it would appear Mother is nicely dealing with the barnacle infestation."

Titus moved to stand at the rail beside Nicholas in time to see Rana reef in the mainsail, and his heart swelled with pride when the small boat rolled onto its side and cut into the choppy sea with the agility of a porpoise—which was nicely exemplified when two harbor porpoise suddenly shot out of the bow wave beside it.

"At least bring one of her sloops from Atlantis," Nicholas muttered.

"She didn't seem to have any problem getting her belongings moved down the mountain to her hovel," Titus said, watching the sun play off his wife's beautiful, spray-drenched face as she wrung every last drop of speed out of the old sailboat. "I'm sure she wouldn't have any trouble getting one of her sloops brought here if she wished."

He didn't have to turn his head to know Nicholas was glaring at him again. "You're lucky she ran away," the warrior said, "instead of getting you drunk and holding a pillow over your face the moment you passed out."

Titus walked back to the wheelhouse. "I wasn't aware our conversation had returned to *your* wife," he said, nudging Duncan away from the wheel. Titus pushed the throttle forward and aimed the bow toward the marina two miles up the fiord. "As for your worry about the colony, Duncan," he continued, "I suggest you hire Niall MacKeage as your chief of police and see if giving the man a *meaningful* way to burn up all that passionate energy might keep him out of trouble."

Chapter Four

"Why am I hearing huffing and puffing?" her daughter asked.

Rana smiled at the road ahead as she reached up and adjusted the volume on the Bluetooth receiver in her ear. "Because I'm walking and talking at the same time."

An exasperated sigh came through the earpiece. "Please tell me you're not walking up Whisper Mountain."

"No, I'm walking to town."

"But you told me the house you bought is two miles down the camp road."

"A mere stroll, even by today's standards."

"And here I thought I've been setting a good example for you to be a modern woman. You need to buy a vehicle, Mom, and have Nicholas teach you to drive. Just make sure you buy a truck, not a motorcycle."

Rana lost her smile. "Now who's acting overprotective?

And for your information, I am quite capable of teaching myself to drive the pickup I *already* purchased. And I might also buy a motorcycle, as I imagine it can't be any more difficult to handle than a thousand-pound horse."

"Horses don't go a hundred miles an hour." The earpiece suddenly went silent, and then Carolina said, "I'm sorry. But in my defense, I can't stop picturing the motorcycle that came racing up the TarStone road last week while I was having lunch with Alec's mom on the ski lodge deck. Sadie choked on her salad and I nearly fell off my chair when the guy took off his helmet and we realized it was Daddy."

It was Rana's turn to sigh. "I can't decide if he bought that motorcycle hoping to impress me or if he's trying to recapture his youth."

"He certainly impressed the MacKeage elders. Greylen and Morgan and Callum all rushed out to the parking lot to admire Dad's new toy, and Alec told me that now his father and Greylen are talking about getting one. Um, Mom? I know you said it's none of my business, but is the real reason you won't tell me why you left Daddy because you're afraid of upsetting me? Maude assures me that just because you had a difficult time in childbirth, it doesn't mean I will."

"Oh, honey, you are the least fragile woman I know."

"Then why won't you tell me what's going on between you two?"

"Because it's none of your business. So," she continued, deciding to change the subject, "have you lovebirds found a place in Spellbound to rent while you build your summer home?"

"Ah . . . not exactly." Rana stopped walking when

she heard her daughter take a deep breath. "Alec got a good deal on a speedboat from a dealer here in Pine Creek," Carolina rushed on, "so we've decided to live at the building site instead of running the length of the fiord every day."

"Caro, you're seven and a half months pregnant."

"So which is it, Mom? Am I fragile or strong?"

"It's not that you *can't* camp out in the wilderness, but rather why would you want to? What's the point of living in this wonderful century if you're going to cook over a campfire and traipse to a privy every time the baby kicks your bladder?"

"Having the *choice* is the point. And besides, I have some pretty fond memories of camping out with Alec."

"And after the baby arrives," Rana whispered so she wouldn't shout, "are you planning to continue living in a lean-to with a newborn?"

"We'll be fine, Mom. So why are you going to town?"

Rana took a calming breath and started walking again, deciding Carolina had inherited her stubbornness from Titus. Because considering how hard their daughter had fought to live in this century, only to ironically *choose* to forego indoor plumbing every summer, the girl was also determined to remain Alec's *girlfriend* right up to her due date. Rana wondered if Alec ever questioned his decision to save "Jane Smith" from her abductors eighteen months ago.

"Mom?"

It took Rana a moment to remember the question. "The ladies are meeting at The Bottoms Up to discuss our progress on the clinic and women's shelter."

"You're meeting in a bar?"

"It's closed at this hour, Caro. Vanetta suggested we

meet there instead of at the Drunken Moose because of the breakfast rush hour."

"Ski season is winding down here, so you can expect me to be a more active member of your little group in a couple of weeks."

"You're going to be busy getting married and *giving birth*. Mayday is less than six weeks away."

"Julia's such a great event planner that all I have to do is show up," Carolina said, blatantly ignoring the last part. "And I want to help with your women's clinic, because I'm planning to start one in Pine Creek when we move back next fall."

"Caro."

"I've already talked to Maude, and she suggested that if I can find a local nurse willing to spend the summer interning with her in Spellbound Falls, she might be able to persuade Dr. Bentley to split his time between both towns."

Rana picked up her pace as she wondered why she was surprised, since Carolina had obviously inherited her love of community service from her. "It took more *divine* persuasion than I'm comfortable with for us to get Roger, and now you want to ask the poor man to open a second birthing clinic almost three hours away?"

A pause as pregnant as the woman on the other end of the line came through the earpiece. "Are you saying Mackie was instrumental in getting Dr. Bentley?"

"I believe it was Olivia's idea for your brother to *gently inspire* Roger to come practice medicine in the wilds of Maine." She gave a soft laugh. "I'm sure our paying off his school loans in return for a five-year contract didn't hurt, either."

"I understand midwives have to be supervised in this century, but I'm still surprised you hired a male doctor."

"That was Olivia and Peg and Julia's suggestion, since the clinic will also offer family medicine," Rana explained. "They pointed out that folks around here are still quite traditional and would feel more comfortable with a man being in charge. In fact, they suggested we look for someone in his late sixties or early seventies, white-haired or balding, with a cranky bedside manner. Oh, and if he has an accent, it better be Canadian."

"Are you serious?" Carolina said on a gasp. "Who wants a cranky doctor?"

"Peg also thought recruiting a hunter or fisherman would be easier than finding a woman willing to move to the middle of nowhere."

"What about the crisis center? Please tell me you aren't searching for a man to run a shelter for abused women."

"Not actively," Rana said. "Olivia claims we can't discriminate on matters of gender or age or race, but she's confident we'll find a qualified *female* administrator."

"A woman who likes to hunt and fish?"

"I seem to recall you went hunting with Alec."

"Just once," Carolina muttered. "It was more boring than fishing. Alec left me sitting on a rock freezing my backside for three hours, and the only critter I saw was an obnoxious red squirrel. It ran up a tree beside me and proceeded to tell the entire forest I was there, until I finally got it to shut up by tossing it bites of my apple. Oh, speaking of men," she rushed on. "Have you heard you're getting a police chief?"

"It's been decided, then? Olivia told me the councilmen from Spellbound and Turtleback were only *discussing* the idea."

"Well, they finally agreed. Duncan called Alec Saturday night and said he tried to hire Rowan or Dante or Micah, but Nicholas refused to give up one of his men. Father suggested he offer the position to Niall MacKeage, but Duncan is against it."

"Why? Niall would make a wonderful police chief. Besides being a laird, he was a great warrior back in the twelfth century. That's why your father brought him here as a potential husband for *you*."

"Yeah, well, Jack Stone had to drag Niall into the police station when some parents complained that he was stalking their sixteen-year-old daughter."

"Stalking?" Rana said in surprise. "But that doesn't sound like Niall. Wait," she said with a laugh. "He would see nothing wrong with pursuing a pretty young lass, as most twelfth-century girls are married and have a babe by the time they're sixteen."

"Yeah, which is why Greylen and Jack had to sit Niall down and explain modern courtship. Anyway, Duncan asked Alec if he wanted the job, but my very wise boyfriend said he was perfectly happy being a ski bum seven months of the year and a supportive husband and doting daddy the other five."

"I hope you realize what a lucky woman you are, Caro."

"Really? I prefer to see myself as smart."

"Yes, I definitely meant *smart*." Rana finally came to the end of the camp road. "I've reached town, so I'm going to hang up and pay attention to traffic."

"Spellbound has traffic at eight thirty on a Monday morning during mud season?"

"*Geriatric* traffic. Apparently the grange ladies are also meeting this morning to discuss their summer project."

A soft groan came through the earpiece. "Any idea what they're planning to spring on the poor townspeople this year?"

"When I was in the Trading Post Friday afternoon, Ezra mentioned that Janice Crupp asked him to keep an eye out for any storefronts coming up for rent that would be appropriate for a historical museum."

"But *you're* trying to find a building in town. And Spellbound needs a women's clinic a lot more than it needs a museum."

Rana turned at the sound of a racing engine to see Christina Richie peering over the steering wheel of the fast-approaching red sedan, even as she recognized Janice Crupp in the passenger's seat beside her. "Preserving a town's history is also important," she said as she scurried into the church's driveway.

"What's that noise? Are you already nearing the waterfall or is that a . . ."

Rana lost the last of Carolina's words when the car suddenly gained speed as it passed by, just as she also spotted a pickup with three women in the front seat crossing the bridge from the opposite direction—both vehicles apparently headed for the one remaining parking space across from the Drunken Moose.

"Mom!" Carolina shouted over the screech of the pickup braking to a halt when Christina Richie shot into the space ahead of it.

"I'm okay," she assured her daughter, only to gasp when the victorious car's right front tire hit the remains of an old snowbank, driving the sedan's nose into the air before finally rocking to a halt at a precarious angle.

"Sweet Athena, what's going on?"

"Two vehicles, one parking space, and some very determined women," Rana said, only to give a squeak and bolt for the closest storefront when the thwarted pickup suddenly shot toward the church's driveway. "Don't worry, Caro," she said dryly. "I definitely won't be purchasing a motorcycle."

"Walking doesn't appear to be any safer. I guess you really do need a police chief, if for no other reason than to write traffic tickets."

"I hope he has balls of brass if he intends to ticket the grange ladies."

"Mother!"

"Because the driver of the losing vehicle just got out and shot Christina Richie a very unladylike gesture. Bye, baby. I'll give you a call this evening and bring you up to speed on our progress."

"Okay. Tell everyone I said hi and that I'll see them in a couple of weeks."

"I will. You give Alec my love. Oh, and be a dear, would you, and tell him I was able to fill his request and that it will be here in plenty of time."

"What request? And in time for what? Mom, what are you and Alec up to?" Carolina asked when Rana said nothing.

Rana pulled her cell phone out of her pocket. "Bye, daughter. Take good care of my grandchild," she said, hitting the END button.

* * *

Joining the small gathering of women sitting at the window table overlooking the Bottomless Sea, Rana shed her jacket and sat down to an interesting conversation.

"Mac told me it's nothing to worry about," her daughter-in-law, Olivia, said to Duncan's wife, Peg. "And until I see otherwise, I have to agree with him."

"But you have to admit that ever since they got a new leader a few months ago," Peg returned, "they've been acting weird. They all started wearing those freaky tunics and baggy pants, and since January, only the men come into town. We never see the women anymore or any children. I'm beginning to agree that the colony looks more like a cult now rather than a simple commune of hippies."

"Near as I can tell, it's people from away who started calling them a cult," Olivia countered. "As far as the locals are concerned, the colonists have been good neighbors for the last four years. Ezra has been selling the organic vegetables they grow at his Trading Post for the last three summers."

"My dad said they canceled an order for clear cedar boards," Julia interjected—Julia being Nicholas's wife and whose father owned a cedar mill a few miles north of town. "They wanted the lumber to build a large communal sauna, but when Dad called them in February to say he'd filled the order, the new leader told him they'd changed their mind."

"Duncan said they're practicing some sort of magic," Peg added. She looked at Rana. "He told me Titus thinks they're trying to create a new god."

"Really?" Rana said in surprise, glancing at Olivia. "Did Maximilian say anything to you about that?"

"He mentioned they were *trying*. But he said it takes a lot of focused energy to make it happen."

"Is that really possible?" Peg asked Rana.

"I don't see why—"

Vanetta Quintana bustled through the door connecting the Bottoms Up with the Drunken Moose, expertly shouldering a tray laden with steaming cups and a large platter of prepared fruit—effectively ending the conversation, since the bar and restaurant owner was the only member of their group who wasn't part of their magical family. She handed out the beverages, set the fruit in the center of the table, then plopped down in one of the chairs with a tired sigh.

Julia moved her gaze from the fruit to Vanetta with an expectant smile. "Is the next batch of cinnamon buns coming out of the oven soon?"

"Sorry, Jules," Vanetta said. "The grange ladies got the last batch."

A heavily pregnant silence filled the otherwise empty bar. "You could have your cook throw together another batch," Olivia suggested sweetly.

Vanetta glanced at Maude, who was Nicholas's mother as well as Spellbound Falls' soon-to-be-official midwife, and then looked back at Olivia. "My cook doesn't have the recipe for those buns. And even if he did, it takes several hours for them to rise." She grinned at the three younger women. "But I have plenty more fruit."

Rana decided that bit of news went over about as well as hearing *who* had gotten the last of Vanetta's infamous cinnamon buns, even as she noticed Peg MacKeage had dropped her scowl to the cup of amber liquid in front of her.

"Um, I have someone else's drink," Peg said, lifting the cup by its saucer and taking a sniff, then looking around the table until her gaze stopped on the steaming mug in front of Vanetta. "You must have my coffee," she said, holding out the cup as she reached her other hand for the swap. "One cream, two sugars," she added more forcefully when Vanetta leaned back in her chair while clutching her mug protectively.

Maude took the cup and saucer from Peg and set it on the table in front of her. "This one is yours," she said with a warm smile, which Rana happened to know was the midwife's secret weapon for disarming expectant mothers. "Ginger tea, no cream, unsweetened," she continued, despite Peg turning her scowl on *her*. "And no caffeine."

"Tea?" Peg repeated, eyeing the amber liquid as if it were hemlock. She glanced at the cup in front of Julia, then at Olivia's identical cup before looking at Maude again and smiling tightly. Or maybe that was desperation, Rana decided as she hid her own smile by taking a sip of her own tea. "I just read an article," Peg told the midwife, "that said it's okay for pregnant women to drink coffee. In moderation," she tacked on.

Yes, that was definitely desperation.

Maude arched a brow. "Do you really want those two darling little boys doing cartwheels inside you all day, Margaret?"

Peg slapped her hands to her chest with a gasp, her vivid blue eyes widening in surprise. "Boys? You think I'm carrying *boys*?"

"I'm sorry. Were you hoping for girls?"

"No. Boys! I want boys." Peg picked up her ginger tea. "I mean, of course I would love girls just as much, but . . ." Her eyes sparkling with excitement, Duncan's wife used her cup to gesture at Julia and Olivia. "We plan to raise all these babies together in a little wolf pack, and the more boys the merrier." But that sparkle suddenly dimmed as she studied Maude through narrowed eyes. "My ultrasound last week didn't show anything even resembling penises."

"Maybe they're shy little boys," Maude said.

Peg snorted. "They're *MacKeages*." She finally took a sip and immediately spit it back into the cup. "Are you serious? This is terrible."

"Trust me," Olivia piped up. "It's an acquired taste."

"So, ladies," Rana quickly interjected when she saw Peg working her way to another scowl. "Where are we in regards to our women's clinic?"

"I mentioned our problem of finding a vacant building to Reverend Peter," Julia said in a rush, apparently also eager to redirect Peg's attention. "And he's offered to let us use the church basement until we're able to find something permanent."

"Well," Rana said, trying not to sound disappointed, "a basement is a bit gloomy for a birthing clinic, but at least it's right here in town. And it is only temporary."

Vanetta gave a negligent wave. "We can brighten it up with a fresh coat of paint and hire Grundy Watts to build some screens to section off exam rooms." She beamed a smile around the table. "As for the women's shelter, I found us the perfect home."

"Where?" Olivia asked. "Is it close to town?"

"It's within walking distance," Vanetta said, her

cheeks flushing when her announcement was met by silence. "It's . . . um, my house. And it'll be vacant just as soon as I finish moving in with Everest. I'm leaving most of my furniture, so we'll only have to buy more beds."

"You and Everest are going to live together?" Peg said in surprise.

Vanetta held up her left hand and used her thumb to push out her banded ring finger, her smile returning at the chorus of soft gasps. "You mean it's not customary for wives to live with their husbands?"

"You guys got *married*?" Julia squeaked. "But when? Or more importantly, why weren't we invited to the wedding?"

"We tied the knot last week when we were in Las Vegas."

"But haven't you and Everest been dating only three months?" Olivia asked, her own cheeks darkening—likely because Vanetta had been dating Olivia's father, Sam, as recently as *four* months ago.

Vanetta picked up her coffee again. "A few days into our vacation, Everest asked me why we were running two households when we could be waking up together every morning for the rest of our lives. Taking that as a proposal, I dragged the man to the first cheesy wedding chapel I could find before he changed his mind."

"Does Daddy know?" Olivia whispered.

"He knows," Vanetta returned just as softly. "And Sam's good with it. In fact, he wished me well, saying he was glad I found someone smart enough to marry me."

"I was hoping *he* would be that smart."

"You and I both know that's never going to happen,

Olivia," Vanetta said gently. "Sam's too much of a loner to be domesticated. So," she said brightly, looking around the table again. "I am officially donating my house for our women's shelter."

"But you could sell it for a fortune," Julia interjected. "Not only is it within walking distance of town, it's right on the shore of Bottomless."

"Which makes it perfect," Vanetta countered. "The women deserve a *beautiful* place to stay while they're getting their lives back on track, and being able to sit by the water is healing." She shook her head. "The real problem will be getting them to leave their abusive husbands and boyfriends in the first place. But thanks to our esteemed councilmen finally getting their acts together, we can promise the women our new police chief will keep an eye on them. And between running the Bottoms Up and the Drunken Moose, I'll be too busy once the tourist season kicks into full swing to help with the everyday operations of the shelter. So for my part, I'm donating my house."

"But that's too generous, Netta," Olivia said. "We decided to raise the funds for the shelter because we want *community* support." She winced. "As well as to include the grange ladies before they come up with any more cockamamie schemes."

Vanetta rested her arms on the table again, her eyes growing haunted as she wrapped her hands around her mug. "Getting this shelter up and running as soon as possible is important to me because it's personal. I begged for a place like this fifteen years ago in rural Alabama."

"You're right, *Mrs. Thurber*," Rana said. "Your home is perfect. And on behalf of the women desperately needing this shelter, we accept. This is wonderful, ladies," she continued, looking around the table again. "We should be able to receive guests in what . . . a couple of weeks?"

"Assuming someone answers our ad," Olivia said. "Even the great salary we're offering doesn't appear to be enough incentive to lure a qualified social worker to the wilderness." She looked at Maude and then Rana. "Are there any women from . . . your island who might like a change of scenery?" she asked with a furtive glance at Vanetta—who had no idea that Atlantis actually existed.

"None who would understand the needs of our shelter residents," Rana said with a sad smile. "Since domestic violence is virtually unheard of on the island."

Vanetta stilled with her mug halfway to her mouth. "Really? *None* of the men in your country ever raise a hand to your women? Well, hell," she continued when Rana shook her head. "Why are we wasting our efforts building a shelter? Let's just ship all the women who come to us for help to . . . to wherever it is you and Maude are from."

"Because running away from a problem solves nothing," Rana said, ignoring the fact that she had run away from *hers*. "Our goal is to offer programs that will give these women the skills to help themselves, and merely sending them someplace safe is in essence treating them like children."

"Yeah," Vanetta said on a sigh. She suddenly brightened again. "Maybe we should send the husbands and boyfriends to your island and let your men teach the bastards how to treat women."

"I second that motion," Peg said, lifting her cup in salute before taking a sip, only to shudder all over as she swallowed. "Curses, that's nasty."

"Curses?" Vanetta repeated.

"I've given up real cussing," Peg explained, aiming an angelic smile at Maude, "because I read that babies start developing language in the womb."

Julia choked on the sip of tea she'd just taken. "You gave up cussing *again*," she said, using her napkin to wipe her chin, "because Charlie ran up to Christina Richie in the Trading Post yesterday and told her that Jacob had taken his *friggin' cock*."

"Clock!" Peg said, her cheeks flushing. "Charlie still has trouble with his *L*s and was trying to say Jacob had taken the *clock* he was looking at."

"Hmm," Julia murmured, her eyes dancing with mischief. "I guess that means he was telling Christina his brother had taken his *flying* clock."

Peg looked at her watch. "Speaking of my sweet little angel," she said, pushing back her chair and standing up. "I promised Duncan I'd meet him at the marina at nine thirty to take Charlie off his hands so he can leave for Pine Creek. He's going to see if he can talk one of his MacBain cousins into becoming our chief of police."

"But I thought he was going to ask his . . . ah, cousin Niall to fill the position," Julia quickly prevaricated, since Vanetta also had no idea that Niall was Duncan's distant *ancestor*. "At least that's what Nicholas told me."

Peg snatched her purse and jacket off her chair and started backing away. "We found out Brodie MacBain just got back from Afghanistan, and Duncan feels it's only fair to give a decorated veteran first dibs."

"I'll walk you out," Rana said, also standing. "I have a favor to ask you, Peg," she said in a whisper as soon as they reached the door.

"What's up?" Peg asked as she slipped on her jacket,

only to sigh when she tried zipping it closed but couldn't. "Dam—darn," she muttered, hiking her purse over her shoulder. "It looks like I'm gonna have to dig out my old maternity clothes already."

"Were you showing at four months with Peter and Jacob?"

"Not this much." Peg smoothed her fleece over her softly protruding belly. "I didn't blow up like the Pillsbury Doughboy until my seventh month, which is why we didn't know I was having twins until Repeat popped out, taking Billy and me *and* the doctor by surprise."

Billy being Peg's deceased first husband, Rana knew. It was Billy Thompson who had given Jacob the nickname *Repeat*, when he had exclaimed in the delivery room, "Hey, it's Pete and Repeat!" The man had died in a construction accident fourteen months later, leaving Peg to single-handedly raise their two daughters and twin boys. That is until Duncan MacKeage had somehow managed to capture the guarded woman's heart, likely by falling just as madly in love with her small tribe of heathens. The newly formed family had expanded nine months to the day after the wedding, when Peg had given birth to a handsome and gregarious second-generation Maine highlander they'd named Murdoc Charles MacKeage. Duncan called the boy *Mur the Magnificent* and Peg vehemently called him *Charlie*.

Rana was looking forward to their upcoming battle to name the new twins.

"Your favor?" Peg reminded her.

"Oh, yes." Rana moved closer, putting herself between Peg and the women at the far end of the room. "I was wondering if you would teach me to drive."

"A car?" Peg said in surprise.

Rana nodded. "A pickup, actually. A rather old one. I was told it's a standard shift, whatever that means."

Peg gave a crooked smile. "It means I hope you have good hand-foot coordination and really strong neck muscles." She suddenly frowned. "What sadistic salesman sold you a standard shift?"

"I didn't purchase it from a dealership, but from the man I bought my house from."

Peg's expression turned to horror. "Are you talking about Pops' old pickup?" She shook her head when Rana nodded. "But that doesn't sound like Gene Latimer. He's the last person I would expect to take advantage of someone who didn't know better, especially a woman. Gene's so straight shooting he makes *Reverend Peter* uncomfortable."

"Gene tried to talk me out of buying the truck," Rana assured her, "but I insisted he include it with the welding equipment. I don't wish to own a new truck, anyway, as it will get ruined when I load it with rusty old iron and steel."

"When you what?"

Rana opened the door and guided Peg outside. "I also purchased Averill Latimer's welding equipment, and Zack is going to teach me how to cut and weld metal into beautiful statues."

Peg went back to smiling, albeit crookedly again. "Wow. When you take off your tiara, you don't mess around, do you?"

Rana smoothed down her shirt. "It kept getting in the way every time I wanted to do something . . . un-queenly."

"Yeah, I could see where that might be a problem. But instead of leaving it hanging on your bedpost, couldn't you have sold it for at least enough money to buy a truck with an automatic transmission?"

Rana looked up in surprise. "You don't think I can drive a standard shift?"

"Oh, no, of course you can," Peg said, nodding vigorously. "And I would love to teach you. When do you want to start? I'm free today until the bus brings my tribe back from school. How about I go get Charlie then swing back here and pick you up? You ladies should be done enjoying your tea and fruit by then, shouldn't you?"

Rana eyed her suspiciously. "Will I see a marina coffee cup in your hand when you pick me up?"

Peg started backing away. "No offense, but Maude is a bit scary."

"But is that not a quality you would want in a midwife? Oh, and Peg?"

She halted. "Yes?"

"The driving lessons will be our little secret?"

"Not a problem. Um, any particular reason you asked *me*?"

Rana set her hand on the doorknob. "Why, I would think the reason is obvious. I assumed any woman who would willingly marry Duncan MacKeage surely must have nerves of steel," she said, stepping through the door when Peg burst out laughing.

Chapter Five

"*This* is why I want boys," Peg said as she led Charlie over to a tree on the back side of Rana's garage. She then positioned the three-year-old in front of her and bent to unfasten his pants. "Potty training them is a breeze, especially if they come in pairs," she continued as she leaned him forward to brace his hands against the tree. "Because just as soon as they realize they can compete to see who can pee the farthest, they don't want to waste their precious body fluids on a diaper. Okay, let her rip, big man."

Rana looked down at the small plastic card Peg had handed her. "You said Duncan . . . made this for me?"

"Yeah." Peg straightened as she continued holding on to Charlie's jacket to keep him steady. "Hey, don't worry; I didn't mention our lessons. I only told him you bought a truck, but that you didn't have an actual license. I swear the man pulled one out of thin air faster than I could say abracadabra," she said, batting her eyelashes, "because he somehow got the notion that seeing him make magic turns me on."

Rana slipped the license in her purse. "Yes, our men do love to impress us with their tricks," she said, walking to her pickup when she saw Charlie had finished drowning the tree. "I'm ready to begin if you are."

"Wait," Peg said, carrying the boy to her SUV. "I thought about it on my way back from the marina, and I think our first lesson should be in my truck."

"How is driving your truck going to teach me to drive mine?"

Peg turned from buckling Charlie into his car seat. "I think you should get used to working a gas pedal and brake before we add in a clutch and shifting. All of which," she added, "you'll have to do at the same time."

Rana glanced at her battered and rusted pickup, then looked at Peg's much newer SUV, which although muddy, was completely devoid of dents. "But what if I hit a tree or drive into a ditch? I would pay to have your truck repaired, of course, but how would you explain the damage to Duncan?" She eyed Charlie in the backseat, just now realizing she might well be putting the child in danger. "Maybe we should do this another time."

"Pfft," Peg scoffed as she opened the front passenger door. "You're not going to hit a tree because you already know how to drive."

"No, I don't," Rana said, rushing around the truck when Peg got in. She opened the driver's door and climbed in behind the steering wheel. "I've never driven a vehicle."

"Sure you have. I've seen you drive snowmobiles and

Nicholas's boat, and you tootle around in the resort carts all the time."

"But those aren't automobiles."

"Same concept, just different applications." Peg pushed a straw into a juice box and handed it to her son in the backseat, then faced forward and fastened her seat belt. "They all have a throttle, a brake, and a steering wheel. Well, except *water* is the brake on a boat." She reached over and turned the key to start the engine, making Rana scramble to fasten her own seat belt. "You have to press on the brake to put the truck in gear, which you do by using this lever," Peg continued, touching the lever jutting from the right side of the steering column. "Pull it toward you and down while watching the letters below those larger dials, and you'll see the light move from *P* for park, *R* for reverse, *N* for neutral, and *D* for drive. You can ignore the numbers because this is an *automatic* transmission," she said with a cheeky grin, "meaning the truck knows which gear it should use. Okay, go ahead and put it—no, wait. Before we start, get a feel for the gas pedal by pressing down on it a few times."

Rana leaned to the side to see her feet. "Which pedal is the gas?"

"Oh, sorry. The tall one on the right is the throttle and the wide one is the brake, just like on the resort carts. The setup is almost always the same on anything with an engine—gas on the right, brake on the left."

Rana pressed on the right pedal, only to yank her foot away when the engine roared loud enough to shake the truck.

"Gently," Peg said with a laugh. "A truck is a lot more powerful than a resort cart. Just think of it as squeezing a horse's sides when you want to move forward. Pressing hard is like kicking it into a gallop."

Rana pressed softly on the gas pedal. "If we're not moving, why is that needle moving?" she asked, pointing at one of the larger dials, which resort carts did *not* have. "See, it drops back when I take my foot away."

"That's the tachometer. It tells you how fast the engine is turning over. You don't need to pay attention to it today, but you will in your pickup. It'll help you decide when to shift to a higher gear. The only dial you should keep an eye on is the one beside it. That's the speedometer."

"Then why does your truck have a tachometer?"

"It's a guy thing," Peg said with a dismissive shrug. "Okay. Press your right foot on the brake, pull the lever down until the *D* lights up, then transfer your foot to the gas."

Rana frowned through the bottom of the wheel at the pedals. "I have two feet, so why wouldn't I use one on each pedal?" She looked over at Peg. "That's how it works on a snowmobile, only with my hands."

Peg shook her head. "You're going to need your left foot to work the clutch in your pickup, so you might as well start training your right foot to work two pedals."

Rana pressed down the brake with a deep sigh. "This is far more complicated than I was expecting. There are so many dials to watch, how does one pay attention to the road? And all the buttons! The resort carts have a key and a light switch." She gave Peg a sheepish smile. "I thought it would be relatively simple, since I've seen your daughters driving with Duncan on the tote roads, and they're only twelve and ten."

"That's a safety thing," Peg said. "Out here we teach

our kids to drive as soon as they can see over the steering wheel, because they could be our only means of getting help in an emergency. Don't worry, driving will become second nature just like your smartphone did. That took you what . . . all of two days to learn? So okay," she said, rubbing her hands together, "let's go see if we can find some grange ladies to run over." Her smile turned sinister. "Extra points if you take out their ringleader."

Rana stilled with her hand on the shifting lever. "You can't mean for me to drive on the main road for my very first lesson."

"Well, you're not going to learn anything idling up and down a camp road. That's why I got you the license."

Sending a silent prayer to Athena, goddess of wisdom and courage, Rana moved the shifting lever to the *D*, then slowly let out on the brake. "Nothing's happening."

"Because you aren't giving it any gas. Gently," Peg said with a laugh when they suddenly shot forward and then jerked to a halt when Rana stomped on the brake.

"Oh, friggin' mess, Mama."

Peg closed her eyes on a groan. "Duncan really needs to start watching his language around Charlie," she muttered, twisting to look at her son. "You're okay, big man," she soothed, pulling her coat sleeve over her hand to wipe juice off the poor child's face. "Let's give it another go," she said, facing forward again. "Or we're gonna miss our chance to flatten those bun-stealing grange ladies."

Realizing Peg was attempting to calm her with small talk, Rana decided she'd made a wise choice for her driving instructor. She checked for traffic and *gently* eased down on the gas, thankful Peg had circled around the garage when they'd arrived so she didn't have to back up.

"Is there a particular reason you're not enamored with the grange ladies?" she asked, guiding the large SUV down the narrow camp road.

Peg gave a soft snort. "The spring Mac brought Henry to Inglenook, the grange ladies were raising funds to send Olivia and Sophie to Disneyworld because her dead husband, Keith Baldwin, was the town's only war hero. But when Olivia said absolutely no way, and Mac suggested they raise money for a *general* widow's fund instead, those busybodies made me and my kids their new pet cause. Um, you're doing great, but you might want to go a little faster than a turtle."

Rana eased down on the gas, pleased to discover that driving a truck was no more difficult than driving one of the resort carts. "But what's wrong with that, Peg? Surely you could have used help providing for four young children."

"They were going to put pictures of my kids on all their friggin' fund-raising jars and stick them in all the stores in Spellbound and Turtleback."

"Oh, how embarrassing. Please tell me you were able to stop them."

Peg suddenly laughed. "I didn't have to. Your son's mountain-moving earthquake nicely redirected their attention."

"Yes," Rana said dryly. "Epic events have a way of doing that."

"When Bottomless Lake suddenly turned into the Bottomless *Sea*, the grange ladies decided the town needed a fancier park more than I needed their charity."

Rana glanced over in surprise. "They really just forgot about you?"

"Well, in their defense," Peg said, "they watched me

go from rags to riches when I started selling my gravel to Duncan to build the road up to Nova Mare. Don't panic," she calmly added when a small red car came racing in the camp road toward them. "There's plenty of room for both of us. Just edge to the side and let him drive by you."

Only instead of continuing past when Rana guided the SUV as close to the trees as she dared, the car stopped beside them and its window lowered to expose Titus frowning up at her.

"The top left button on your door lowers your window," Peg said.

Rana gently pressed on the gas pedal and drove off, stifling a smile when Peg gasped in surprise. Only they hadn't gone more than a hundred feet when the engine suddenly shut off. Rana lifted the shifting lever into park with a resigned sigh, which was lost in her passenger's laugh.

"I'm torn between admiration and pity," Peg said, "when I think of you being married to him for *thousands* of years. You want me and Charlie to walk up the road to give you a little privacy?"

Rana reached over to stop Peg from unbuckling her seat belt. "That isn't necessary. But listen closely," she added, patting Peg's arm, "and maybe you'll learn an impressive trick of your own for the next time Duncan starts flexing his muscles at you." Rana then pressed the button to lower her window when the small red car backed up and stopped beside them again. "If you're heading to Missy Maher's," she said to her glowering husband, "I don't believe she's returned from her grange meeting yet."

"What makes you think I'm going to Ms. Maher's?"

"I can't imagine why you would be driving down this

road other than to show off your fancy new car to the most eligible spinster in Spellbound Falls," Rana said, reaching over and squeezing Peg's arm when the woman started choking.

"I'm down here to see *my wife*."

"Oh, I'm sorry. I must have missed your *phone call*."

He had the good grace to look contrite. "It appears I left without my phone this morning. Therefore," he went on when she tried to speak, "I decided to simply ask you in person to have lunch with me today."

"I'm rather busy today, Titus," she said as she started raising the window. "Try *calling* me later on in the week." But she suddenly stopped the window halfway up as she made a point of running her gaze over his newest purchase. "Did the motorcycle turn out to be a little too spirited for you?"

"I purchased this car so you would be comfortable on our *dates*."

"Oh," she said with a pronounced pout. "I was looking forward to our zooming through the countryside on that motorcycle together. You remember how I used to wrap my arms around you and hold on for dear life, don't you, my love?" she said in a husky purr as she slowly started raising the window again, "when I'd sneak away to meet you in the meadow and we would race the wind on your powerful warhorse?" She started the truck, then gave the slack-jawed blackguard a jaunty wave as she headed out the camp road at the speed of a racing turtle.

"I want . . ." Peg cleared her throat. "I want to amend what I said earlier. I don't know whether to admire or pity *Titus*."

"I specifically asked him not to drop in unannounced,"

Rana explained, only to mutter a curse—in Greek, for Charlie's sake—when the truck stalled again.

"Are you sure you don't want me and Charlie to take a hike?" Peg drawled when Rana's window lowered *without* her touching the button.

"Why are you driving the MacKeages' vehicle?" Titus asked when he halted beside them again. His eyes suddenly widened. "Zeus's teeth, you don't drive!"

"Of course I do. I've been driving for nearly four years."

"Electric carts on resort *paths*."

"Same concept, different applications," Rana said. "We're leaving on our errands now, and I would appreciate it if our vehicle continued running."

"Wait. You didn't say why *you* are driving."

She gave a negligent shrug. "Peg was kind enough to let me try out her truck to see if this is the model I should buy." She made a production of running her gaze over the small red sports car again, wondering how the man had folded himself inside it. "But maybe I'll buy myself something more fun. Good-bye, my love. Enjoy this beautiful day."

"Thank you," Peg murmured when Rana started driving down the road again.

She glanced over in surprise. "For what?"

"For making *my* day. So, how about we drive to Turtleback so I can pick up a couple of bags of chicken feed? That way we'll be killing two birds with one stone."

Rana gently braked to a stop when they reached the main road. "You expect me to drive all the way to Turtleback Station? It's over thirty miles one way," she added, frowning. "And what two birds are we killing?"

"One, you'll be driving like a pro by the time we get back," Peg said. "And two, we really will be doing errands, so you didn't just lie to your husband."

"If a woman can't lie to her husband, who can she lie to?"

Peg's beautiful blue eyes widened. "We're *supposed* to lie to them?"

"Every chance we get." Rana glanced in the rearview mirror to make sure Titus wasn't behind them, then lifted the shifting lever into park. "In fact," she continued as she unfastened her seat belt and pulled her cell phone out of her jacket pocket, "it's our duty to lie to them."

"It is? Why?"

"To kill two birds with one stone."

"Um, which two birds are *you* talking about?"

"The first reason is to keep them from taking us for granted." Rana tapped a picture, hit the speakerphone button, then smiled at her gaping passenger. "Oh, I'm sorry, sweetheart," she said when Titus answered with a hesitant although expectant *hello.* "I seem to have accidently called you. But aren't you glad to discover you didn't forget your phone after all? Talk to you later, my love," she finished, tapping the END button on his silence. She refastened her seat belt and pulled the shifting lever back into drive. "And that, my friend, is bird number two."

"Ohmigod," Peg said behind her raised hand. "I can't believe you just did that."

"What can't you believe?" Rana asked, pulling onto the main road in the direction of town. "That I knew Titus was lying about forgetting his phone, or that I let him know I knew he was lying?" She gave an exaggerated sigh. "Sometimes I can't decide whether to admire or pity *myself*." She shot Peg a wink. "But the majority of the time I feel like the luckiest woman on the planet."

"Cinibums!" Charlie suddenly cried as Rana idled through town watching for determined grange ladies. "Mama, cinibums!"

Peg muttered something under her breath and turned to her son with a huge smile. "The cinnamon bun fairy is taking a nap, Charlie. But I bet if you take a nap, too, you'll see her in your dreams and she'll give you a bun."

"Lying to children, however," Rana drawled when Peg faced forward again, "will *always* come back and bite you on the behind."

Titus stood on his wife's beachfront, facing the large metal whale rising out of the wind-driven waves, and wondered yet again what Rana was hoping to accomplish by leaving him. Any fool could see that needing a breath of fresh air was merely an excuse to mask the real reason for her little rebellion, because last he knew, loving wives did not abandon their *loving* husbands while continuing to call them "sweetheart" and "my love." Nor did they blatantly flirt—at least not in front of others—much less allude to their youthful and decidedly passionate antics. As for her desertion being a means to force him to explore the everyday wonders of this world . . . well, that was an even more futile attempt to direct his attention away from the real problem.

Studying the detailed features layered into the rusted patina of the twenty-foot whale, Titus couldn't help but appreciate what a feat it must have been to set the massive statue in place. Either Averill Latimer had enjoyed a good challenge or he'd loved his grandson very much to have wrestled that supporting post into the granite seabed, which would only be exposed for short periods of time during low tide.

Titus smiled at the realization that he at least knew why his wife wanted to create beautiful works of art under the tutelage of young Zachary, as the teenager really was quite talented. And early in their short courtship, he had discovered that Rana had been the driving force behind her father redesigning the utilitarian utensils he forged by encouraging him to keep in mind the women who used them, which had smartly elevated the humble blacksmith to that of artisan.

But Rana needn't have run off in order to try her hand at metalwork; she need only have asked to set up a workshop at Nova Mare or at home on Atlantis. And she very well knew that. So despite alluding to it during his visit a few days ago, recapturing her youth was no more convincing than her needing a breath of fresh air.

Titus sat down on a boulder and rested his arms on his knees. Despite being only fifteen at the time, the beautiful and spirited and surprisingly astute maiden he had fallen in love with the moment he'd looked into those big brown eyes had agreed to marry him only if *he* agreed never to use his magic on her. He'd nearly broken that vow when she'd given birth to Carolina, but even then the woman had been adamant that Providence be the one deciding her fate. Well, he thought with a humorless laugh, Providence and Rana's own determination not to leave her two precious children in his care.

His beautiful wife was not, however, averse to using the magic when it suited *her* purposes, such as turning a blind eye when Olivia had asked Maximilian for help persuading Roger Bentley to come practice medicine in Spellbound Falls. Nor was Rana reluctant to dip into her husband's bottomless satchel of money whenever she needed funds for one of her projects. Or to purchase a crooked house and a tired old sailboat, he thought with a groan. But then, whatever was his was hers, as he could deny her nothing.

Titus stared down at his clasped hands dangling between his knees and decided the woman must be hiding something so horrifying, she had felt the need to—

He suddenly straightened. Horrifying, yes, but only because it concerned him!

"Poseidon's teeth," he quietly growled. "She's *protecting* me."

Rana feared nothing, not even dying. And that meant the only thing with the power to make her run was if she thought she was protecting him. But he was virtually invincible. Hell, the combined power of the gods hadn't been able to defeat him in the thousands of years he'd been championing mankind.

Surely the woman didn't believe he was in mortal danger. She not only knew the width and depth of his power, she also understood the more subtle nuances of the magic he commanded. In fact, they had been married only a few months when his still relatively young wife had begun serving mankind right alongside him—though she tended to focus more on women's issues.

So if Rana truly was protecting him, it must be from something she felt had the power to destroy him. And that put *her* in harm's way as well, because if he was sure of anything, it was that his wife would not sit idly by while his enemies rose against him.

But which enemies?

And more importantly, how had Rana sensed the threat when he had not?

Titus cradled his head in his hands and stared down at the incoming tide lapping the toes of his boots. Rana had no command of the magic, which meant her female intuition had sensed he was in danger, and she had apparently decided running away was her only means of protecting him.

Not that she'd run very far. But if that were the case, then purchasing a house in the same town, not to mention the same century, didn't make sense. Unless she wanted to be nearby when . . . No, it simply didn't make sense. And no matter how confounding she might be sometimes, Rana was *always* sensible.

He was no closer to figuring out what was going on than when he'd found himself crawling into an empty bed seven nights ago. At this rate, hell would be frozen solid before—

Titus snapped his head up, then rose to his feet when the massive whale breached dangerously close to shore. "Leviathan," he called in surprise as the ancient warrior slapped back into the water. No sooner had the splash settled when a handful of orcas surfaced, the largest of the sea wolves breaking away from the pod and speeding toward shore. "Kitalanta, no!"

Frantically looking to see if any neighbors were around as well as scanning the water for nearby boats, Titus raised his arms to capture the percussion he knew was coming and muffled the boom of the orca's transformation as it slammed onto the gravel beach. "You accursed beast," he said tightly, striding toward the four-legged, fur-covered wolf stumbling to catch its footing. "You know you can't pull this kind of stunt in broad daylight within sight of mortals."

Only instead of becoming submissive, the large northern timber wolf turned to face the water, its hackles raised as it gave a menacing growl. Titus stiffened and also looked out at Bottomless. "What is it?" he asked just as Leviathan surfaced, the whale emitting a series of low-frequency clacks.

Titus muttered a curse and began undressing. "You will stay and guard your queen's home," he instructed the wolf as he shed his jacket, his focus now on the storm squall forming to the south. "Stay hidden and do not let so much as a mouse on the property." He sat down and took off his boots, stood up and looked around again to make sure they were alone, and took off his shirt. "Any threat will be coming by sea, though I doubt whoever it is will dare venture this close to Maximilian's magic." He unbuckled his belt. "I will leave half your pod to patrol out front and send the other half to guard the entrance to the fiord. All of you are to remain on duty until you hear from me personally." He dropped his pants and walked into the water up to his waist, then stopped and looked back. "And Kitalanta? Mortals are not the threat, so don't eat any of them, especially my wife's young employee, should he show up."

Confident his orders would be obeyed, Titus turned and dove into the sea—only to have his urgency change to that of curiosity when he sank below the surface and felt a new and unfamiliar energy pulsing through the water.

Chapter Six

Rana tightened her grip on the steering wheel when a gale-force wind suddenly buffeted the truck just as lightning lit up the trees to their left.

"Wow, where did this come from?" Peg said as a curtain of heavy rain swept over them from the direction of Bottomless. "That second lever on the left side of the steering column turns on the wipers. Just twist the end of it."

Rana felt for the switch, not wanting to take her eyes off the ominously darkened road. "Maybe I should pull over and let you drive."

"Naw," Peg said above the sound of the pummeling rain and frantic slap of the wipers. She touched a button on the dash, which Rana assumed was the defroster when warm air pushed up from the windshield toward her. "It's not cold enough to freeze, so the road won't get slippery.

And this is just an ordinary old rainstorm. Um, isn't it? I mean, we don't usually get thunderstorms this time of year."

"I'm sorry," Rana said with a laugh, hoping to mask her own alarm. "You seem to have me mixed up with the men in our lives. I wouldn't know an ordinary rainstorm from an epic event, since I'm usually hiding under the bed when either one arrives."

"You mean that even after being married to Titus all these years you still can't tell the difference? Well, bummer," Peg said when Rana shrugged in an attempt to appear nonchalant. "I was hoping Duncan's magic would eventually rub off on me and I'd be able to start doing . . . stuff." She held up her left arm and pulled back her jacket sleeve to expose the wide metal cuff on her wrist. "This thing doesn't do anything unless Duncan wants it to. Or his mountain feels like freaking me out and starts making the stupid thing vibrate for no reason." She dropped her arm. "I'm never going to be able to do *anything*?"

"Sorry, I'm afraid magic-makers have a monopoly on—" Rana stomped on the brake, the tires chattering on the wet pavement as the truck jerked to a stop. "Sweet Athena, what is that?"

"It . . . they look like . . . those are friggin' *trees* running toward us," Peg said over the racing thump of the wipers.

The truck rocked on another gust of wind just as the two-legged tree in front of no less than a dozen other trees suddenly spotted them and also halted, then held out two leaf-covered branches to stop the small . . . grove and apparently say something to them. The group suddenly split, with half bolting into the forest toward Bottomless and the other half—including the leader—into the woods on the opposite side of the road.

Rana heard her passenger heave a relieved sigh. "I know what they are. Or rather, *who* they are," Peg said. "We're not far from that colony of weirdos that Duncan has decided are just a bunch of nature nuts. Probably beechnuts and acorns," she said with a snicker, waving at the woods. "They must dress up like trees when it rains and run around being one with nature." Peg checked on Charlie in the backseat, then faced forward again. "Too bad he's sleeping, because I bet the little guy would have loved to tell his brothers and sisters he saw a whole herd of tree fairies. Ah, you might want to get going," she added, gesturing behind them. "And next time *not* stop in the middle of the road, especially in a storm. Unlike the resort paths, you're likely to get rear-ended by some-one going sixty miles an hour."

Rana quickly started down the road again as fast as she dared, considering it was still raining hard enough to keep the wipers on high, and decided a bit of small talk might help calm her own nerves as she kept an eye out for more two-legged trees. Because in truth, she was fairly certain this was not an ordinary rainstorm. "So, Peg, have you made peace with Providence for giving you another set of twins?" she asked. "Seven children are a few more than you planned on having, isn't it?"

Peg looked over in surprise, then smiled. "Can you keep a secret?" she asked, only to tap herself on the forehead. "What am I saying? You're the queen of secret keeping."

"Yes," Rana said dryly, "everyone knows how much I love secrets. So what's yours?" she quickly added, realizing she may have sounded sarcastic.

"Well, if you want to know the truth," Peg said hesitantly. "I wouldn't mind having a dozen little heathens."

Rana frowned out the windshield. "But did you not have an operation after Peter and Jacob were born to prevent you from having more children?"

"Yes, I did," Peg drawled, sounding more than a little sarcastic herself. "But apparently nobody told Providence—or Duncan, either—that having your tubes tied is supposed to prevent pregnancy." She sighed again. "Billy would have loved to have more children, but four were all we could comfortably afford. But now that money is no longer the deciding factor, and seeing how Duncan wouldn't mind having *two* dozen, we've decided to . . . Well, if it's a choice between abstinence and letting Providence decide how many we end up with, I'm going with Providence." Rana glanced over to see Peg shake her head. "I know people in town are whispering behind my back," Peg continued, "and wondering if I'm an idiot for getting pregnant again, but I don't care. I *like* children, and I'll damn well have a big family if I want to."

"Good for you, Peg. I hope you have—" The truck suddenly shuddered as if something had slammed into the rear of the driver's side, making Rana jerk them to a stop again. "What did I hit?"

"No, something hit us," Peg said, twisting in her seat to look back. "Ohmigod, it's another one of those weirdos, only—ohmigod, he's *huge*."

Rana shoved the lever into park and unfastened her seat belt to the sound of branches scraping the truck, and twisted around in time to see a blur of leaves rush past the rear window.

"That's not a man!" Peg yelped, hitting a button on her

door that snapped all the locks—which apparently unlocked whenever the shifting lever was put in park, Rana realized. "That was a *real* tree," Peg continued. "Only I swear it had a face."

"Did the face appear to be in pain?" Rana asked, watching out the rear window and seeing what definitely looked like a tree disappear into the forest. "Was it grimacing?"

Peg checked her still-sleeping son and faced forward again. "I don't know. But I do know we're not chasing after it to find out," she said, gesturing for Rana to also face forward. "I vote we call Mac and have him come down and find out what that thing was. Preferably *before* Duncan gets back from Pine Creek," she added, pulling out her cell phone.

Rana refastened her seat belt, then started driving down the road again. She listened to Peg explain to Maximilian what was taking place on the road halfway to Turtleback Station, the one side of the conversation she could hear suddenly stopping and the interior of the truck turning silent but for the racing thump of the windshield wipers.

"What do you mean, you have no intention of doing anything?" she heard Peg ask in disbelief. "Mac, there are friggin' *trees* running around out here. Real ones. Well, one of them was real," she said more softly, obviously attempting to sound calm. "He—it—was nine or ten feet tall and had a trunk the size of . . ." She fell silent again, and Rana took her eyes off the road long enough to see Peg looking incredulous as she clutched the phone to her ear. "Okay. Yeah, thanks for nothing," she muttered as she lowered her hand and tapped the phone's screen.

"What did he say?" Rana asked as Peg silently stared out the windshield.

"Nothing I didn't already know, other than that he's not going to do anything. But it appears Duncan's more worried than he's been admitting to me about the colony practicing some sort of magic."

"It's not unusual to practice magic, Peg," Rana said gently, "even in this century."

"But a *new* god? Is that even possible?"

"As I had started to say when Vanetta walked in, I see no reason why it *wouldn't* be possible. All mythical gods were created in men's minds before they actually came to exist. They were *imagined* into being, Peg."

"Even . . . even Titus?"

Rana smiled over at her wide-eyed friend and nodded. "Even Titus."

"Could . . ." Peg cleared her throat. "Could he be un-created? I mean, could people suddenly un-imagine Titus *out* of existence?"

"Although unlikely," Rana said with another nod as she watched the road for more trees, "it *is* possible." She looked over with a smile. "But not by un-imagining him, as the very act of thinking about something gives it presence. Titus would have to be completely forgotten. But if even one man, woman, or child believes a god exists, then it does. Don't worry," she said, reaching over and patting Peg's arm. "Titus will not suddenly vanish, because I will always believe in him."

"But . . . but you're eventually going to die," Peg whispered.

"I am mortal," Rana agreed. "But my children are not. Nor are my grandchildren. The Oceanuses will be around for a long, long time. Oh, look, the rain has stopped," she said brightly, wanting to calm her friend's worry. She turned off the wipers with a small laugh. "This certainly has been an eventful driving lesson."

Rana didn't stomp on the brake this time, but she did slow to a turtle's pace at the sight of several cars parked on both sides of the road, no less than two dozen men and women standing around them holding what appeared to be hand-painted signs.

"Don't stop," Peg said. "And whatever you do, don't make eye contact with any of them."

"Who are they? What are they doing?"

"That road on the left leads down to the colony, and these people started hanging out here a couple of weeks ago in protest. Don't slow down too much or they'll jump out in front of you and start preaching that something a lot worse than an earthquake is going to happen if we don't get rid of the 'pagan devil-worshippers.' I know, because they caught me last week."

"But pagans don't—" Rana was forced to stomp on the brake when one of the men darted into the road in front of her, the cardboard sign he was carrying slapping onto the hood of the truck when she stopped only inches from him.

"Well, shit," Peg growled, twisting to check on Charlie—only to reach out and stop Rana from lifting the shifting lever into park. "Don't unlock the doors and definitely don't roll down your window. I don't recognize any of them, so we'll just stare straight ahead and you start slowly creeping forward until they get out of the way. Then you kick this horse into a gallop."

"Hey, lady," a man said, making Rana flinch when he rapped on her window as several people crowded around him. "You gotta hear what that cult is trying to do," he shouted through the glass.

"Is Charlie still sleeping?" Rana asked, staring down at the dials on the dash. "I could blast the horn, but I don't want him to wake up and be frightened."

"Try inching the truck forward," Peg suggested as she stared down at her fists balled on her lap. "*This* is why we need a police force. Most of those cars are wearing out-of-state license plates. People from away can't just come up here and tell us what we're supposed to think, and they sure as hell can't ambush innocent people by blocking the road and forcing us to listen to their—"

The rest of what Peg said was cut short by the simultaneous arrival of a brilliant flash of lightning and an earsplitting clap of thunder, the ensuing deluge of wind-swept rain effectively sending the protestors scrambling to their vehicles.

"That worked," Peg said with a laugh when several signs were ripped from their grasp as people held them over their heads like umbrellas. "Probably better than a police siren. So let's get out of here."

Rana turned on the wipers and headed down the road *again*. "For the love of Zeus," she muttered. "What will we encounter next, a parade of penguins?"

Not penguins but *Titus*, she discovered when the rain stopped two minutes later. Rana pulled onto the gravel edge of the road, put the truck in park and shut off the engine, then dropped her head onto the steering wheel with a silent curse. "All I wanted was a simple driving lesson, and I get a comedy of errors."

"No offense," Peg said, "but instead of practicing your driving, maybe you should work on learning some magic tricks. That way you won't—wait, how'd he get down here ahead of us?" she asked, only to suddenly gasp. "Was he responsible for that storm?"

Rana lifted her head to see her husband walking toward them. "He most likely was responsible for the second one."

"Then I vote we be nice to him," Peg said, grabbing Rana's arm when she reached to start the truck again. "And give him a ride. Hey, what's he wearing?"

"You mean other than that proud-of-himself grin?"

"Yeah, besides that," Peg said with a laugh. "I don't think I've ever seen him so . . . wrinkled. Well, except for where that tunic is pulled tight across his chest. He's dressed like the colonists, only everything looks two sizes too small. Where do you suppose he got those clothes, anyway?"

"I imagine he got them from the same place he does every time he unexpectedly goes swimming—off someone's clothesline."

"He swam here?" Peg said, this time in a whisper because Titus was standing beside Rana's window. "Ah, the key has to be turned on for the windows to work," Peg added, reaching over and turning the key, but apparently not far enough to start the engine.

Rana pressed the button to lower her window. "Is there a reason I'm seeing more of you than I did when we were living together?"

That got rid of his grin. "I need a ride back to my car."

"I'm sorry," she said, gesturing out the windshield, "but our errands are in the opposite direction."

He reached for the back door handle. "I don't mind accompanying you."

"No, wait. You can't . . . I don't . . ." Rana released a

heavy sigh. "Very well," she said, opening her door to get out. "I'll ride in back."

Titus caught her door and slowly closed it. "I wouldn't dream of interrupting your test drive. I'll ride in back with young Murdoc."

"Good heavens, no," Peg said, unfastening her seat belt and opening her door. "There's barely enough room for my kids back there. You ride up front."

Rana grabbed Peg's arm the moment Titus headed around the rear of the truck. "You drive, Peg, and I'll ride in back with Charlie."

"I'm not putting you in the backseat, either." Peg patted Rana's hand on her arm. "Hey now, you're driving like you were born holding a steering wheel. And this is your chance to wear a proud-of-yourself grin of your own."

Glancing in her side mirror to see Titus had stopped and was studying the rear fender of the truck, Rana scowled at Peg and let go of her arm. "Well fine then, I'll drive the friggin' truck."

Peg spun back with a gasp, her hands going to her mouth.

"What?" Rana asked, looking around for more two-legged trees or protestors.

"I've corrupted you, too!" Peg splayed her hands over her face and shook her head. "I'm going to hell for my contagious cussing."

"There is no hell," Rana snapped, twisting the key to start the truck, "unless you count being married to a frig-gin' magic-maker for forty years."

Chapter Seven

Titus couldn't remember the last time he'd spent a more enjoyable afternoon, although some of that may have had to do with the fact that he couldn't remember the last time he had seen his wife so flustered. In truth, she reminded him of a beautiful young maiden he'd known long ago who had found herself the sole focus of a man determined to make her his queen. At present, however, he was more interested in wooing the even more beautiful woman back into his bed.

Rana had left it to Peg to carry most of the day's conversations, although that hadn't appeared to be a problem for Duncan's wife, who had more questions than a three-year-old about the magic in general and how a new god was called forth in particular. Titus had remained vague in his answers, often suggesting she ask her husband, even as he'd worried he might develop a permanent crick in his neck from constantly smiling into the backseat as Peg had excitedly told him about the colonists running around dressed like trees. And the protestors. And the giant *real* tree with a face that had slammed into their truck—the latter relieving Titus of the worry that Rana was responsible for the dented rear fender.

Not really being dressed to appear in public, he'd offered to stay with Murdoc while the women did their shopping, assuring them he was fully prepared to entertain the young highlander when he woke up and help him drown a tree if need be. And if Peg had been excited before, she had become downright exuberant on the return trip when Titus had directed her attention away from the magic by asking what names she and Duncan were considering for their new twin sons.

Confirming their genders had gotten him a grateful smile from Rana.

But despite the pleasantly relaxing afternoon, Titus found himself yawning as he got out of the truck in Rana's driveway. He was surprised he was tired, since he'd taken a nap with Mur after he and the boy had wolfed down a large takeout meal at one of their many errand stops. Not that Rana had ever returned carrying any packages, whereas Peg was in danger of sinking her pontoon boat with all her purchases—including several bags of grain—when she crossed the fiord to go home.

He hadn't been aware the MacKeages owned a veritable zoo of farm animals, which had Titus worried that he *had* been too self-absorbed lately to notice the simple, everyday happenings around him.

"Let me go get my clothes," he said as Peg climbed

behind the wheel of her truck, "and I will follow you to the marina and help transfer your purchases to your boat."

"Oh, thank you," she said, waving away his offer as she reached for her seat belt, "but I have a whole tribe of heathens getting off the bus who can help me." She stopped from closing the door, her eyes lighting with mischief as she shot Rana what appeared to be a conspirator's smile. "I hope our little ride today helped you decide which vehicle you want to drive."

His wife darted a quick glance across the road, and Titus stifled a groan when he saw the tired-looking pickup parked beside the garage.

"Yes, I will definitely consider getting one like yours," Rana said, her own eyes sparkling in the low-hanging sun. "Especially if it's smart enough to lock its own doors."

"Well, if I don't catch you in town before then, I'll see you Wednesday morning when we start fixing up the church basement. Wave good-bye, Charlie," Peg said as she also waved before starting the truck and backing out of the driveway.

"Why does she object to the noble name of Murdoc?" Titus asked as he stood beside Rana, watching the large SUV head out the camp road much faster than it had come in. "Murdoc is Celtic for 'protector of the sea,' which is fitting for Duncan's son."

"I don't believe she objected until all you men started calling the boy 'Mur the Magnificent.' " Rana eyed his car parked in her driveway. "Does your newest toy have an automatic transmission?"

"No, it's a five speed."

She looked up at him, her big brown eyes unreadable.

"Is it very hard to shift through five speeds while paying attention to all the dials as well as the road?"

"It quickly becomes second nature," he said, eyeing the old pickup across the road and disguising a shudder by turning away. "I'll go get my clothes off your beach-front," he added, stifling another yawn as he headed toward the side of the house, only to be surprised when Rana fell into step beside him.

He was even more surprised when her hand slipped into his. "Thank you," she said, giving him a squeeze.

"For what?"

"For many things, not the least of which was your restraint from commenting on my driving. Especially when I stopped a little too quickly backing up to the grain store loading dock and I heard your head bump your headrest."

He gave her hand a return squeeze. "The first time I got behind the wheel of a modern vehicle, I'm afraid I scared several years off Henry's and Sophie's young lives when I drove down to the turnoff to pick them up from the school bus. In fact, they both got out and walked most of the length of the Inglenook road." He gave her a wink. "But then, I hadn't even driven one of the electric carts, but went straight to a vehicle with the power of hundreds of horses." He stopped and turned to face her, lifting her hand to hold it against his chest. "What else do you wish to thank me for?"

She stared at her captured hand. "For rescuing us from the protestors, for entertaining Char—Murdoc all after-noon, for calming Peg's worries about the new god, and . . ." She looked up, gracing him with a beautiful smile. "And for not taking an unguided tour of my home while I was away."

He arched a brow. "What makes you think I didn't let myself in and—"

"Are you two going to spend what's left of the afternoon smiling at each other?"

Titus turned to see Maximilian standing with his hands on his hips next to a small campfire on the beach, Kitalanta standing beside him.

"Or are you going to come tell me all about today's little adventure?"

Titus gave Rana's hand another squeeze, then tucked her arm through his and continued down the lawn. "Did Peg not say she called Maximilian and explained in detail what happened?"

"Yes, but *your* son told her there was nothing he could do about it."

"He damn well could have gone down and calmed your fears."

"I wasn't afraid. Well, not of some silly new tree god." Rana pulled him to a stop. "The protestors did worry me though, because I truly didn't want to run over any of them."

"Why didn't you call me instead of rushing down there alone?" Mac asked as he strode up to them, his glare aimed at Titus.

"Odd that I don't recall," Titus said dryly. "When exactly did I die and leave you in charge of protecting the world? Or is it your belief that I've simply become too feeble of mind to do *my* job?"

Rana stepped away with a laugh, giving her now-scowling son a pat on the arm before continuing down to the beach. "Ah, Kit, how nice to see you again," she said when the wolf ran forward and fell into step beside her.

She gave his broad head a pat. "Is this an impromptu visit, or did your king press you into service guarding my home from that scary new god?"

Titus returned his attention to his son. "Get lost."

"Excuse me?"

"Go back up your mountain. If you couldn't be bothered to make sure your mother and your friend's wife were not in danger this morning, then you have no right to question my not calling you."

"But I did check on them. I only acted unconcerned for Peg's sake, then rushed there the moment I ended the call." His son crossed his arms over his chest, making a point of running his gaze over Titus's borrowed clothes. "In fact, I arrived just in time to see you climbing into the passenger seat of Peg's truck. So," he continued before Titus could say anything, "having *made sure* they were not in danger, I followed the storm."

"And what did you discover?"

Mac suddenly grinned. "It appears the colonists can't form a consensus on what attributes their new deity should embody. The poor entity was half god, half goddess, part tree, and some tender plant." He shrugged. "There was even an unidentifiable animal thrown into the mix."

Titus ran a hand over his face to hide his urge to yawn again, lest his son have him retired and lounging on some beach sipping coconut milk.

"My guess is," Mac continued, "the male colonists are trying to call forth a god as big and strong as an oak, but the women believe the new *goddess* should personify the docile side of nature and have pictured it possessing the essence of flowers." He dropped his arms and shook his head. "The confused wretch was already dying when

I caught up with it. But hearing several of the colonists searching the woods, I put it out of its misery and sent it back from whence it came."

"And just where would that be?"

His son grinned. "Surely you're not too feeble of mind to remember your own origins."

"Go home," Titus repeated as he headed for the beach, "and enjoy the company of your children before they grow too big for *their* britches. Kitalanta, come," he said as he approached the campfire, not having to look back to know Maximilian had silently disappeared. He crouched down and cupped the wolf's head. "You and your pod are relieved of service, warrior, but you have my blessing to spend time as Rana's companion if you wish. Only you must travel to the secluded point of land guarding the fiord whenever you come and go from the sea to feed." He stood, then nudged the wolf with his knee. "Go fill your belly, orca."

Kit glanced toward Rana picking up clothes on the beach, then tore off up the lawn toward the camp road. Titus walked to the campfire their son had built while waiting for them to return just as Rana walked over with her arms full of clothes.

"Thank you," he said, taking them from her. "I think I'll change before I head up the mountain," he added, turning toward the boathouse to hide his smile. His wife was back to being flustered, if he'd read those beautiful brown eyes correctly. He stopped and pulled his jacket from the pile, then turned and spread it on the ground. "We could sit together and enjoy this lovely campfire for a while," he said, gesturing for her to sit on the jacket. He gave her a wink when she eyed him suspiciously. "Since I'm fairly certain watching the sky turn magnificent colors with the sunset is one of life's simple, everyday pleasures."

He strode to the small shed without waiting to see if she would sit, only to sigh when he heard footsteps racing toward the house. He turned upon entering the shed and closed the door on the sight of Rana rushing onto her porch and disappearing through the door—which she apparently hadn't bothered to lock.

He took his time changing, wondering what in Poseidon's name the woman had to be flustered about. It was almost as if she expected him to— Titus stilled with the borrowed shirt halfway off. By the gods, she wanted him. Queen Rana Oceanus, the embodiment of grace and a lady to the core of her being, was lusting after her husband.

Apparently she didn't care to be crawling into an empty bed any more than he did. In fact, she likely hadn't had a good night's sleep since leaving him, considering she always spent several minutes trying to find a comfortable position and never settled down until he bundled her tightly up against him with her nose buried in his chest. And that was why she hadn't dared enjoy the sunset with him; obviously afraid her resolve would weaken and she would ask him to stay for dinner.

And then ask him to spend the night.

Titus grinned the whole time he finished dressing, pleased that Rana was no happier than he was for them to be living apart. And that interesting little piece of knowledge, he decided as he sat on a dusty old trunk and put on his socks and boots, just might be the key that let him back into the castle.

He stilled again, then dropped his head onto his hands with a groan. Sweet Zeus, he was no better than Nicholas for comparing a romantic pursuit to mounting a war campaign. But then he smiled, realizing how successful that approach had proven to be for the mythical warrior, as Julia did appear quite happily captured. As to whether the woman remained happy when she finally realized she was never having a daughter . . . well, only time would tell that tale.

Titus tiredly scrubbed his face, then lowered his hands to his knees and pushed to his feet. He stretched, glad to be back in pants that fit, and snagged the borrowed clothes off the floor and rolled them into a ball. He left the shed, intending to toss the clothes into the sea so Leviathan could deposit them on the beach near the colony's clothesline, only to stop in mid-step—his fatigue vanishing when he spotted Rana sitting on a blanket spread out next to the campfire, pulling what appeared to be food out of a half-crushed cardboard box.

"Did Kit leave?" she asked as he approached. "I brought him a can of tuna."

"He's gone to sea to feed," Titus said, making sure not to let his own lust show as he walked to the edge of the water. Damn, his wife was a fine-looking woman. She'd obviously taken time to run a brush through her hair, she'd exchanged her jacket for a thick pink fleece that nicely matched her blush, and she no longer appeared to be wearing one of those accursed modern brassieres. "I told Kitalanta he's welcome to continue visiting with you," he said as he tossed the clothes into the water before turning to her. "If that is okay with you."

She eyed him suspiciously. "As a companion or a watchdog?"

He walked up to the edge of the blanket and grinned

down at her. "I believe I used the term *companion* when I gave my permission."

She dropped her gaze and patted the blanket beside her. "Come sit down and have some dinner. Well, what will have to pass for dinner, as I still haven't fully stocked my cupboards. That is, what cupboards I can actually open."

"I could open them for you," he offered, sitting down and reclining back on his elbow. "Why would Averill Latimer put puzzle locks on his *interior* doors?"

She took a few more items out of the box. "He only put diabolical locks on the places he wanted to keep Zachary out of," she said, "such as where he kept his liquor." She suddenly frowned. "And also on the entrance to a small chamber under the stairs. Zach has no idea what might be in there."

"I could get you inside that chamber."

"Thank you," she said, pulling a bottle of wine from the box, "but for now I'm enjoying the mystery of not knowing. You can open this for me, though," she said with a cheeky grin, handing him the wine and then standing up.

Titus straightened and also started to stand when he realized she was going to the small woodpile. "I'll feed the fire."

"I'm the hostess and you're my guest." She gave him another cheeky smile. "Not that you're a very good guest, as it appears you didn't bring your hostess a gift."

He began taking the foil off the top of the wine bottle. "So you don't consider that car parked in your driveway an appropriate gift?"

She straightened while holding two pieces of wood. "You purchased that for me?"

"Not quite," he admitted. "I would worry myself sick

knowing you were traveling these roads in something that small. It was my intention for you to drive it when I'm with you, so neither of us will have to worry about your being crushed by a loaded logging truck."

She tossed the wood on the fire. "Thank you—I think." She then stood staring at the clothes being carried away on the outgoing tide. "Titus, did the world get a new god today?"

"It almost did," he said, nodding when she turned to him. "But apparently the good people of the colony haven't decided exactly what they need in a god. Maximilian found their first attempt dying in the forest and helped it back to Providence," he explained as she sat down beside him again. "They'll get it right eventually, although we're likely going to experience more turbulent storms this summer."

"And will this new god be good for mankind?"

He shrugged and leaned over to look in the box for a corkscrew. "It will be what it will be." He looked up, then reached out and cupped her face, placing his thumb over her lips when she tried to speak. "Probably better than anyone, you know it's not our place to judge mankind's desires," he said gently, "or interfere in their actions. As long as the Trees of Life are not threatened, we can only sit back and watch."

"But why here?" she asked when he caressed her cheek with his thumb. "Why does this new god have to come to *this* peaceful corner of the world?"

He dropped his hand to the wine bottle. "Because Maximilian thinned the veil between reality and imagination when he brought the magic here." He shrugged again. "We expected this to happen, so we're not exactly surprised."

"Do you know anything about the new god?"

"Only that I didn't recognize his energy. Did you bring a corkscrew?"

"No."

He arched a brow. "Is that why I've been invited to dinner? Because you had a thirst for wine but no corkscrew?"

"No," she murmured as she tore open a package of crackers with her teeth. "You were invited because I believe *you* are in need of some wine after dealing with Murdoc all afternoon." She set down the opened crackers and picked up a package of cheese. "I will make sure I have Scotch available the next time you come visit. So, do you think I could learn to drive your motorcycle?"

"No," he said, despite knowing his answer might prevent there ever being a next time. "It's not that you *couldn't* learn, but that I probably wouldn't survive teaching you. Have you spoken with Carolina lately?"

"As a matter of fact, *Jane* called me this morning," she said, smiling smugly when she got her expected scowl from him. "Do you know *your* daughter is planning to spend the summer camping out at their building site?"

"Even after she has the baby?" he asked, only to flinch when the cork shot out the end of the wine bottle he realized he was squeezing.

"And before," Rana said. "I don't know if she truly is that naïve or if she's simply determined to drive us both nuts."

"Is *Alec* aware of her intentions?"

Rana shrugged. "Apparently the man is as clueless as our daughter about how much work a newborn is." She suddenly laughed. "Carolina will change her mind the first time she finds herself washing dirty diapers in a pot of water over a campfire."

He poured wine into the paper cup she was holding. "I don't suppose you've talked her into moving up the wedding date to *before* her due date?"

That got him another laugh. "Don't be so old-fashioned," she said, nudging his shoulder with her own. "Carolina won't be the first princess—in modern or ancient times—to walk down the aisle pregnant."

"I haven't attended a wedding with one *waddling* down the aisle," he muttered, guzzling his wine and quickly refilling his cup. "The way my luck has been running lately, *your* daughter is liable to go into labor halfway through the vows."

"Yes, well, about those vows," Rana said, making him still with the cup halfway to his mouth. "I hope you realize they're not exactly going to be . . . traditional."

"Then what exactly are they going to be?"

"I'm not certain. But I hope you're not expecting to hear Carolina promising to *obey* Alec."

He downed the contents of his cup. "Just as long as I don't hear Alec making that promise to her." He wiped his mouth on his sleeve, then reclined back on his elbow again. "Let's talk about something besides you—our daughter. So," he continued, taking the tiny cheese and cracker sandwich she handed him, "have you begun cutting and welding metal into beautiful works of art yet?"

"Zack is coming by after school tomorrow to give me my first lesson." Rana looked at the large whale statue and softly sighed. "I'm not sure where I got the notion that I'm any sort of artist. Or why I chose to work with metal." She gave him an endearingly shy glance, then looked down at the sandwich in her hand. "Watercolors and needle and thread are more feminine mediums."

"But nowhere near as exciting," he said after eating his sandwich in one bite. He began assembling a new one. "And you've already proven yourself in paint and needlework, and are smart enough to take advantage of having a master metal craftsman at your disposal."

"Zack did an amazing job, didn't he?"

"If I didn't know better," Titus said, also looking at the statue, "I might think Leviathan was his model."

Rana's musical laugh shot straight to his groin when the vainglorious old whale under discussion suddenly breached not two hundred yards past the statue, Leviathan's body arching in exact mimic of his metal counterpart before splashing back into the water. Titus downed the last of his wine when he realized that if he didn't leave now he might not leave at all, then stood up and walked around the blanket. He bent to one knee, cupped his wife's face in both hands, and smiled into her big brown eyes. "Thank you for the lovely afternoon," he whispered just before kissing her, being careful not to reveal how much he missed her.

Her response was immediate and far more encouraging than he expected, making Titus realize he hadn't thought beyond tasting her sweetness again—although he did wonder if he might be better served to give her a taste of her own medicine and be the one running away. He reluctantly broke the kiss, then pressed a finger to her lips to keep her from speaking. "I wish you sweet dreams tonight, wife."

He grabbed his jacket off the ground and stood, then headed up the lawn at a brisk pace, breaking into a broad grin when he heard a distinctly feminine voice mutter a very un-queenly curse.

Chapter Eight

Looking forward to a breakfast of more than just toast and tea before spending the day figuring out how to transform the church's basement into a women's clinic, Rana entered the Drunken Moose to find it was standing room only and that Vanetta was two waitresses short. Unable to simply watch her friend and one harried waitress struggle to keep up, she shed her long winter coat and donned an apron, grabbed a pad and pencil, and strode into the chaos.

Looking up from clearing dishes off a table half an hour and a few wrong orders later to see it was still standing room only, Rana was surprised at how much she was enjoying herself—likely because she couldn't remember the last time she'd felt so *useful*. Oh, she helped Titus when he needed feminine input on whatever project or disaster he happened to be working on, but serving mankind from a distance wasn't nearly as exhilarating as rolling up her sleeves and getting physically involved. Nor was it as lucrative, Rana realized, staring down at the five-dollar bill in her hand.

"I know you know what a tip is," Vanetta said, balancing a tray of dirty dishes on her shoulder as she stopped next to the table, "because you're always generous with my girls when you come in."

Rana leaned closer. "But I can't take money from these hardworking people," she said, trying to stuff the bill in Vanetta's apron pocket.

The restaurateur stepped away with a laugh. "You keep giving the customers that winning smile, and maybe you'll earn enough tips to pay for the massage you're going to need about an hour from now."

Rana stuffed the money in her own apron pocket with a sigh of defeat, gave the table a good scrubbing, and set out fresh utensils and napkins just as four of the waiting patrons rushed over and sat down.

"No need for menus, darlin'," one of the men said. "Coffee for everyone and I'll have a number five."

Rana plucked her pencil out of her hair, flipped the pad to a blank page and drew a square on it, then wrote the number five on the right side of the square. She looked at the man sitting to his right. "And you?" she asked, her pencil posed to write as she gave him a winning smile.

"I'll have a number two, but leave off the ham and double up the bacon."

She wrote the number two on the top side of the square, made a note next to it about the meat, then looked at the gentleman on his right. "And you, sir?"

The man seated beside her suddenly snorted. "Sir?" he repeated, leaning back on the rear legs of his chair and grinning up at her. "You gotta be new here, 'cause everyone knows the only thing Cecil ever hears calling him *sir* is the handle end of a shovel. You can give me a number six." He gave her a wink and reached over and patted her backside, catching Rana so off guard that she froze. "And then you can give me your phone number, Brown Eyes, and I'll give you a—"

Whatever the lech was about to offer changed to a shout of surprise when his chair suddenly skidded out from under him, making Rana scramble away from his windmilling arms as he landed on the floor hard enough to shake the building. "And you, sir?" she asked Cecil again, lowering her voice in the sudden silence. Well, it was silent but for the curses coming from the man standing up and righting his chair.

"I'll have a number two," Cecil said, his grin broader than his puffed-out chest.

Rana nodded, writing both breakfast numbers on the pad as she headed behind the counter. She rewrote the orders on a sales slip and handed it to the cook's helper, then started to reach for the coffeepot, only to be stopped by a hand on her arm. "Well played," Vanetta said, a gleam in her eyes as she nodded toward the table Rana had just left. "I don't suppose I could interest you in a job?" She leaned closer, that gleam intensifying. "If not as a waitress, I could use a bouncer at the Bottoms Up."

Rana blinked in surprise. "I didn't kick his chair out from under him."

"Yeah, okay," Vanetta drawled. She nodded toward

the kitchen just as the cook slid several plates teeming with food onto the serving shelf. "I have to go next door and take the book club's orders, so could you run those to the table in the corner for me?" Her gleam returned. "Try not to knock any of those men on their butts, okay? They're really big tippers," she said as she rushed off, only to stop and turn back. "Oh, if any more people come in holding Nooks or Kindles, send them over to the Bottoms Up."

"Nooks or Kindles?"

"Digital book readers," Vanetta explained, only to laugh at Rana's quizzical look. "When I noticed women standing on the town dock day after day, even when it was below freezing, I finally went out and asked what they were doing. And when they told me they have to drive into town to get a reliable cell tower signal to download books and magazines, I installed Wi-Fi in the restaurant and bar, started a book club, and offered a group discount on breakfast if they meet here Wednesday mornings." She started backing away. "We're up to sixteen men and women in only two months, with more joining every week as word spreads."

Rana frowned at the astute entrepreneur rushing off to tend to her latest community service, then grabbed a tray from under the counter and began loading it with the waiting food. Spellbound had monthly visits from a traveling bookmobile, and she knew Ezra sold a small assortment of magazines at the Trading Post, but now that she thought about it, she hadn't seen a bookstore in either Spellbound Falls or Turtleback Station. So that meant if anyone living in the wilderness wanted to read, they had to ask the bookmobile to bring them specific titles, make the three-hour drive to Bangor, or download digital books over the Internet and cell phone towers.

Seeing there were more plates than she could safely carry in one load, Rana stopped at three and a couple of side dishes, then headed around the counter. Maybe she should suggest the grange ladies raise funds for a library instead of a museum this summer or find some way to combine the two.

Rana stopped beside the hall leading to the restrooms, realizing why Vanetta had gotten a gleam in her eye when she'd told her not to knock any of the big-tipping men on their backsides. She took a fortifying breath, plastered a winning smile on her face, and brought her husband and son, Nicholas, Duncan, and Niall MacKeage their breakfasts. None of whom appeared surprised to see her wearing an apron and carrying a tray of food, which meant they had been watching her running around like a harried woman for the past half hour. Which also explained someone's chair mysteriously—or rather, magically—being kicked out from under him.

Niall immediately stood up when he saw her approaching. "Your high— Mrs. Oceanus," he said as he looked around to see if anyone had heard him. He took the tray from her, clearly uncomfortable to have her serving him. "This is too heavy for ye. Here, let me go get the rest of the food."

Rana had to forcibly pull him to a stop. "Are you trying to get me fired?" she said, glancing over her shoulder as if looking for Vanetta and surprising Niall enough that it took very little effort to push him down in his chair. "I've already messed up two orders, and my boss thinks *I'm* the one who kicked that chair out from under that poor man," she continued, darting Titus a glare for good measure. "Now I'll probably get stiffed on my tip, and I'm trying to save up to buy a motorcycle." But upon seeing the highlander's stricken expression change to horror when she mentioned the motorcycle, Rana laughed and patted his shoulder. "I'm teasing, Niall. I'm helping Vanetta this morning because two of her waitresses called in sick." She began handing out plates, not really caring which of the grinning fools got which breakfast. "And I've already purchased a vehicle. It might not be pretty, but I was told it has a solid frame."

"Does that mean you don't want the electric cart we brought you?" Nicholas asked as he swapped plates with Duncan.

Rana held the tray to her chest, moving her gaze to Maximilian, then to Titus, then back to Nicholas. "Why would you bring me a cart? I can't drive it on public roads."

"It was Peg's suggestion," Duncan said, drawing her attention. "She thought you could use it on the camp road to come to town."

"But it's only a two-mile walk."

"It will seem like six if you're carrying groceries," Nicholas said, "or it's raining." One side of his mouth lifted in a grin. "It's already parked behind the church."

"Hey, brown eyes! How's that coffee coming?"

Niall stood up again, and Rana stepped into his path when he started toward her backside-patting patron, only to gasp when she heard a shout and turned in time to see the falling man's windmilling arms catch the tray of the waitress scrambling out of his way, which brought the entire load of dirty dishes down on top of him.

"There goes my motorcycle," she said, darting a glare over her shoulder at her innocently grinning husband as she headed back into the chaos.

"So, Niall," Titus said when he realized the highlander was thinking of helping Rana's obnoxious customer leave *without* opening the door first, "how has the twenty-first century been treating you?"

The twelfth-century warrior turned back to the table and sat down. "I can't complain," he said with a shrug. "Although I could do with fewer rules. Society has come up with a bloody lot of laws in nine hundred years."

"It's going to be your job to *enforce* those laws," Duncan growled, driving his fork into his plate of food, "not bend them to suit *your* sense of right and wrong."

Niall returned Duncan's glare. "You expect me to arrest a man simply for asking a bonnie lass to have dinner with him?"

"You will if he's thirty and she's *sixteen*."

Niall looked at Titus. "Another thing I find confounding in this century is how young men and women are treated like children long into their teens, their parents coddling them and making excuses for why they're roaming the streets at all hours of the day and night instead of working. Just last week I stopped to help a woman I saw dragging large bins of trash out to the road, only to discover she had a teenage son sitting in the car waiting to be driven to school."

"Blame the mother," Mac interjected. "Children are what they've been taught."

"I was tempted to teach that particular boy a lesson on respecting his mum."

"Thank you," Titus said when Vanetta brought their two missing breakfasts.

Only instead of leaving, the restaurant owner eyed Niall, then suddenly grabbed a chair from a nearby table, sat down with them, and looked at Duncan. "Peg mentioned you were bringing back one of your cousins from Pine Creek to be our chief of police. Would that be you?" she asked, looking at Niall and then thrusting out her hand when he nodded. "Vanetta Quintana—I mean Thurber," she corrected with a laugh. "I'm still getting used to being married."

"Niall MacKeage," the highlander said, shaking her hand.

"So, Niall, where do you plan to live?" She looked at Duncan again. "Because if he stays with you across the fiord, it'll take him just as long to respond to a call as it does the sheriff. And finding a rental anywhere near town is all but impossible."

Duncan leaned back and folded his arms over his chest. "Are ye wanting to rent him a room upstairs, Netta, to get yourself a little added security for your bar and restaurant?"

Vanetta straightened in surprise. "Hey, I like that idea. Maybe I will remodel the upstairs for one of our new deputies." She shook her head. "But that's not what I had in mind for Niall here," she said, giving him a warm smile before looking at Duncan again. "I don't know if Peg told you, but I've donated my house for the women's crisis shelter. It's less than a mile down the road Rana lives on, and there happens to be a bunkhouse on the property that could easily be turned into an apartment for our new chief of police."

Titus filled his mouth with a forkful of egg to hide his grin. He'd thought Olivia's father, Sam Waters, had been an idiot to let Vanetta get away, and here was another example of why. The sharp restaurant and bar owner definitely wanted a little extra security, but for the women's shelter rather than her businesses.

"Talk is you were planning to put an apartment over the police station," Vanetta continued before Duncan could respond. "Only now the councilmen have decided we need a new municipal building to house a full-time fire station as well as the town offices and police station. But at the speed they operate, it'll take them a month of Sundays just to buy that land beside the post office they've been eyeing, and nearly a year to get the place built." She stood up, pushed her chair back to the nearby table, and looked at Niall. "Not only would you be living right on the shore of Bottomless if you take my offer, you'd also be within rock-throwing distance of a house full of women who probably bake better pies than I do. I bet they wouldn't mind earning a few bucks taking in laundry and doing some housekeeping, either." She glanced over her shoulder at the sound of a ruckus in the kitchen, then looked at Duncan again. "Will you think about it?"

Duncan nodded. "Is the bunkhouse unlocked, so we can go take a look?"

"Yes. Everest should be there moving the last of my stuff," she said as she started backing away. "And I already told him you'd be stopping by today," she added, shooting a smug smile over her shoulder as she rushed off.

"What is a women's crisis shelter?" Niall asked.

"It's a safe house for women who have left their abusive husbands or boyfriends," Duncan explained.

"It's settled then," Niall quietly growled, stabbing his omelet. "I'll take the rental."

And that, Titus decided with a smug smile of his own, was exactly why he'd invited the powerful warrior to this century eighteen months ago.

"What happened to your hair?" Peg asked when Rana walked in the church basement and took off her coat. "Some of the ends look frizzy, like they're burned."

Rana reached up and pulled the tortoiseshell clip from the remains of her bun, then blindly started arranging her hair into a twist while making sure to fold under the singed ends. "I had my first metalwork lesson yesterday," she murmured around the clip in her mouth. She clamped the clip over a new bun that she hoped looked better than it felt, then tugged down her fleece. "They apparently call it a cutting *torch* for a reason. And if you think my hair looks bad, you should see what's left of my jacket."

"But Zachary Latimer knows better than to let you near welding equipment wearing anything flammable," Peg said. "Surely there was some of Pops' old gear hanging around that you could have put on."

Rana smoothed down her fleece when she felt her cheeks heating up. "It appears Averill Latimer was a small, wiry man, and his welding jacket wouldn't button across my bosom. I assured Zack that my jacket was cotton, but apparently the waterproof coating is highly flammable." She looked up with a sheepish shrug. "We didn't immediately notice when some sparks caught my sleeve on fire, as we were both wearing protective masks with very dark glass. Zack threw a bucket of muddy water on me, then spent the next ten minutes apologizing as he made me a list of protective gear, which he said I'll have to purchase before he'll give me another lesson."

Peg's laughing gaze dropped to Rana's size *D* bosom, then lifted to her hair again. "I could trim the singed ends if you want, or drive you up to Nova Mare to the resort salon."

"She might as well get it all chopped off," Maude said as she walked over, a distinct sparkle in her eyes, "if she's going to insist on playing with torches."

"One of the items on Zack's list was a welder's cap," Rana explained as she protectively touched her hair. "And a leather coat, gauntleted leather gloves, chaps, and . . . It's a very long list."

Maude tapped the notebook she was holding tucked against her size *B* bosom. "I bet it's not nearly as long as my list." She glanced around the drab basement, then blew out a sigh. "I hope you thought to grab a satchel of money when you ran away from home. I want to start seeing women the moment Roger arrives, which gives us one week to have this place turned into a clinic."

"You're not even going to give the man a couple of days to settle in?" Peg asked.

Maude smiled tightly. "Since I am now officially licensed to practice midwifery in the state of Maine, it appears I can't even talk to patients unless we have a doctor in residence." She looked at Rana. "I've already been approached by several women who heard we're opening a birthing clinic, and I've told them to be here bright and early *one week* from tomorrow."

"Did Olivia deliver on her promise to find you some administrative help?"

Maude's smile turned genuine. "Your daughter-in-law said, and I quote, 'You owe me big-time for this,' because she offered us Inglenook's activities director. And if my interview yesterday was any indication, what Gloria Smith lacks in medical knowledge she makes up for in enthusiasm and organizational skills." Maude shook her head. "I felt comfortable going to Inglenook to meet Gloria because the resort hasn't opened yet, but I nearly turned around and walked out when I saw the activities center she'd created and the fully stocked equipment room. Everything was so beautiful," Maude said in a reverent whisper, "that I wanted to sign up as a guest."

"I went to high school with Gloria," Peg interjected, "and she was class president our last three years. Everyone voted for her because after our freshman class trip to a friggin' *paper mill*, Gloria talked Principal Halley into letting us go to fun places, like down to Bangor to attend the symphony and to TarStone Mountain Ski Resort our senior year." Peg gave Maude a quizzical look. "So how'd you get Gloria to give up what had to be her dream job to come work at our little clinic?"

"Olivia had already asked Gloria if she might be interested, and promised that we'd match her salary and benefits. But I suspect what sealed the deal is that Miss Smith has a thing for doctors." Maude's eyes took on a sparkle again. "Especially if he happens to be handsome and is willing to live in the middle of nowhere."

"She's got a thing for a doctor she hasn't even met yet?" Peg said. "Heck, for all she knows, the guy could look like a troll."

"Well," Maude murmured, brushing something off her notebook, "since Olivia had mentioned that Gloria was single, I might have had a picture of Roger mixed in with my interview questions, which I may have accidently dropped in Gloria's office."

Peg turned widened eyes on Rana. "I want to amend what I said the other day," she whispered, giving a barely perceptible nod in Maude's direction. "She's *a lot* scary."

"And I'll stand by what I said," Rana said, giving Peg a wink. "So where is our esteemed new clinic director?" she asked Maude.

"Gloria is handing over the reins of the activities center to her newly promoted assistant today. She promised to be here bright and early tomorrow with her sleeves rolled up and a long list of medical suppliers."

Rana nodded. "Good. Have her order whatever equipment and supplies you need, tell her to hire some painters and carpenters—or steal them from Nova Mare if she can't find any—and I will go home and search the boxes I haven't unpacked until I find that satchel of money."

"I'm late," Olivia called out as she rushed through the door while juggling a bulging tote, an equally heavy purse, and her sobbing daughter. She came to a stop, looked at Peg, then looked around the basement before looking at Peg again. "Where's Charlie?"

"Mom and Aunt Bea took him for the day."

"Seriously?" Olivia said on a groan, dropping her tote and purse on the floor and bouncing her daughter in her arms. "I was hoping he'd be here to play with Ella."

She kicked the tote with her foot. "I brought toys and snacks."

"What happened to your small army of babysitters?" Peg asked.

Olivia rubbed her sniffling daughter's back. "They're quitting faster than Lucy can replace them, because," she said in a heated whisper, "according to Lucy, everyone is suddenly afraid Ella will go missing on their watch."

"Oh, come on," Peg scoffed. "She's *three*. How fast can the kid run?"

Olivia shook her head. "I don't know how she's doing it, but two days in a row she's somehow managed to slip into the secret tunnels. Yesterday when the babysitter couldn't find her and called Lucy in a panic, and Lucy ran to me in a panic, I ended up having to send Nicholas after her. And when he finally caught up with the little imp, she was almost down to the fiord." Olivia looked at Rana, her pale complexion accenting the fear in her eyes. "Do you think . . . did Mac and Carolina show signs of . . ." She protectively pressed her daughter to her shoulder, holding her hand over Ella's exposed ear. "Please tell me she can't work the magic already."

"Not in any meaningful or dangerous way," Rana said with a laugh, stepping forward and taking Ella, who immediately buried her sniveling nose in Rana's neck. "But she likely can sense her father's energy glowing in the tunnels and simply went searching for him."

"Ohmigod," Peg said behind her raised hands. "Is Charlie going to be able to work the magic?"

"I have no idea how it manifests in the MacKeages," Rana said. "Ladies," she continued brightly, giving them what she hoped was a reassuring smile, "you're both experienced mothers whose babies will get into *typical* childhood trouble."

"But Winter and Matt Gregor's daughter started traveling through time at *six months old*," Peg said, now clutching her throat. "And Duncan told me their grandson, Talking Tom, visited them as an old man *before he was even born*."

"Fiona is the child of two very powerful drùidhs, Peg." Rana smiled at Olivia to include her. "Like me, you are both mortal women who happen to be married to magic-makers, so your children won't develop any real power until they reach puberty."

"But that's even worse," Peg said on a gasp. "Raging hormones *and* the magic!"

"Then I suggest when they hit their teens that you hand them to their fathers to finish raising," Rana said as she transferred Ella to Maude. She looked at Olivia while she put on her coat. "I'm not afraid of losing the cherub, so I can watch her today. The men brought me one of your resort carts, so we won't have to walk home. Thank you for that idea, Peg." She then turned her smile on her skeptical-looking daughter-in-law. "After Ella and I pick up a few things at the Trading Post, we'll go home and bake cookies."

"Are you sure, Mom? She's starting to get really sneaky."

"I can't tell you how glad I am to hear that, because she's going to have to be very sneaky to hold her own against her father and grandfather." Rana slipped her purse onto her shoulder then took Ella again. "You want to come home with Grammy, little miss? Kitty will be there for you to torment."

"Go Grammy's," Ella chortled as she clapped her hands, whatever had caused her tears apparently forgotten. "Hug Kitty!"

"Wait," Olivia said when Rana headed for the door. "Don't you want the toys?"

"What little girl needs toys," Rana said without bothering to stop, "when she has a powerful sea wolf to play with? We'll be fine, so don't rush through your day."

"Rana," Maude said, following her into the parking lot.

"What's up?"

"I've been trying to decide if you thought I wouldn't notice your little weight gain, or if *you* haven't noticed it," the midwife said dryly, actually giving Rana her disarming smile. "Or if you're simply refusing to acknowledge it," she said, her smile disappearing when she realized it wasn't being returned. She touched Rana's arm. "Did you honestly believe you could hide this from me, considering I've been tending to your health since Carolina was born?" She darted a worried glance at Ella, then lowered her voice even more. "We need to discuss this, if not as healer to patient, then as friends."

"We will, but not until we absolutely have to." Rana turned so Ella was no longer between them and lowered her voice. "My concern right now is that Titus not know."

"You think you can keep this from your husband?"

"Your word of honor, Maude, that he won't hear it from you. I will tell him when I am ready."

"But in the meantime," Maude said, nodding agreement but not conceding, "you mustn't shut *me* out."

"Grammy, I wish go see Kitty now," Ella said, clasping Rana's face to look her in the eyes. "I'm anxious to torment the orca."

Maude gasped in surprise. "She knows who Kitalanta is?" Her eyes narrowed. "And why is she suddenly talking like a much older child?"

Rana gave Ella a bounce, answering Maude by addressing her granddaughter. "Because you've figured out that talking like a ten-year-old scares your mother, haven't you, baby?"

Her large green eyes solemn, Ella nodded. "It scares the bejeezus out of Mum."

Rana leaned her forehead against Ella's with a sigh. "Being smart doesn't give you license to be crass, Princess."

"Rana, you have to warn Olivia," Maude whispered. "The woman needs to know her daughter will mature faster than other children." She suddenly snorted. "Not that anyone told *me* what I was getting into when I adopted Nicholas."

"Well, Olivia's not going to hear it from me," Rana shot back, "because I refuse to be one of those meddling mothers-in-law who tell their children how to raise *their* children. It's Maximilian's place to tell Olivia."

"If I remember correctly," Maude countered, "your mother and father weren't so circumspect about how you dealt with *their* grandchildren."

That made Rana smile. "They never said another word after Maximilian sank the ship they were on when he conjured up a storm trying to hurry their journey to Atlantis. And if *I* remember correctly, Nicholas was his partner in crime."

"That boy scared the bejeezus out of Mathew and me."

"Mrs. Maude," Ella said, a distinct Oceanus twinkle in her eyes. "Being crass is unbecoming."

"I give up," Maude said with a laugh, heading toward the church—only to stop with her hand on the knob. "Rana," she said, utterly serious. "We'll talk soon?"

"Soon," Rana agreed with a nod. She set Ella down and grasped her hand. "Come on, little miss smarty-pants, let's go see if your great-grampy Ezra has the ingredients for gingerbread cookies. And after you and I take a nice long nap, I have a cupboard you can open for me."

Chapter Nine

Rana sat in the old wooden love seat above her beach, watching Kitty wrestle a large piece of driftwood out of the brisk surf, and thought about how *not well* the second week of her campaign to misdirect her husband's attention had gone. She tugged her hat lower over her ears, pulled up her collar against the April breeze, and burrowed her hands into the pockets of her new jacket.

She'd completely misjudged Titus's reaction to her leaving, having expected him to become more stubborn and self-contained, or even resort to playing the victim of a wife who had obviously lost her mind in hopes of rallying family and friends to his side. But instead of openly sparring with her as she had hoped, Titus had dusted off his youthful charm and set out on a not-so-subtle campaign to win her back. Hence the realization that not only had she misjudged him, she had also underestimated her own ability to battle a man notoriously known for using any and all means at his disposal—be they fair or foul or friggin' magical—to ensure he came away the victor.

Rana slid her gaze to the sleek racing sloop bobbing on its mooring and blew out a sigh, knowing now that she should have recognized its appearance four days ago to be a change in tactics. No longer dropping in unannounced, Titus had come up with . . . other ways to keep himself foremost in her mind, such as the shiny new red SUV—with self-locking doors—she'd found parked in her driveway three mornings ago, and the utterly feminine mask she *hadn't* purchased mysteriously appearing in the box of welding apparel she and Peg had driven all the way to Bangor to get. But it hadn't been until this morning, when she'd walked downstairs and spotted Averill Latimer's huge old Christmas cactus in full bloom that she'd sat down on the bottom step, buried her face in her hands, and burst into tears.

The dirty-fighting rogue; even though he couldn't stop himself from trying to impress her with grand gestures—such as a boat, a truck, and a hot pink welding mask—Titus had reverted to a tactic he'd employed during their courtship, when he'd discovered that whimsical little miracles were the surest route to her heart.

Forget holding him at bay a few more months; how in Hades was she going to survive even a few more nights of not falling asleep in his big strong arms and waking up to his tender kisses every morning. Yes, the blackguard knew her well, and had begun calling her each evening to see how her metal-sculpting lesson had gone that day, telling her interesting resort gossip and funny grandchild anecdotes, and always ending their conversation by wishing her sweet dreams.

Although he still hadn't asked her out on a date, thank the gods.

Nor had he refrained from mentioning her glowing beauty when he happened to accidently run into her in town—to which she always refrained from asking if the two more pounds she'd gained might have anything to do with that glow. She'd actually had to buy new bras and slacks when she'd been in Bangor—Peg politely not noticing the pants had elastic waists.

"Permission to come ashore, Grandmother!"

"Permission granted, Master Henry!" Rana shouted back, standing up with a laugh as her grandson positioned his kayak to ride a building swell onto the beach. She quickly sobered, however, when she realized the wave was actually Leviathan. But recalling an eerily similar scene some thirty years ago, Rana decided not to shout a warning, curious to see if Henry was indeed his father's son.

Kitalanta, however, wasn't about to let the mischievous old whale ambush their young prince, and splashed into the surf with a threatening growl.

Frowning at the wolf racing toward him, her grandson yelped a very adult curse when he suddenly shot forward, the impact lifting the nose of the kayak out of the water before it crashed into a second frothing wave created by Leviathan's slapping tail.

Rana couldn't have been more proud when Henry burst into exhilarated laughter and used the wave to his advantage by surfing it to shore. He climbed out of the kayak as soon as it scraped bottom, speared the paddle onto the beach, then turned and stood knee-deep in the frigid water with his hands on his hips facing the sea. "You try that again, you lumbering behemoth," he shouted at the bump of gray floating next to the racing sloop, "and you best start sleeping with both eyes open!" He turned and gave Kitalanta a pat on the head when the wolf ran up and started nosing him. "How noble of *you* to warn me, Kit," he said, shooting Rana an imperially arched brow before dragging the heavy kayak across the beach and dropping it above the high tide mark.

"What, and ruin your chance to impress me?" Rana said, throwing her arms around him the moment he straightened. "So, to what do I owe this surprise visit?" She squeezed him tightly. "Not that I'm complaining."

"Can't a kid paddle over to see his gram?" he said as he hugged her back. He stepped away, his smile similar to those she'd seen on Maximilian more times than she cared to recall. "Since you can't seem to come up the mountain to see me."

Rana dismissed his not-so-subtle scolding by sliding her arm through his and starting toward the house. "You want some hot cocoa and gingerbread cookies?"

"Not if the cherub helped bake them." He redirected her back to the wooden love seat, sat her down, then dropped down beside her. "So, Gram, how about we climb in that fancy new truck of yours, you impress me by driving up the mountain, and the two of us have dinner at Aeolus's Whisper?"

Okay, maybe Olivia *shouldn't* let Maximilian finish raising Henry, seeing how the boy was already too much like his father. "Or," she drawled, "how about you say what you came here to say while I cook us dinner in my crooked hovel?"

His deep green eyes narrowed suspiciously—his expression once again eerily familiar—before he looked out at Bottomless. "I'm here to ask you to come home and save Granddad from the women," he said quietly, still staring at the water.

"What women?"

"Any number of single women in town who've heard you left him." He looked over with a frown. "Ms. Maher in particular."

"Missy?" Rana said in surprise, even as she shook her head. "I'm not certain Missy likes . . ." She in turn narrowed her eyes at him. "If this is an attempt to get me to move back," she went on when he tried to speak, "it's a very lame one." She nudged his shoulder. "You should have asked me to save *you* from the ladies."

That got her the scowl she was looking for. "It's not a complete fabrication," he said, his chin taking on a stubborn tilt as he dug his cell phone from his pocket. "I have proof." He tapped the phone's screen, then shielded it from the sun as he held it toward her. "See, this is the text Granddad sent me two days ago. It says," he went on when she squinted at the screen, " 'come save me.' " He lowered the phone to his lap, giving another scowl when he caught her fighting a smile. "I found him in the barn trying to politely extricate himself from one of the resort's female guests."

Rana could no longer contain her laughter. "Henry, Henry, Henry," she said, shaking her head. "Your grandfather has been saving *himself* from unwanted female attention for several millennia."

"On my honor, Gram, he required my assistance. He was in the barn brushing Phantom because Nicholas is away, and the lady trapped him in the stall." Henry gave her a sidelong glance—to see if she wasn't at least a little outraged, Rana assumed. "The woman wanted him to take her riding on the fiord trail to see the spectacular views she'd heard about. But she claimed she was afraid to ride her own horse, and asked if she couldn't ride with him. That's when he hid behind Phantom and texted me."

"Oh, the poor man," she murmured, brushing something off her knee. "That should teach him to be tall and handsome and rich. Wait," she said, her amusement vanishing when she realized what Henry had said. "What do you mean Nicholas is away? Is he gone on a mission?"

"Now, Gram, you know no one ever tells me anything because I'm just a kid."

"Then what have you heard *eavesdropping*?"

And there was that imperial raised eyebrow again, accompanied by one side of his mouth lifting. "I may have *accidently* overheard Dad and Granddad and Nicholas discussing the new god trying to come here, and Nicholas muttering something about it better not be a goddess shortly before he left."

"But he didn't take Phantom? What about Micah or Dante?"

"Dante's gone missing, too. But not hearing any sudden claps of thunder, I don't believe they actually *went* anywhere." He leaned closer. "I think they're both still here, but have gone undercover."

Rana looked out at Bottomless, specifically toward the western shoreline, despite the colony being too far away to see.

"They're not in any danger, Gram. It's a simple mission to find out what sort of god the colonists are trying to call forth."

"The mission last November was supposed to be simple," she said, still staring out at the water. "Nicholas barely made it back, and then he was nearly as dead as Sampson." She looked at her grandson and smiled sadly. "I am aware your father has begun letting you participate in some of his and your grandfather's work, which means you know that they only involve Nicholas when a mission is anything *but* simple."

Henry stood up and pulled her up beside him, making Rana wonder if the boy hadn't grown another inch in the last two weeks as she found herself looking him level in the eyes. "You're going to have to drive me home," he said, clasping her hand and starting up the lawn, "as I can no longer feel my feet."

"Is it my fault you got out of the kayak before you reached shore?" She pulled him to a halt and touched his young chest. "I'm not going home, Henry, at least not yet." She gave him a reassuring pat. "But I promise I won't stay away forever."

"Why stay away at all?" he quietly growled. "Why won't you simply *tell* Granddad what's wrong so he can fix it?"

She gave him another pat, this one a bit firmer. "I do not need anyone fixing anything for me, especially not your grandfather. And you, young man, need to learn that women are not helpless and we don't appreciate men—" Rana shut up when she realized the more she said the broader his grin got, and she dropped her head with a sigh. "You are so much like your father."

"Thank you."

She snapped her head up. "That wasn't a compliment."

He took hold of her hand and started up the lawn again. "Actually, it's quite safe for you to come to Nova Mare and have dinner with me tonight. Granddad left for Atlantis this morning, so you don't have to worry about bumping into him."

Rana pulled Henry to a stop again. "Did someone contact him? Is everything okay on the island? Is he sailing or did he leave in a hurry?"

"You know, Gram," he said with a chuckle, leading her off again, "I never realized how you always imagine the worst. There's no emergency, and your old relic of a ship is still in its hidey-hole inside Whisper Mountain. Granddad said he was going home to conduct some island business and that he'd be back in a few days." He shot her a wink. "And he asked me to personally keep an eye on you while he was gone."

"Very well," Rana said, picking up their pace. "Prepare for me to impress the both of us, because this will be my first time driving a steep, winding mountain road. Don't worry," she drawled when she felt him take a misstep. "I'm sure Titus gave me a truck with plenty of air bags."

Henry came to a halt at the edge of the house. "Have you driven at all?"

"In general or my new truck in particular?"

"Gram."

"I drove it all the way to Bangor and back the other day. But I did switch places with Peg when we neared Bangor, because I didn't want my first driving lesson involving stoplights to include that much traffic. Do you know that one stoplight near the mall has five lanes going in each direction? Oh, come on, Henry," she said when she couldn't budge him. "You just faced down a forty-ton whale. Surely you can ride up a mountain road with me."

"I was at the helm and I can swim," he shot back. "But I can't *fly*."

"You're immortal."

"But you are not." He shook his head. "And now that I think about it, I don't want you driving back down the mountain alone, especially in the dark."

Bless his young heart; Henry was a few months shy of his eleventh birthday, and he was already an overprotective male. "Then spend the night with me."

"I can't. Duncan is taking Pete and Jacob and me brook fishing tomorrow, so I'm staying at the MacKeages tonight because we're heading out at dawn. Ah, what's that?" he asked, gesturing at the trees beside her driveway.

"It's a turtle," she muttered, trying to lead him toward her truck.

Only instead of cooperating, he gently shrugged free and walked over to the small clump of woods and crouched down.

Rana sighed in defeat and followed. "It's a leatherback."

"No," he said as he touched the metal. "It isn't even close." He looked up with a frown. "This wasn't made by the same artist who sculpted the whale out front, because *that person* obviously knows marine life."

"I'm the artist who made the turtle."

Henry's jaw slackened and he turned away to look at the turtle again, but not quickly enough to hide the two flags of red on his cheeks. "It's beautiful."

She crouched down beside him. "It's the saddest-looking

turtle I've ever seen, and making it was probably the hardest thing I've ever attempted. But Zachary Latimer, the young man who's teaching me how to cut and hammer and weld steel, apparently has the patience of a saint. This was his grandfather's house," she continued, waving at her crooked hovel, "and Averill Latimer was a metalworking genius." She stood up, pulling Henry with her. "I can drive you to the parking lot and you can probably catch one of the resort shuttles up the mountain."

"Or maybe Mum is still at Inglenook," he said, pulling out his cell phone. "I'll see if she can come pick me up."

"No, let me drive you to Inglenook," Rana offered, only to then remain silent while he spoke to Olivia.

"Mum was just leaving, so she'll wait for us at the turnoff," he said, walking around the front of Rana's truck and opening the passenger door. "You left the key in the ignition," he said as Rana climbed in behind the wheel. "Sweet Zeus, you left your purse in here, too," he growled, picking up her small tote off the floor.

Rana grabbed her purse from him and set it on the floor of the backseat. "It's more convenient to keep the key in the truck than having to hunt through my tote for it."

"This isn't Nova Mare, Gram. There's no security down here. Anyone could steal your truck and get the added bonus of a wallet full of cash to pay for their getaway." He pulled the key from the ignition just as she was reaching for it, then fiddled with the key chain. "If you're determined to leave your belongings in here, at least keep the fob in your pocket and lock the doors. And get in the habit of putting the key in this cubby," he went on, tapping one of the cubbyholes in the dash, "so anyone looking through the window won't see it."

Rana sat with her hands folded on her lap as Henry slid the naked key back in the ignition, and wondered when she'd traded places with her grandson. She knew children grew up and started parenting their parents—such as Maximilian giving his father a hard time for racing down to rescue her and Peg last week—but she hadn't expected Henry to start bossing her around at the advanced age of ten.

And really, it wasn't as if she had one foot in the grave already.

A heavy sigh broke the silence. "I'm sorry, Gram. I had no business speaking to you like that."

"I am aware of how hard it is for you, your father and grandfather, and even Nicholas, to see me living down here on my own," she said gently, still looking out the windshield, "where you don't have complete control of my safety." She looked over at him and smiled sadly. "But loving someone who doesn't behave the way you think they should *is* hard." She reached out and rested her hand on his arm. "And loving them anyway is . . . well, if we don't ever leave our comfort zones, Henry, we might as well not even bother getting out of bed in the morning." She looked out the windshield again. "I was fifteen when I married Titus and went from my father's house to my husband's. Can you imagine spending your entire life having someone provide you with shelter, food, money, and safety, and always trying to fulfill your every wish? Do you think that would be wonderful?"

"No. It would become stifling."

She nodded. "I love Titus with all my heart. And he is letting me do this because he loves me with all of *his* big immortal heart. And someday, Henry, you're going to love someone, too; so much that it's going to hurt every time you have to stand aside and watch them leave their comfort zone."

"I already do," he whispered.

"Trust me," she said with a laugh, "it will be a whole different kind of hurt when the person behaving badly is your wife." She fastened her seat belt and started the truck, turned to put her hand on his seat to back up, and shot him a wink. "But just know that I intend to have a long chat with that lucky lady *before* she pledges her troth to you to make sure she understands what loving an Oceanus means."

His eyes widened, even as they took on an Oceanus twinkle. "Is that a promise or a threat?"

"Definitely a threat," she said, checking for traffic before backing into the road, then heading toward town as if she'd been driving all her life. "So just remember that every time you start getting overprotective of me, my chat with your intended will get ten minutes longer."

"Did you have a chat with Mum before she pledged her troth to Dad?"

"Your father got married without telling us. He didn't tell Olivia, either, until after the fact." She shot him a glare. "But I'm a lot older and wiser now, so don't think I won't be watching you more closely."

"Did you even hear the part where I said I loved you?"

"I love you, too."

"Blackmailing me into not being overprotective is a moot point, anyway," he said, sounding way too smug as he gestured at all the pickups parked in Vanetta's driveway as they passed by. "Or it will be when Niall MacKeage gets back from Pine Creek."

Rana frowned out the windshield, utterly confused.

"What's Niall got to do with my blackmailing you? And I thought Duncan hired him over a week ago?"

"He did. But he thought a twelfth-century highlander might need a crash course in modern law enforcement, so he's making Niall ride around with Jack Stone. It's worked out well, actually, because Duncan said it's going to take his crew all this week to remodel Miss Vanetta's bunkhouse into an apartment for Niall."

Rana stopped at the main road and looked over in surprise. "Niall's going to be living at the women's crisis shelter?"

Henry nodded. "Dad said Miss Vanetta approached them at the Drunken Moose and suggested Niall could live in the bunkhouse in exchange for keeping an eye out for angry husbands and boyfriends."

Rana pulled onto the main road toward Inglenook. "Why am I not surprised she came up with that idea? It's brilliant."

"Granddad thought so, too, right before saying that Grampy Sam was an idiot to let her get away."

"Sam's loss was Everest Thurber's gain," Rana said dryly. "You heard Everest and Vanetta got married a couple of weeks ago?"

"I heard. There's Mum," he said, unfastening his seat belt when Rana turned into the Inglenook road.

She stopped the truck, then grabbed Henry's arm when he opened his door. "Wait. I'm still confused. Why is your being overprotective a moot point now?"

He leaned over and gave her a quick kiss on the cheek. "Because you're about to get an equally protective highland warrior for a neighbor," he said, an eerily familiar chuckle trailing behind him as he escaped.

Chapter Ten

Rana sat in her idling truck at the end of her camp road, undecided whether to turn right toward Nova Mare or left toward town. But wanting to think she was smart enough to take her own advice about people needing to venture outside their comfort zones, she absolutely was *not* turning around and going home. Because staring up at the ceiling rafters last night, once again finding it hard to fall asleep without a strong heartbeat in her ear, Rana had realized she hadn't been stretching the truth three days ago when she told Henry she had spent her entire life being taken care of. And this morning she had awakened to the disheartening realization that she was a coward.

All these years of feeling strong and brave and at times even invincible had been nothing but an illusion, a trick she'd played on herself by thinking she was as powerful as her mighty, magical husband. But apparently the best cure for arrogance was a healthy dose of reality, especially when it carried the bitter taste of defeat. Sweet Athena, she couldn't even drive to Turtleback Station for fear of being stopped by that mob of people protesting the colonists. And she *had* been postponing going to Nova Mare; not because she didn't want to run into Titus, but because she was afraid of driving up that steep, winding mountain road.

Even having several strong, independent, twenty-first-century women for role models didn't appear to be enough to bolster her courage. How had Peg, widowed at the tender age of twenty-six, managed to raise four children all by herself? And how had Olivia dared to risk her heart again and fall in love with Maximilian despite knowing *what* he was? And Vanetta, who had suffered at the hands of a violently abusive husband; where had she found the courage to marry again? And Julia had knowingly married an ancient mythical warrior. Even Carolina, born of a time when women expected they would be fed and sheltered and protected, had fought for and was now embracing her independence—having settled for nothing less than falling in love with a man who admired her for it.

Rana looked over at the lupine eyes staring at her from the passenger seat and released a heavy sigh. Forget underestimating her ability to battle Titus; she was having a hard time doing something as simple as taking care of herself. Heck, even Kitalanta's courage to ride in a truck only served as another reminder of her cowardice.

Rana flinched and Kit gave a startled yip when a horn sounded behind them. "I'm sorry," she said into her rear-view mirror, raising her hand to wave at the man in the pickup behind them as she quickly checked for traffic and turned toward town.

"We're going to Turtleback," she told Kit with a decisive nod—aimed more at herself than him. "And if those protestors jump in front of us, you have my permission to growl at them. Zack's not coming this afternoon," she continued conversationally, finding that talking—albeit to a wolf—was calming. "He has to study for an important test, because he said if he doesn't pass chemistry with at least an A, he could lose his slot in the pre-med program he signed up for. I think it's wonderful he's going to train to be a doctor, don't you? Although I believe he's doing it more to please his parents than for himself. Personally, I think Zack would prefer a career in metalwork, but as an artist rather than welding truck frames and logging chains."

Having made it through town without running over any bun-stealing grange ladies, Rana picked up speed. She touched a button on her door handle to lower the passenger window, smiling when her panting passenger immediately stuck his head into the breeze. "There, I bet that feels better. You're so brave, Kitalanta. Not only have you left the safety of the sea to keep me company, you jumped in a vehicle with only a little cajoling and now you're going nearly fifty miles an hour," she said, trying to sound excited. "And if your pod mates don't believe you when you tell them, you just send them to me and I will set them straight."

Rana fell silent when Kit rested his head out the window and closed his eyes against the drool blowing off his lolling tongue. She could do this, she told herself firmly. She would go to the furniture store she had noticed the day she'd driven to Turtleback with Peg and Charlie *and Titus*, and buy something for her new home—even though she wouldn't be living in it three months from now. But maybe the people she sold the house to would appreciate having a couch that didn't bite them on the ass every time they sat down.

Rana stiffened when she rounded a curve and saw several cars in the distance, along with a mob of people gathered in a tight group near the road leading down to the colony. She lowered her speed to thirty, figuring that was slow enough to be safe but too fast for anyone to jump out in front of her. "It's okay, Kit," she said, worried the wolf sensed her tension when he sat up with a whine.

"It's okay," she repeated as she drew nearer, noticing Kit's gaze was locked on the gathering. She frowned, also noticing that none of the protestors were carrying signs or even looking her way, but rather seemed focused on a small, battered-looking car stopped in the colony entrance. "Oh, no!" she cried, slamming on her brakes when she saw the obviously frightened woman struggling to pull her driver's door closed as the mob surrounded her car.

Rana shoved her truck into park and got out. "Come, Kit," she said, breaking into a run when she realized one of the men was trying to drag the woman out of the car. "Get away from her!" she shouted, pushing through the crowd. "Let her go! Now!"

Although their attention had remained focused on the car, it quickly changed when Kit charged past her, his loud, guttural snarls effectively scattering everyone except for the man still tugging on the woman. Rana grabbed his arm and gave him a vicious yank. "Back off," she snapped when he spun toward her.

She didn't know if it was the threat in her voice or his finally noticing Kit that made the man step away, but

Rana immediately moved to stand in the open door with her back to the woman. "Keep your distance or risk getting bitten," she said when Kit moved in front of her, his hackles raised and his lips rolled to expose his teeth.

"You back off, lady. You got no call to come charging in here and threaten to sic your dog on us."

"I have more right than you have to be terrorizing this poor woman."

He pointed at the car. "She belongs to that devil-worshipping cult."

"We're trying to save her," one of the women in the crowd said.

Several people nodded and crowded closer, but immediately scurried back when Kitalanta gave another deep growl.

"That dog bites any of us," a different man said as he pointed at Kit, "and we're pressing charges."

"You'll have to get in line, because I'll already be there pressing charges against *you*. Keep guard, Kitalanta," she said, finally turning to the car, only to ball her hands into fists when she saw the frightened, tear-filled eyes of a young lady barely into her twenties. "You're okay now, honey," Rana said, crouching down to touch her trembling shoulder. "No one is going to hurt you. Do you want me to drive you home?"

"Th-The car stalled," the young woman whispered as she groped for Rana's hand and then held it in a death grip. "Please don't leave me. Can you give me a ride to town?" She dropped her head, her tears spilling onto their clasped hands. "I-I can't go back there."

Rana stood but stayed bent over when the woman's

grip tightened. "I won't leave you, I promise. I'll take you wherever you want to go."

The girl finally released her, but fell back with a gasp when she got caught on the steering wheel as she tried to get out of the car. Barely stifling a gasp of her own when she realized the young woman was pregnant, Rana helped her out and immediately tucked her up against her side. "We're leaving now," she said to the mob, stepping around the door and heading for her truck. "And I suggest you all go home before the sheriff responds to the emergency call I made when I saw what you were doing," she continued while looking straight ahead, knowing Kitalanta had her back. "What's your name, honey?" she asked, giving the girl a squeeze when she felt her trembling.

"M-Macie."

"What a beautiful name. So, Macie," she said casually as she continued to the passenger side of her truck. "Is there someplace in particular you would like me to take you? To your family or maybe a friend?"

"I don't know anyone." Macie hesitated when Rana opened the door, and after a nervous glance at the people silently rushing to their vehicles as Kit watched from the front bumper, she turned her still-frightened, hazel-gold eyes on Rana. "This is only the second time I've left the settlement since I arrived. I don't know anyone."

Rana helped her climb in, then held out her hand. "Yes, you do. You know me. Rana Oceanus."

The girl took her hand with a shy smile. "Macie Atwater."

"Well, Macie Atwater, now that we're friends," Rana said soothingly as she handed Macie her seat belt, "I know exactly where to—"

A blaring horn sounded, and Rana looked up to see a large truck loaded with logs struggling to slow down as it rounded the curve behind them. She closed Macie's door with a muttered curse and rushed around the front of her SUV. "Come on, Kit," she said on her way by, waving at him to jump in through the door she'd left open. She shoved the wolf over the console into the backseat as she scrambled behind the steering wheel, closed her door, then immediately yanked down the shifting lever and kicked her truck into a gallop.

She didn't slow down until she had a safe distance between themselves and the logging truck, then finally fastened her own seat belt and shot Macie a wink. "I forgot I'm not supposed to stop in the middle of the road. So," she went on, watching for a place to turn around, "if you don't know anyone in town, what was your plan?"

Macie took a shuddering breath. "I didn't think beyond getting out of there and making it someplace safe. The settlement members wouldn't dare drag me back in front of townspeople."

Rana glanced over, specifically down at the soft bulge spilling over the seat belt beneath the girl's loose-fitting tunic. "Is there a particular reason you decided to leave today, Macie?" she asked gently. "Is your being pregnant a problem for the col—the settlement members?"

"I kept it hidden as long as I could," Macie whispered, "while I tried to figure out what to do. I didn't know how they'd react, because two other women who got pregnant left with their husbands shortly after everyone found out. And those who already had kids left this past January." She looked out the side window. "But two days ago,

Sebastian—he's the high priest—walked in the women's bathhouse just as I was stepping out of the shower." Rana saw Macie hug herself. "I grabbed a towel, but he dragged me to the main house without even letting me get dressed, then locked me in one of the back rooms."

"You said two days ago. Did you only just escape today?"

Macie nodded. "A new guy joined the settlement earlier this week, and he . . . Men are allowed access to all the buildings, and he snuck me in some clothes the first night, but told me not to put them on or let anyone see them until he came for me. And that I should act submissive to Sebastian until then."

Spotting a dirt road ahead, Rana checked her rearview mirror, then slowed down and pulled into the road, glancing over her shoulder just as the logging truck went zooming past with another blare of his horn. She looked for other traffic, backed into the main road so she was facing Spellbound Falls, then started off again. "But what were you doing out here in the middle of the day?" she continued. "I would have thought the man would help you escape at night, when you had the cover of darkness."

Macie smiled slightly. "He said the guards are more alert at night, and that it would actually be easier if I just walked across the yard during the day like I was supposed to be there and climbed in one of the cars and casually drove away. He came in and unlocked my door just before lunch today and told me to get dressed. He said when I heard a commotion in the dining hall, it was my cue to leave." Her smile disappeared. "I thought I was home free, but those people jumped in front of the car when

I reached the main road, and the engine stalled and I couldn't restart it. Do you know why they were there? I saw them carrying signs that said *devil-worshippers*, and they kept shouting something about cults and . . . and evil," she ended on a whisper, hugging herself.

"They're nothing more than uninformed, overzealous protestors," Rana said with a dismissive wave, deciding to direct the conversation back to Macie's escape. "Where were you planning to go if your car hadn't stalled?"

"The man who helped me said to drive to Spellbound Falls, but to keep going another nine miles until I came to a sign that said Nova Mare. Then I was supposed to drive up that road another mile until I came to the guard booth and ask the guard to contact someone named Julia Salohcin." Rana looked over to see Macie staring down at her hands. "I might have worked up the nerve to steal one of the cars," the girl said, shaking her head, "but there's no way I could drive into some fancy resort." Rana heard her take another shuddering breath. "I guess I'm not as brave as you are."

Rana sputtered on a laugh. "What on earth gave you the idea I'm brave?"

The young woman looked over in surprise. "You pushed right through those people and shouted at them to leave me alone, and you even grabbed one of the men and pulled him away."

"Only because I knew I wasn't in any danger."

"You were outnumbered twenty to one."

"No, *they* were outnumbered twenty to one hundred pounds of lethal wolf," Rana said with another laugh, gesturing at the backseat. "Kitalanta is the brave one in this truck."

Macie's eyes widened as she glanced over her shoulder. "He's a real wolf?"

Rana nodded, leaning closer. "He likes to think he is," she whispered, "and I don't have the heart to tell him differently. So it will be our little secret, okay?"

Macie faced forward. "Where are you taking me?" she asked. "To your house?"

"The gentleman who helped you steal the car and told you to go to Nova Mare; was he unusually tall, with deep blue eyes?" Rana asked instead of answering. "Did he happen to tell you his name?"

"He is tall, but he has green eyes. And when he showed up at the settlement a couple of days ago, he told us his name is Dan." She shrugged. "If he has a last name, I don't know what it is. He may have told Sebastian."

"Was he alone when he arrived?" Rana asked, thinking that Dante had green eyes. "Or did he show up with a friend?"

"No, just him."

Well, Rana supposed that made sense, as the colonists might have recognized Nicholas from town, as he definitely was memorable. And since it usually took a herd of horses to drag Dante off the resort, it also made sense that he was the one Nicholas had recruited to go undercover. And knowing Dante, he wasn't about to sit back and watch a woman being bullied even at the risk of blowing his mission.

"Dan just walked in from the main road a few days ago," Macie continued, "and told Sebastian that he wanted to be part of what we're doing."

"What exactly are you doing?" Rana asked, slowing when they reached town.

"I thought we were trying to save the world. At least, that's why I came here last summer."

"Save the world how?"

"By trying to tap into whatever happened here four years ago and using it to stop wars and starvation and global warming and . . . and stuff like that. It was all over the Internet that an earthquake had turned Bottomless Lake into an inland sea. But when scientists couldn't explain how or even why it had happened, some of the blogs started saying that something supernatural was going on up here."

"Or something *uniquely* natural," Rana offered.

"I suppose it could have been a plain old earthquake," Macie said. "Anyway, I read that a group of people had started a settlement on Bottomless because they believed magic was responsible. The website said they were hoping to tap into what must be *good* energy, since nothing had been damaged in the earthquake, and try to harness it to save the world. And it was wonderful at first, with everyone working together for a common cause. But then it . . . only everything . . ."

"But then what?" Rana gently prodded.

"Everything changed when Sebastian showed up in January and started talking about *gods*." She looked over, her nose scrunching in aversion. "You know, those mythical gods like Zeus and Apollo and Atlas? Sebastian said we needed to be better organized and persuaded everyone to elect him our leader. Or rather," she said dryly, "he had secret meetings with the men and persuaded *them* to elect him. But there were several more men than women living at the settlement, so they carried the vote."

"None of the women voted for Sebastian?" Rana asked softly.

"Most of us didn't trust him." Macie's chin lifted militantly, and Rana was pleased to see that instead of fear, the woman's eyes now held anger. "We were right, too. He made everyone start wearing these ugly 'vestments,' divided us into five 'cells,' and put five hand-chosen men in charge of each one. And then he started the rituals."

Rana didn't have to ask what some of those rituals might involve, since Titus had brought her in to help with the aftermath of his dealings with charismatic, egotistical leaders like Sebastian more times than she cared to recall. Yes, her un-interfering husband was also notoriously known for breaking his own rules. And if history wasn't telling her what this modern-day cult was in all likelihood practicing, seeing her passenger protectively cup her softly rounded belly certainly did.

"Did the women not have any say in these rituals, Macie? Or were you not allowed to leave if you didn't like what was happening?"

"Some of the women left when Sebastian was elected, along with several of the men. Everyone with kids did. I stayed because the guy I'd come to the settlement with promised me everything would be okay." She covered her face with her hands. "Only it wasn't. Sebastian made Johnny one of the five priests, and the power went to his head. And when I got mad and tried to leave, he . . . Johnny got . . ."

"Shh, it's okay," Rana crooned, patting Macie's leg. "It's done, and you'll never have to go back there. Easy now," she rushed on when the girl gasped as Rana turned at the Nova Mare sign. "I'm taking you to the safest place in the world, Macie. My daughter-in-law owns this resort, and Julia Salohcin works and lives here." Rana gave her one last pat, then stopped at the guard house and rolled down her window.

"Mrs. Oceanus," the guard said, doing a terrible job of hiding his joy to see her heading home as he turned and punched some buttons on his computer. "Could you make sure your resort radio is on?"

"I don't think I have one, as this is a new truck."

"I'm pretty sure it had one when your husband drove it down here last week," he said, leaning out his window to look inside her truck. He smiled and pointed at the center of her dash. "It's right there under the navigation screen. Nicholas found a company to build us radios that could be permanently installed in the trucks and limos." He then pointed at a spot in the overhead console. "The microphone is up there. You don't have to touch any buttons if we call you about an accident or emergency on the road; it works just like a cell phone speaker. But if you want to call us, just tap that call button," he said, pointing down at the dash again. "Oh, and these new radios automatically come on when you start the vehicle." He smiled again. "It's just going to take us a while to get out of the habit of asking you if it's on. You're good to go then. Have a nice day, Mrs. Oceanus," he finished, waving her on.

"Wait," Rana said, making him turn back to her. "Can you tell me if I'll meet very much traffic on the drive up?"

He tapped a few keys on his computer and read from the screen. "You should meet a limo in a couple of miles, a delivery truck soon after—assuming the guy didn't stop for a cigarette break at one of the turnoffs—followed closely by a black Lexus sedan. A shuttle bus just left the summit, so if you don't speed," he said with a grin, "you should meet it just before the road starts getting steep."

"Thank you," Rana said with a nod. "Do you know if Julia Salohcin is at the resort, or is she in town with clients?"

"She hasn't come down the mountain on my watch, and I started at six this morning," he said as he checked his computer again. "She passed the summit guardhouse at eight this morning, so you'll probably find her at the event pavilion."

"Could you do me a favor . . . Jason?" Rana asked, reading his name tag, "and call Julia and tell her I'm coming to her office?"

"Sure thing, Mrs. Oceanus," he said, apparently too polite to ask why she wasn't calling Julia herself. He was also circumspect enough not to have reacted when Rana had noticed *he* had noticed the woman beside her was wearing colony attire. "I'll tell Mrs. Salohcin to expect you in about forty-five minutes."

"Make that an hour, as I believe I might stop for a cigarette break," Rana said, laughing at his stunned expression as she drove off.

"I . . . I'm not so sure about this," Macie whispered, looking frightened again as she glanced back at the guardhouse.

"My word of honor, Macie; you won't have to steal a car if you want to leave after meeting Julia and my daughter-in-law, Olivia. One of us will drive you anywhere you want to go, even if that's all the way to Bangor. And Julia's mother-in-law happens to be a midwife, so you might wish to see Maude while you're here, if only to assure yourself that your child is doing well."

"Why are you doing this for me? Why did you charge into a group of twenty people to save a complete stranger, and then bring me home to your family?"

"Would you not do the same for me if our circumstances were reversed?"

"I . . . Yes, of course."

"Yes, of course," Rana repeated with a nod, "because women help women." She leaned closer. "Which, I believe, is what makes us stronger than men."

And that, Rana decided as she fearlessly drove toward Whisper Mountain, would become her mantra: She was brave simply for being a woman.

Chapter Eleven

Titus stopped in midsentence when he realized his son and Nicholas were no longer listening, and turned to see what had caught their attention. "By the gods," he said when he spotted Rana's truck at the summit guardhouse, "it's about time."

"Don't get too excited," Nicholas said with a chuckle. "She's not here for you."

"I was referring to her making the drive up here, since she's had that truck for nearly a week. Is her passenger the woman she rescued from the protestors?"

Nicholas nodded. "I was just about to intervene when I noticed a red SUV approaching. Rana slammed on the brakes the moment she saw what was happening, and ran into the mob shouting for them to back off. She even pulled one of the men off the woman and started giving him hell."

Mac closed his eyes on a groan. "Sweet Zeus."

"Someone," Nicholas drawled, "might want to mention that she's not supposed to park in the middle of the road." He sobered. "I'm just glad Kitalanta was with her, as I'm afraid she would have charged in there even if she'd been alone."

"Of course she would have," Mac said as he glared at Titus. "Because *someone* has spent the last forty years letting her believe she's invincible."

Ignoring his son—which he found himself doing a lot lately—Titus watched his wife get out of her truck and let Kitalanta out before rushing around to the other side. After finally coaxing her obviously hesitant passenger to get out, Rana put her arm around the young woman and headed toward the conference pavilion just as Julia came rushing outside. "You might as well leave Dante in place, since he's already established himself," Titus said to Nicholas. "But I see no need for you to continue shadowing him. Dante can warn us if anything important is about to occur." He grinned, gesturing toward the pavilion. "We seem to have acted in haste, as it appears my wife just brought the inner workings of the colony to us."

"She wouldn't have been able to if Dante hadn't already been there," Nicholas pointed out. "Although I'm more worried about the protestors than I am the colonists. Someone needs to rout those idiots before they go from merely being zealous to dangerous."

"When is Niall returning?" Titus asked.

"Too soon for Duncan's peace of mind," Mac said with a chuckle, "and not soon enough for Jack Stone. Apparently Laird Niall isn't all that enamored with modern law, and suggests that instead of putting people in a comfortable jail cell, Stone should take the bastards on a one-way ride to the end of Pine Lake, claiming a long trek through the wilderness might better serve to help them find the error of their ways."

"Can't say that I disagree with him," Nicholas muttered.

"Niall will be back in a couple of days," Mac added, "with his badge and gun and all his *passionate energy* focused on protecting the fine citizens of Spellbound Falls and Turtleback Station."

"Good," Titus said, starting up the path to his cottage. "Then the protestors can be his problem."

"Are you not going to go see Mother?" Mac asked.

"She knows where I live." Titus stopped and looked back. "I would appreciate it if neither of you mention that Nicholas witnessed her little adventure today."

"Why not?" Mac asked, even as he and Nicholas nodded agreement.

Titus said nothing, merely giving a negligent wave over his shoulder as he started toward his cottage again. But in truth, he was curious to see if his wife might simply forget to mention her recklessness or tell him herself. Either way, he was proud of her for not only rushing to the woman's rescue, but for driving up Whisper Mountain despite her terrible fear of heights. And since one particularly steep section of the winding road was cut into a cliff sheer enough to test the courage of most men, Titus found himself grinning at the prospect that Rana had been too busy being a hero to be afraid.

Actually, Kitalanta was probably the one needing a

stiff drink. He'd have to remember to give the orca another tattoo for his valor.

Titus stepped into his empty cottage with a tired sigh and closed his eyes on the deafening silence. He was long past trying to figure out why Rana had left him and nearing the end of his patience for waiting her out. He was, in fact, considering taking up the MacKeage practice of stealing their women, as the highlanders apparently felt that spiriting them off to an isolated cabin in the woods was a good way to get their undivided attention.

He snorted, remembering how he had wasted two weeks making a complete fool of himself trying to impress the beautiful maiden who had caught his eye that long-ago summer by following her home from the tournament—his large entourage in tow—and showering her with gifts befitting a queen. All to no avail, as each ambassador he sent forth had always returned still in possession of his gifts. It hadn't been until he'd politely ambushed her equally beautiful mother in town that he'd learned his grand gestures were actually repelling Stasia. Instead of being seen as tokens of esteem, the astute woman had boldly explained, her daughter believed that a man of his power and wealth must be touched in the head to be sending a lowly blacksmith's daughter jewels and scented oils and priceless works of art.

He'd gone back to his encampment and disbanded his entourage but for a handful of warriors, shed his tournament finery in favor of plain britches and shirts, turned his horse to pasture, and taken up his pursuit on foot. He hadn't gone so far as to throw the baby out with the bathwater, however, and had kept a few magic tricks tucked up his sleeves.

The fair-haired maiden hadn't immediately recognized him the first time their paths had crossed in town, and he'd been able to get close enough to press a heart-shaped pebble into her delicate hand before she had once again escaped into the crowd. And although Aaron Proust might only have been a lowly blacksmith, that hadn't stopped the well-muscled and fiercely protective father from paying Titus a late-night visit to *respectfully* suggest he get lost.

And he might have started questioning his pursuit, Titus remembered with a chuckle, if he hadn't found himself lingering in the woods outside of Stasia's home the following day when she'd been hanging clothes on the line, and had watched her pull on a leather lacing tied around her neck to see his heart-shaped pebble emerge from her bodice. It had taken him another two weeks of secretly—albeit sometimes magically—presenting her with equally simple tokens of his esteem before he'd been able to have an actual conversation with her, and another week of cajoling to persuade her to meet him in a nearby meadow that he might take her horseback riding.

His beautiful maiden had shown up wearing britches.

He had shown up leading *one* horse and wearing his heart on his sleeve.

Aaron Proust had shown up not ten minutes later, carrying a double-edged felling axe and wearing a scowl fierce enough to turn back an army.

But it had been the arrival of Mrs. Proust—carrying a picnic basket and wearing a smile that apparently had the power to bring the blacksmith to his knees—that should have warned Titus who would be wearing the britches in his own marriage once he did indeed win the beautiful maiden's love.

He'd do it all again in a heartbeat: make a complete fool of himself, give up his wealth and power and even his kingdom, and drop to his knees in defeat just to hear his wife sigh his name when he turned to her in bed.

"Grampy!" came a shout as tiny footsteps scrambled onto the porch, followed by urgent knocking on the cottage door. "Grampy! Hurry! You're going to miss her!"

Titus opened the door in time to catch the explosion of blonde curls and flailing arms as Ella hurled herself at him. "Whoa, little cherub," he said with a grunt as he swept the squirming toddler against his chest. "What are you caterwauling about?"

She clasped his face in her tiny hands to look him directly in the eyes. "Gram's here," she whispered excitedly. "You must go tell her that you love her and miss her and want her to come home."

"I must?"

She nodded solemnly. "And if she won't listen to you, then steal her truck keys so she can't leave."

Titus arched a brow. "You believe I should force her to stay?"

Ella looked down with a fierce frown. "No," she said, her large, troubled green eyes lifting to his again. "Then *beg* her to stay, Grampy."

"Oceanuses—male *and* female—do not beg," he growled in an attempt to stifle his laughter.

"You are so stubborn," she growled right back at him, squeezing his face for emphasis—only to suddenly get a familiar gleam in her eyes. "Then *kiss* her."

Titus rested his forehead against hers in defeat. "Where's your mother?"

"Working."

"Then where is your brave new Atlantean tutor?"

She straightened away with a shrug. "Likely searching for me."

He walked out onto the porch and scanned the path, then gave Ella a stern look. "A princess does not sneak off like a common thief in order to shirk her duties. And at three years old, your most pressing duty is to be good for your mother and tutor."

Her eyes narrowed. "Don't change the subject. Are you going to go tell Gram you love her and miss her, or not?" She suddenly threw her arms around him in a fierce hug. "She's living in a crooked old house, Grampy," she whispered, "and all her furniture is lumpy." She leaned away just enough to eye him again. "Do you think she misses Atlantis, and that's why she went to live by the sea? Because if it is, then you must go live in her crooked house with her so she won't be alone." Ella nodded, apparently liking her plan. "Henry and Sophie and I promise to visit."

Titus pressed her head against his shoulder to hide his grin and walked down the steps. "Or," he said as he started toward the resort offices, "you could leave courting your grandmother to me and concern yourself with being a *well-behaved* princess."

"Ella! Where in Hades are you?"

Ella straightened with a gasp. "Sweet Zeus, Mum sent Nicholas after me!" She clasped Titus's cheeks again. "Please, Grampy, don't let him make me sweep all the cobwebs out of the tunnels. They go on for *miles*."

"There you are, you little termagant," Nicholas muttered as he jogged up the path toward them. He stopped and pulled a small resort phone from his pocket. "I have her, Olivia," he said into the phone. "She's with Titus." He suddenly grinned. "No, that's okay. She can spend the rest of the afternoon with me, and I'll bring her back in time for dinner. But she's probably going to need a bath when she gets home," he drawled, "and you might have to burn her clothes."

"Grampy," Ella squeaked, her arms tightening around his neck when Nicholas shoved the phone back in his pocket. "You must save me."

"Come on, princess," Nicholas said, holding out his hands. "I believe there's a broom with your name on it waiting for you."

Titus must not have disguised his amusement quickly enough when Ella leaned away to give him one of her well-practiced pouts, because she suddenly made a sound of disgust and wiggled for him to put her down. "Well, fine then," she snapped as she stormed past Nicholas with all the dignity of a haughty princess. "I'm not afraid of any stupid spiders."

Nicholas turned to watch the little cherub stride away, and Titus saw the warrior violently shudder. "I almost feel sorry for Mac." He glanced over his shoulder and shot Titus a grin. "Almost," he repeated, shoving his hands in his pockets and whistling a merry tune as he followed.

Concluding that Kitalanta had decided to run down the mountain rather than ride back with her, Rana gave up waiting for the wolf and climbed in her truck. "You are brave simply for being a woman," she said aloud, fastening her seat belt with a decisive click. "And besides, you'll be on the *inside* of the road for the descent."

But despite her pep talk, she couldn't seem to start the engine. Drat it to Hades; it was different driving the mountain alone, with no one to keep her mind off the fact that she was higher than most birds flew. She should have persuaded Macie to come home with her instead of letting Olivia give the still-shaken woman a hotel room, complete with room service and the security of knowing she was safe from Sebastian and Johnny and anyone else who might come after—

What was that smell? Rana took several deep sniffs as she looked around the interior of the truck, only to stiffen when her gaze stopped on the passenger seat and she saw a small towel wrapped around something that appeared to be the size of a—

Finally placing the scent, Rana snatched up the bundle with a squeal of delight and peeled back the towel to reveal an oversized peach that she knew for a fact was perfectly ripe and juicy and unbelievably sweet. "Sweet Athena," she groaned, holding the peach to her nose on an indrawn breath, "I don't care how you got here, only that you're all mine."

She took a huge bite, closing her eyes on the explosion of juice and groaning again at being instantly transported back to her palace garden. "Ohhhhmigod," she hummed as she squished the sweet pulp into every corner of her mouth and used her fingers to capture any escaping juice, not wanting to miss even a drop. She rotated the fruit and took another bite, chewing and humming and groaning—then nearly choking when she heard a tap and snapped her eyes open to see Titus staring at her, his intense green eyes locked on her mouth.

She turned the key and rolled down her window.

"One?" she mumbled past her mouthful of peach as she shook the fruit at him, making him lift his now-laughing eyes to hers. "You brought back only *one*?"

He plucked the peach out of her hand, took a *really large* bite, then handed it back to her. "I have more," he said around his own mouthful, arching a brow as he quickly swallowed without even having the decency to savor it. "But knowing their value, I decided to put them up as a prize." He gestured at the peach oozing juice all over her hand, his eyes gleaming with challenge. "That one was merely to whet your appetite for a little wager. Say, an entire bushel of Atlantean peaches to the winner of a race between that pretty racing sloop of yours and my new boat."

Rana took another bite as she thought about having a whole bushel all to herself, seeing how Titus didn't have a single boat in his little fleet that could touch her sloop. In truth, it would be like taking candy—no, taking *peaches* from a baby.

"And," he added roughly when she started licking juice off her fingers, "if you somehow manage to beat me by at least half a league, you will also win . . ." His eyes lifted to hers. "One favor from me."

She stopped licking. "What sort of favor?"

"Your any wish will be my command."

She looked down at the peach in her hand. "And if I should lose this wager?"

"You will give me your first metal sculpture."

She shot him a smile. "Then prepare to be—"

"And," he continued, "grant me one favor."

She stopped smiling. "What sort of favor?"

His eyes dropped to her mouth again. "My choice."

Rana took another huge bite to disguise her scowl. The

dirty rotten scoundrel; he knew how much she loved peaches, and was only using them to get what he really wanted. She shoved what remained of the fruit at him. "Here, you've obviously overestimated the value of your prize and underestimated me."

"Forgive me, madam," he said, his eyes lighting with laughter again as he took the peach. "I thought I was challenging the reigning queen of the regatta, not some shy young maiden who hadn't even *boarded* a boat until she sailed off on her honeymoon."

Rana snatched the peach back before he could sink his teeth into it. "Well, fine then," she snapped, hitting the button to lift her window. "Consider yourself challenged." She stopped the window halfway up. "And it had better be a *full* bushel."

"Wait," he said when she clamped the peach in her teeth and reached down to start the truck. "The weather is supposed to be warm tomorrow with a stiff breeze. Shall we meet at the point of land guarding the fiord at ten A.M. and lay a course down Bottomless, around its most southern island, and back?"

Still sucking on the peach, she merely nodded and hit the window button again.

"Wait," he repeated, his eyes turning serious as he gestured behind him, where she only just noticed his motorcycle parked beside her truck and realized she must have been too busy humming and groaning and *savoring* to hear him arrive. "I was just on my way to the Drunken Moose for dinner," he continued, "and wondered if you would mind following me down the mountain."

Now what was he up to? Rana pulled the peach from her mouth and batted her eyes at him. "Why?" she murmured, running her tongue over her lips and stifling a smile when his gaze dropped to her mouth again. "Are you hoping to impress a shy young maiden with your prowess for handling a hundred horses on a winding mountain road?" Seeing he was still staring at her mouth, she pouted. "Or do you hope to throw me off my game tomorrow by giving me a glimpse of your recklessness tonight?"

And there was that gleam again when his gaze lifted to hers. "It's a hundred and sixty horses, and I was hoping to impress a beautiful—" He went silent when she started sucking her sticky fingers, and turned away with a very un-kingly curse. "Just try not to run me off the mountain," he growled as he strode to his motorcycle.

"Take that, you blackguard," she muttered, starting her truck as she scowled at him slipping on his helmet. "Thinking to trick me with your little wager, were you? Let's see how clever you're feeling tomorrow afternoon, when I'm sitting in my crooked little hovel with my bushel of peaches and you're *swimming* back to the marina."

But her scowl soon turned into a smile when she pulled up to the guardhouse behind the shiny red motorcycle and realized she wouldn't be descending the mountain alone after all.

Chapter Twelve

Rana stopped tightening her jib line when she spotted the tall mast traveling behind the narrow peninsula separating the fiord from the main body of Bottomless, and frowned that she didn't recognize the brightly colored sails—only to gasp when the fast-moving vessel rounded the point. She then watched in utter and complete awe as the *modern* catamaran caught the strong sea breeze and one of its pontoons lifted clean out of the water, exposing a narrow, mid-hull dagger and equally long tiller.

For the love of Zeus, forget his being a blackguard and scoundrel; she was married to a no-good-rotten *cheater*.

Rana scrambled to finish tightening her jib, then rushed back to the helm and turned her sloop to catch the wind, planting her feet against the steep cant of the deck as the boat rolled onto its side and surged forward. She glanced over her shoulder at her competition and realized that even though their sails were nearly equal in size, her sloop was probably twenty times the weight of that catamaran. And two skinny fiberglass pontoons—even with both of them in the water—had very little drag compared to an *ancient* wooden mono-hull.

Where in the name of Hades had he gotten that boat? "New," she whispered. "I was so busy savoring that damn peach that I didn't even notice when he slipped the word *new* into his challenge." Sweet Athena, not only had he known exactly how to distract her, he had actually had her acting like a fifteen-year-old starry-eyed maiden. Forty years of marriage and she was *still* falling for his tricks.

"Good morning, wife!" the no-good-rotten cheater shouted as he pulled up off her port side as effortlessly as if she were dragging an anchor. He loosened the line on his mainsail to dump some of the wind so he would keep pace, then reached into a large dry bag lashed to the trampoline, pulled something out, and sank his teeth into—

A peach! He was eating one of her peaches!

"That better not be from *my* bushel!" she yelled.

Despite the distance between them, she could see his brow arch as he chewed and grinned and nodded. "Pretty damn sure of winning, are you?" he said around his mouthful of sweet, succulent peach.

"That's not even your boat!"

"It is now," he said, licking the juice running down the side of his hand. "Care to put that pretty sloop back on its mooring and spend the day on a real racer? I'll let you drive, and I might even be persuaded to share my prize," he magnanimously offered, gesturing at the bag on the trampoline.

"You can't share something you haven't won yet," she called out, even as she adjusted her course to fill her sails with wind again. "Play fair," she shouted over her shoulder as she angled away, "and perhaps I'll share my prize with you!"

Rana laughed when her husband straightened in surprise, only to gasp when he tossed the half-eaten peach in the water in order to reef in his mainsail.

And with that, the race was on. Titus might in theory have a faster vessel, but Rana knew from personal experience that skill and timing and even plain old simple luck could just as easily carry the day. So with that knowledge fueling her determination, she set a course toward Spellbound Falls.

Surrounded by mountains covered in spruce and pine and various hardwoods, Bottomless was more than fourteen miles wide at its northern end and, not counting the fiord, stretched thirty-nine miles south to Turtleback Station. The large inland sea was dotted with islands varying in size from small exposed ledges to several hundred acres, its seemingly endless shoreline coiling in and out of the rugged terrain to narrow the waterway to only a few miles in several places.

As Titus had predicted, today couldn't have been more perfect for sailing if it had been custom ordered. The air temperature flirted with sixty degrees, which was veritably *balmy* for northern Maine in early April, and a stiff breeze hovered around fifteen knots. After a glance back to see her competition had apparently decided to tack southeast rather than follow her, Rana altered her course to avoid a raft of kayakers paddling out from town. Satisfied the few fishing boats scattered about were holding steady courses, she locked the wheel to run parallel to the shoreline, then relaxed back against the stern with a sigh of delight to be at the helm of her beloved sloop again.

Probably the thing she loved most about sailing—right behind feeling powerful to be controlling the wind—was the solitude. She enjoyed being alone with her thoughts at sea; her senses sharpening to the task at hand, no one but Mother Nature demanding anything of her, and time seeming to stand still as the rest of the world simply faded away.

She often found it hard to believe she'd never set foot on a boat until she had met Titus, no more than she could believe she had spent the entire first day of her honeymoon throwing up over the side of his beautiful sailing ship. However, that might have had less to do with the rolling swells and more with her being the fifteen-year-old bride of a rich and powerful and very magical young warrior.

"If only you hadn't been so handsome," she murmured past her smile, "I might have stood a chance." And charming. And humorous. And so very tender. "Well," she said with a laugh, "tender when you were certain no one was looking."

And persistent. Sweet Athena, the man had skulked around for weeks trying to catch her eye. And once he'd gotten her attention, he'd gone after her heart.

It scared her sometimes to think that she might have missed out on a lifetime of loving Titus but for her mother's wisdom. Annabelle Proust hadn't seen wealth or power or even the magic when Titus had introduced himself to her; she had seen a man desperately needing to be loved.

What mother encouraged her mere mortal daughter to marry a god, Rana remembered crying in dismay. A mother, Annabelle had quietly answered, that had raised a daughter who was brave enough not to let *what* he was stop her from marrying the man her love would make him.

It had been known far and wide that Titus Oceanus preferred living with mortals rather than in the ethereal world, and that he in fact had little stomach for the violent wars the gods constantly waged against each other at mankind's expense. Within a year of marriage he'd started making plans to do something about it, but little had Rana realized his decision to champion humanity would eventually send him—and her and young Maximilian—into exile.

It was then she'd learned that not only was Titus capable of being just as violent as his fellow gods, but that her mighty husband was really quite devious. While slowly gathering mankind's knowledge into what he referred to as the Trees of Life, he'd also set about building a secret island upon which to safeguard the mystical grove. He had then scoured the earth to find a small, hand-chosen army of intelligent and courageous mortals, personally trained them in the ways of the magic, and charged those first drùidhs with protecting the Trees while nurturing—and sometimes nudging—mankind's conscience.

But not three months before Carolina was born, the gods finally caught wind of what he was doing and Titus had been forced to move his young family into his partially completed palace, scatter most of his Trees and drùidhs around the world as an extra precaution, and sink the island and everyone on it into the ocean. And thanks to her devious husband and now Maximilian, mythical

Atlantis had remained out of reach of the gods and demons bent on destroying it, and out of sight of unbelieving mortals.

Becoming aware that she could hear the fast-approaching catamaran cutting through the water, Rana continued looking toward the western shoreline to hide her smile, and even managed not to flinch when Titus crossed her stern close enough that she could have reached out and touched him. She did yelp in surprise, however, when a big, fat, juicy peach landed on her lap, then burst into laughter when she picked it up and saw a bite had been taken out of it.

He immediately turned into the wind, nearly stalling as he changed tack before his mainsail and jib snapped taut and he surged forward again. "You're not going to win by daydreaming," he shouted as he cut across her bow, this time looking over his sail as the pontoon he was now *standing* on rose out of the water.

Rana also stood and ran forward to get a better look at the harness he was wearing. There appeared to be a cable running from high up on the mast down to his waist, allowing him to brace his feet on the flying pontoon and use his body as ballast to stop the boat from capsizing. Which made sense, she realized as she took a bite of peach, since there wasn't a weighted keel to offset the push of the wind.

Oh, she really needed to sail that catamaran.

And then she needed to find a way to steal it for her fleet.

"Sweet Zeus, woman, tack!" Titus shouted, the pontoon he was standing on dropping like a stone when he released his mainsail, making him have to scramble onto the trampoline to keep from falling in the water and getting dragged by the harness.

Rana snapped her head around and saw she was closing in on one of the small ledges. Clamping the peach in her teeth, she broke the line on the jib and scrambled back to the helm, unlocked and spun the wheel and locked it again, ducked the boom as it swung from starboard to port, then ran forward and hauled in the line to retighten the jib. And then she ran back and flopped down behind the wheel, pulled the peach from her mouth, and huffed and puffed to catch her breath.

Wow, why was she winded?

Oh, that's right; she was lugging around ten extra pounds.

"Are the peaches making you homesick?" Titus asked, his sharp green eyes studying her face as he returned to keeping pace beside her again. "Near as I can tell, you've spent the last hour daydreaming."

She tucked some escaping hair inside her hat and relaxed back against the stern. "They're not making me homesick, exactly." She shot him a lopsided smile. "I was just remembering how you charmed my mother into persuading my father to let you marry his little girl."

"You're thinking of your parents?" he said in surprise, his eyes darkening with an old, familiar pain. "Why, Stasia?"

"No, not in a sad way," she quickly assured him. "I was thinking about something Mom said when she was persuading *me* to marry you."

He edged his boat dangerously closer. "What did Annabelle say?"

Rana stood up at the wheel and shot him another

smile—this one smug. "The answer will cost you *one catamaran*," she said, turning the sloop tighter to the wind and surging away to his booming laughter.

They spent the morning tacking back and forth down Bottomless like two drunken sailors, all while avoiding a seemingly suicidal old whale and frisky pod of orcas—Kitalanta at the front—bravely running interference in an attempt to level the playing field for their queen. Her only real worry was for the fishermen who thought they were safely trolling open water only to find themselves on a collision course with a fast-moving catamaran. Apparently unaware of how agile a cat could be, she would watch in dismay as the shouting fishermen quickly reeled in their lines and sped away.

Rana was the first to round the southernmost island, but only because she had very unsportingly sailed past her capsized husband—twice!

Hey, she had *waved.*

She'd also thrown the peach pit at him. She had good aim, too, and had hit him right on his regal head of wet white hair just as he was struggling to pull the catamaran back upright.

But was it her fault he was making her feel fifteen years old again?

"I wish to call a time-out!" Titus shouted as he raced past her starboard side. "I need a nap."

"Oh, thank the gods," Rana whispered, turning into the wind to stall the sloop. Not that she was about to admit *to him* that she'd spent the last hour fighting to keep her eyes open. It must be the extra pounds making her tired and not the fact that her muscles certainly didn't feel fifteen years old.

"Drop your anchor and loosen your sails," he said as he approached her port side and released his own sails. "I'll come aboard and let the cat drift off your stern."

"I'm sorry," she said, brushing down the front of her spray-drenched jacket, "but I don't allow no-good-rotten cheaters on my boat."

He grabbed the sloop to hold them drifting together. "I come bearing gifts."

She shrugged. "I've gotten my fill of peaches."

"Are you over your fondness for figs, too?"

She snapped her gaze up to see him pull a small burlap sack from the dry bag lashed to his trampoline. "You brought some of Mathew's figs?" she asked.

"Mind telling me what you were thinking to give Olivia our royal gardener? The boy he left in charge had already eaten half our crop."

"I couldn't very well move Maude here and not her husband." She stepped up to the rail. "If I let you come aboard, do you promise to behave?"

He set the figs on the pontoon precariously close to the edge and reached in the bag again. "I also raided our wine cellar," he said, pulling out a bottle and *not* answering her question, she couldn't help but notice. He tucked the wine between his legs and, while still holding on to her boat, reached in the bag again. "Your goat herd is exploding with new kids this spring," he continued, pulling out a small container of what she knew for a fact was the most delicious goat cheese on the planet.

Rana lifted onto her toes to lean over the rail. "Did you happen to stop by the kitchen and steal some of Michelin's bread before you left?"

"At great risk to life and limb," he said with a chuckle

as he set down the cheese and pulled a cotton bread sack out of the dry bag. "Our staff has been eating better than we have." He glanced up—his gaze lingering on her hips and even longer on her bosom before lifting to her face—and chuckled again. "I imagine you and I alone are keeping the Drunken Moose solvent."

Rana dropped to her heels with a gasp. "You brought back healthy foods because you think I'm getting fat."

"What? No." He grabbed the cheese and held it up with the bread. "All of this has been your diet for centuries."

She leaned over the rail and snatched the two items out of his hand before he could pull them away. "Go find your own island to nap behind. This one is taken."

"Ah, wife," he said with a laugh as he picked up the sack of figs and gently tossed it onto her deck, "but you do please—"

What felt like a solid wall of wind suddenly caught the sails of both vessels, forcing Titus to let go of her boat in order to keep the light catamaran from capsizing, and making Rana scramble after the line of her flapping mainsail.

"Leviathan!" Titus roared over the howl of the wind, the urgency in his voice making Rana stop in mid-hoist. "Come to me now!"

She started to glance around to see what had him worried, but instead lunged toward the mast when the sea began to froth like a cauldron of boiling water, making the sloop heave wildly as bursting bubbles filled the air with a musty smell she couldn't identify. Clinging to the mast, she finally looked at where Titus was looking to see dark, roiling thunderclouds sweeping toward them from the south.

"Rana! Do *not* lash yourself to the mast!" her husband shouted as a driving rain engulfed them—her last sight being of Titus standing on his trampoline as he studied the churning water beneath him and then roared Leviathan's name again.

"No magic!" Rana yelled. "Titus! Don't use your magic on me!"

Something rammed the sloop with enough force to make her fall to her knees, and she stayed kneeling on the wildly heaving deck as she continued to hug the mast, sighing in relief that Leviathan was here—only to scream when she realized the dark shadow rising out of the frothing water was *not* a whale.

Her second scream was drowned out by a loud crack followed by the sound of wood splintering, and Rana pushed away from the vibrating mast just as the top half of it crashed to the deck and trapped her in a tangle of ropes and rain-soaked canvas.

"I have you," Titus said as she felt his strong hands encircle her. "Close your eyes, little one."

"No," Rana rushed out, clasping his face just as she felt the sloop begin to tilt. "Please, Titus, you can't use your magic on me."

His arms tightened around her. "I must!"

"No. You can't. It will—" There was a loud groan of splintering wood and the sloop gave another violent shudder. The deck tilted sharply, the shifting mast and sail dragging them both into the frigid water. Titus pulled her even deeper to get away from the snare of ropes and canvas, and Rana thought her lungs would burst before he suddenly shot upward.

"You'll drown if I don't," he snapped the moment they

surfaced into the churning waves and driving rain. "Or freeze to death first!"

"No magic!" she cried again when she felt him tensing in preparation. "It might kill our baby."

His grip on her momentarily slackened before he growled a curse and suddenly hauled her back underwater just as she heard a deep groan and felt something brush against her. The sloop was sinking, she realized, clinging to Titus as he kicked away before it sucked them down with it. He pushed her to the surface again then held her steady in the churning waves as she gasped and sputtered trying to catch her breath—until she stopped breathing altogether when she realized they'd surfaced right in the middle of a fierce battle.

"No, don't look," he said roughly, pressing her face against his shoulder as he turned and started swimming away.

Although the storm was making it nearly as dark as night, the flashes of lightning had allowed her to catch a glimpse of the huge shadow she'd seen earlier, which now appeared to be fending off repeated attacks from what she *had* recognized were several demons. Rana kept her eyes closed as her husband's powerful legs carried them away from the horrible battle, but she couldn't close her ears to the blood-curdling screams of the demons and the gut-wrenching roars coming from the shadow.

Titus stopped swimming and pressed his mouth to her cheek. "You're not going to make it to shore," he said, his lips feeling like burning embers against her cold skin. "I need to get you to safety."

"I-I can make it," she whispered, shivering uncontrollably. "P-Please don't—"

"I will not lose you!" he growled as she felt the telltale sign of him tensing.

She dug her fingers into his shoulders. "You don't n-need the magic, Titus. You're powerful enough t-to save me and our child without it."

His grip tightened as he hesitated for several pounding heartbeats before he turned with another curse and started swimming again. Too lethargic to cling to him anymore, Rana closed her eyes on a shiver, knowing she couldn't be in safer hands. She did give a weak scream when something bumped her leg, however, and tried to kick it away.

"That was Leviathan," Titus said, shifting his hold on her without slowing. "He's guiding us to the closest land."

"K-Kit?"

"The orcas are guarding our backs. Conserve your strength."

She could still hear the screams of the demons and terrified roars of whatever they were fighting mixed with nearly continuous thunder and the howling wind, but she could tell Titus was quickly putting distance between them and the battle.

Was the shadow another new god or goddess trying to come forth like the one that had run into Peg's truck last week? Had the demons been sent to stop this one before it fully manifested? Because she couldn't imagine many of the established gods would be too overjoyed to have new competition.

Unlike her husband, apparently.

She really didn't know why Titus seemed unconcerned about what the colonists were doing. Even though he'd sent Nicholas and Dante to spy on them, she suspected that was more to see if the other gods intended to interfere rather than become involved himself. Had Dante told Titus and Maximilian what Macie had told her, which was that the colony was trying to use the magic for the good of mankind?

She smiled, thinking she wouldn't mind having another god in their corner, only to gasp when Titus suddenly stood up and swept her into his arms.

And then she flinched when he muttered another curse and scaled the rocky shoreline. "You've stopped shivering," he said roughly, running into the forest.

She was pretty sure that should alarm her, but she really couldn't remember why. Because honestly? She didn't feel cold anymore. She tried to tell him that she actually felt wonderful, but her voice didn't seem to want to work. So she tried patting his shoulder to let him know how proud she was of him for saving her without the magic, except her arm kept flapping down his back like it belonged on a ragdoll. And then she felt herself falling, but quickly realized he was setting her down on soggy moss, just before she was engulfed in an equally wet but familiar-smelling jacket that covered even her head from the driving rain.

"I'll be back shortly," her life-saving husband said as he rolled her onto her side, folded her knees up to her chest, and tucked the jacket around her. "Don't move."

She probably should promise she wouldn't move an inch, but she was too busy forming an apology for throwing that peach pit at him, considering how he had gallantly saved her life. Yeah, just as soon as he got back, she would tell him what a brave and powerful husband he was even *without* the magic.

* * *

Titus couldn't remember ever being so scared in his life. No, that wasn't true; he had been all but paralyzed with fear when Rana had lain dying in their bed after giving birth to Carolina. He had, in fact, threatened Providence that he would personally destroy every damn last Tree of Life if he lost her.

"Leviathan!" he shouted when he reached the water, squinting into the driving rain at the battle still going on—not that he had any trouble hearing it. He walked into the waves up to his waist. "Kitalanta! Come!"

The old whale surfaced nearby. "Bring me my boat," Titus instructed. "Kit," he said the moment the orca appeared, "bring one of your warriors to land and set the others on patrol just offshore."

His orders given, Titus tensed against the assault he knew was coming and began pulling the energy of the inland sea into his body, then stretched his hands to the wind-whipped waves and called forth the great whites. "Send those demon bastards scurrying for their lives," he instructed when a dozen dorsal fins began circling, one of the larger sharks coming close enough to brush his leg. "And leave the new entity untouched. By the gods, Leviathan!" he shouted when he saw his capsized catamaran floundering in the waves. "Hurry the hell up before your queen dies!"

Titus glanced over his shoulder in the direction of Rana, but decided he didn't dare summon more of the energy for fear of killing her himself. Even whole and hearty, her mortal body could withstand only small doses of the magic.

The catamaran slammed onto the rocks, shattering one of the pontoons and snapping the mast like a twig. He waded over and ripped off the mainsail and ropes, tore the dry bag off the twisted trampoline, then took off the jib.

"Leviathan!" he called out after climbing to shore with the gear balled up in his arms. "Go alert Maximilian and Nicholas to what is going on." He hesitated, then said, "Tell them we are safe, but do not tell them where we are. I will let you know when we're ready to go home. Assuming we go home at all," he muttered as he turned and ran back into the forest.

For in truth, if his wife did not leave here alive, neither would he.

Chapter Thirteen

Rana woke to the sound of gentle rain hitting some sort of material and the feel of heat from a crackling fire on her face, but it was the strong, steady heartbeat inside the warm, naked chest she was lying on that made her sigh in relief that she was alive and well and exactly where she belonged.

She assumed her sigh is what made the arms around her tighten, and she in turn melted into her husband's life-saving embrace. "I love you," she said without opening her eyes, even as she wondered why she sounded hoarse. Oh, that's right; she'd nearly drowned. "I love you," she repeated a bit louder when he didn't respond, thinking he might not have heard her.

She sighed again when he stopped her from tilting her head to look at him, and instead smiled at the brightly burning fire when she realized he was angry. Not at her directly, but rather at her almost dying. Yes, her big strong magical husband didn't like being reminded he was in love with a mortal woman, especially one who couldn't even travel through time with him without throwing up. Add to that the shock of having just learned he was going to be a father again, and . . . well, she really hadn't intended to shout her news at him, especially not in the middle of a horrible battle and definitely not while he was busy saving her life.

Come to think of it, she was rather angry herself. Those vile demons had ruined her plan to cook Titus a wonderful meal in her new home, after which they would stroll hand-in-hand down to her beachfront and sit in front of a wonderful bonfire, where she would gently tell him that their deep and abiding love had created another wonderful new life. Only she hadn't intended for that to happen for two or three months, because she'd wanted a little more time *not* being smothered by his concern and treated like an invalid, considering how badly he'd been fussing over her ever since she had nearly died giving birth to Carolina.

Titus was still the handsome, charming, and tender man she'd married forty years ago, and she loved him dearly, but she was also very much aware to what lengths he would go in order to protect her. For hadn't he made a pact with his enemies to keep Carolina safe until she could marry an intelligent mortal brave enough to love her? And hadn't he shown no mercy to Henry's uncles when they had tried to kill Maximilian in order to keep control of their magical nephew? But like all the men in her family, Rana also felt honor-bound to ensure mankind's continued existence, which could be in jeopardy if her husband decided to . . . well, she really didn't want to think about what he might do to keep her safe. Oh, yeah; her mother had been right about what sort of man her love would make Titus, and the responsibility that came with *his* loving *her* could at times be overwhelming.

She felt his lips touch her hair. "How did this happen?" he quietly asked.

Knowing he wasn't talking about the storm, Rana propped her chin on her hands on his chest and smiled into his unreadable eyes. "I believe in this century they call it make-up sex."

"I've always gone to great lengths to ensure you never got pregnant again."

"Yes. But sometimes you get . . . distracted by my response to you."

"Do you know how far along you are?"

"Eight or nine weeks."

"Have you seen Maude?"

"No. But she's not blind and suspects I'm with child."

His eyes narrowed, though they remained unreadable. "Then you're not really certain. You're of an age," he continued, his embrace tightening when she tried to sit up, "that you may have merely reached the end of your childbearing years."

"I am in the *prime* of my life. And," she snapped when she saw a hint of a smile, "I know my own body."

He pulled her coiled fingers out of his chest hair and trapped her hands against his sides, then cupped her head back to him. "What did you hope to accomplish by leaving me?"

"This," she said in exasperation, wiggling her trapped hands. "I wanted a few months of experiencing what it's like to take care of myself for once, before you became even more overprotective."

"Forgive me. I hadn't realized my love for you has been such a burden."

She tried to look at him, only to sigh again when he wouldn't let her. "I went from my father's care to yours, Titus—from being a dutiful daughter to being a dutiful wife. Don't get me wrong, I wouldn't change anything. Well," she said brightly, hoping to lighten his mood, "I might have made you work a little harder to catch me."

"As it was, you were one day away from succeeding."

She popped her head up before he could stop her. "You were going to give up on me? What stopped you?"

"Remember that heart-shaped pebble I pressed into your hand when I bumped into you at the market? Well," he said when she nodded, "I knew I had you when I saw you pull it from your bodice when you were hanging clothes on the line."

"You were hiding in the woods *spying* on me?"

Apparently deciding that was a rhetorical question, he merely arched a brow. Rana laid her head on his chest and stared into the fire just beyond the colorful sail he'd stretched between two trees like a tent. She could see all their clothes hanging on branches under the sail to dry, and guessed he must have had the heavy flannel shirt she was wearing in his dry bag.

"We can hold off sailing home until after Carolina has her baby," she said when he remained silent, fighting to keep her sorrow out of her voice. "Or maybe a few weeks after, so we can have some time with our new grandchild? I . . . I'm not that far along."

She closed her eyes when he still didn't respond, and fought back tears when he covered her head with his big masculine hand and brushed his thumb over her cheek. She was going to miss the births of Olivia's and Peg's and Julia's babies, as well as Henry's eleventh birthday and Sophie's and Ella's. And knowing Titus, he wouldn't let her travel again until their child was several months old, which would be a whole friggin' *year* from now.

Yes. Well. He could stay silent until the cows came home, for all she cared. Having known that the moment he learned she was pregnant he would hustle her back to Atlantis, she didn't feel the least bit guilty for scheming to spend the summer here.

He'd really almost given up courting her?

Titus slowly sat up, sitting her up with him, and Rana disguised wiping her eyes by making a production of tugging the oversize shirt down over her legs. He lifted her off his lap and set her on what she realized was his jib sail, then stood up—utterly and magnificently naked—and walked to the fire and began feeding it branches that he must have gathered . . . sometime.

"Are you hungry?" he asked, turning, still crouched, to look at her.

She toyed with a button on the shirt. "Not really." She looked toward where she thought Bottomless was, uncertain because Titus had apparently wanted to make camp far from the sea. "Do you know if the demons . . . if they won?"

"I only know they found themselves battling an army of great whites shortly after we reached shore." He shrugged. "I have no idea if the new entity survived."

Nor did he particularly care, judging by his tone. "Did you send Kitalanta or Leviathan to tell Maximilian what happened? We should be rescued shortly, shouldn't we?"

Titus stood up, pulled his clothes off the branches, and started dressing. "Kit and one of his pod mates are patrolling nearby and occasionally bringing us firewood, so don't be alarmed if you hear a noise or they suddenly appear."

"So you sent Leviathan to Nova Mare, then?" she repeated when she realized he hadn't answered her question about being rescued.

Titus pulled on his pants. "He's gone to report to Maximilian and Nicholas what happened and that we are safe, but I instructed him not to tell anyone where we are."

"You . . . why would you do that?"

He slipped on his shirt. "Because I wish to spend some time alone with my wife," he said, finally turning to her—his eyes unreadable again. "And knowing how much you enjoy camping, I've decided we'll walk back." He shrugged. "It should take only a few days."

He was serious. And why wasn't she surprised he hadn't asked if *she* wanted to walk back? Rana glanced at the surrounding woods again, not that she could see very far, since the sun had obviously set, and worried she had slept quite a long time. Oh, yeah, she must have really, really scared him. "Are we on the western shore?" she asked, knowing there was nothing but wilderness on the east side of Bottomless.

"We're on the eastern shore." He sat down and began dressing his feet. "My guess is we're about thirty or thirty-five miles from Duncan's house."

"And you want to walk there," she stated rather than questioned.

He stopped lacing his boot and smiled at her, although she couldn't help but notice it didn't reach his eyes. "A mere stroll for a woman in the prime of her life."

Oh, yeah, the man was royally pissed. Only she was beginning to worry he was actually angry at *her* rather than the fact that she'd nearly drowned. And he expected them to spend the next few days *strolling* through the wilderness together?

"Are you forgetting I'm with child?"

"I haven't forgotten," he said, standing up.

"What are we going to eat? Or wear? You expect me to live in the same clothes for several days?"

"You have before."

"When I was nineteen," she snapped. "And we didn't have a *choice*."

"You don't have a choice now, wife." He pulled her socks off a branch and tossed them onto her lap. "You should cover your feet to keep from getting chilled again. But don't bother dressing," he said as he turned away, "because I'll just have to undress you again when I get back."

And with that parting shot, he disappeared into the darkness.

Rana picked up the socks and started to throw them after him, but then dropped her hands to her legs. She had *known* he'd be angry when he learned why she'd left him, so she couldn't very well be angry back at him, could she? Because honestly? If their roles were reversed and he'd kept that kind of secret from her, she probably wouldn't be acting half as civilized as he was.

She slipped on her socks, then lay down on the sail and curled up inside the thick fleece-lined shirt. Maybe Titus was right and living in this century really had put ideas in her head, such as the foolish notion she was a fearless, capable, modern woman. The only problem was she didn't think being modern gave her license to be deceitful, any more than it had given her instant courage. But then, visiting this century a few weeks a year for the last four years, and even living here for the last five months, didn't automatically make an ancient woman *modern*, now did it?

Sweet Athena, she'd made a mess of things. If she were as mad at Titus as he appeared to be at her, she'd probably walk home without him.

Not that he would ever consider leaving her out here alone. Because he loved her—even if she didn't particularly love herself at the moment.

Titus stood deep in the nighttime shadows watching Rana wind back her arm to throw her socks after him only to lower her hands to her lap. Barely able to breathe for the tightness in his chest, he saw her scowl as she appeared to have a conversation with herself while putting on the socks, then watched her curl up inside his shirt and stare unblinking at the fire as she obviously fought back tears.

He scrubbed his hands over his face to keep from roaring in frustration, then ran his fingers through his hair with a tired sigh. How in the name of Hades had he allowed her to get pregnant again? For all these years he had managed to keep her in good health, safe from their enemies, and sheltered from the heart-wrenching aspects of the world, and in the end it very well might be his love—and lust—that ultimately killed her.

Assuming she was even pregnant, as it was still possible she had misread the signs and merely reached the end of her childbearing years. And although he knew women often had a difficult time accepting the undeniable proof that they were aging, at least she would be *alive* to voice her displeasure that men missed out on that wonderful transition.

Titus felt the beginnings of a smile at the notion he'd managed to sneak a bit of the magic into their marriage, though he suspected Rana had known all along he had subtly been slowing her aging process. Which was why despite being in her mid-fifties, she had the physique of a woman in her early forties. But being an intelligent woman, she had never broached the subject to him, apparently having decided it was something she could live with. Although if she had asked, he truthfully could have told her he'd never broken his vow, as it had been *time* he'd manipulated, not her.

Only once had Rana wanted something from the magic for herself. And of all the things she could have asked for, it had been the one thing he hadn't been able to grant. He'd made sure Annabelle and Aaron Proust had been blessed with good health and fortune—although not on a grand scale, as was their wish—but he hadn't been able to protect them from an invading army bent on destroying anything and everyone in its path. And by the time news of the tragedy had reached Atlantis, it had been too late to return her parents to his heartbroken wife.

Kitalanta appeared out of the darkness as silently as a ghost, jarring Titus out of his musings. He instructed the wolf to make his presence known to Rana and keep her company until he returned and, after a glance to see her still staring into the flames, he quietly turned away and walked through the pitch-black forest toward the sea.

He actually chuckled, remembering Rana asking if he remembered she was with child when he'd told her they would be walking home. He knew she was expecting him to get *even more* overprotective, whereas in truth, he suspected she was more worried about her pregnancy than he was. But they happened to be living in the twenty-first century at the moment, and had access to medicine not even imagined when Carolina had been born, which was why they were *not* sailing back to Atlantis like she assumed.

Which he would tell her, once he recovered from the scare she'd just given him.

In the meantime, he intended to have her undivided attention for the next few days. And while he had it, he thought as he reached Bottomless and began undressing, he should probably let her in on *his* life-altering little secret.

Chapter Fourteen

"You and your warrior may go feed," Titus said softly when he reached camp, which made Kitalanta immediately rise from being pressed up against Rana's back. "But return to us in the morning. And Kit," he added, making the wolf stop and look back. "Bring your entire pod and have your bellies full enough for a four-day overland hike."

Titus would swear the wolf actually grinned just before it turned and bolted into the darkness. He stashed the items he'd salvaged from the sunken sloop under the end flap of the makeshift tent, then crouched to his heels and added branches to the fire his sleeping wife had let burn down to embers. He sat down with a tired sigh and took off his boots, pulled off his shirt, then sat staring into the slowly building flames.

Some days—especially days like today—he wondered

how much longer he could go on pretending he cared. He'd so far managed to fool everyone except most likely Rana, probably because she was so intimately tuned to him. In fact, he wouldn't be surprised if she'd noticed him growing tired of dealing with the incessant petitions of mortals looking for easy solutions to the messes they kept making, and the reason she'd run off really had been to force him to remember what truly was important.

But for the love of Zeus, there were tens of thousands of years of accumulated knowledge sitting in the Trees of Life, available to *anyone* willing to journey inward. Yet mankind continued to grow dangerously closer to destroying the planet; if not by smothering its air and oceans, then by blowing it to Hades in mindless disputes born of self-righteous arrogance and fueled by the ridiculous notion that progress was desired only if it didn't require *change*.

Could mortals truly not understand that *nothing* was static, not even the very universe they were but a small part of? Change was inevitable. It was also the energy behind the magic, which thankfully went about its business whether or not people believed. Atlantis couldn't exist if it didn't.

Then again, neither could he.

"Were you able to discern if the new entity survived?" Rana asked softly.

"It appears to have escaped," he said, adding branches to the fire. "Though I don't know if it will survive what I suspect were fairly vicious wounds."

"Do you know if it was a god or goddess?"

He shrugged. "Even the great whites couldn't tell." He reached into the supplies he'd brought back, grabbed the wine bottle—which he'd guzzled down when he'd come ashore—and handed it to her. "I found a spring not too far from here. You must be thirsty from your salty swim."

She took the bottle and pulled out the half-seated cork, and there was enough light from the burning fire for him to see her arch a brow. "You drank all the wine and brought me water?"

He made sure to stifle his grin. "I believe they established sometime in the last century that wine is not good for pregnant women."

She suddenly sat up. "Do you think that may have been my problem with Carolina? I drank as much wine as water back then."

Titus rested back on his elbow and let his smile burst free as he shook his head. "It supposedly hurts the child, not the mother, and I don't see that it harmed Maximilian or Carolina in any way," he said with a chuckle.

She frowned at the bottle in apparent thought, then took a long drink. "Perhaps," she said slowly, wiping her mouth on her sleeve as she looked down at him, her expression neutral, "this is a good century in which to have a baby."

Well, no one could ever accuse his wife of being slow of mind. "Perhaps," he agreed with another shrug. "Are you hungry?"

She scowled, apparently not caring to have the subject changed. "I'm still full from swallowing half of Bottomless." She nevertheless looked over at his stash of supplies. "If you were able to recover the wine, what else did you get?"

"The figs and container of goat cheese, but I'm afraid the fish are feasting on Michelin's soggy bread." He gestured at the stash. "Knowing you always kept a change of clothes in an oiled canvas bag onboard, I managed to salvage them as well. And this," he said, reaching in his pocket and then holding out his hand to her.

"A comb!" she cried, lifting one hand to her hair as she reached for the prize. "Oh, thank you for even thinking of it," she said, clasping the comb to her bosom as the firelight reflected in her grateful eyes.

He lowered his gaze. "It was more for my benefit than yours, as I wasn't looking forward to spending the next several days with a troll."

She smacked his shoulder with the comb. "You're always saying you love me most when I'm a disheveled mess," she said, her musical laugh allowing him to take his first decent breath since the storm had hit.

"I believe we both know," he said, giving a grunt as he pushed himself to his feet, "that I'm usually referring to your appearance after a night of lovemaking." He took off his pants. "Not that I can remember the last time that happened."

"Yes. Well," she murmured, becoming very busy working the tangles out of her hair, "I guess that's what happens when one grows too feeble of mind to remember what happened as recently as a *month* ago."

He dropped to one knee beside her and clasped her chin to look at him. "Am I ever going to see you disheveled that way again, Stasia?"

She stared up at him in silence, and he saw her lower lip start to quiver and her eyes well up with tears before she suddenly tossed the comb away and lunged at him. She hid her face in his chest with a loud sob as Titus fell to his side, so damned glad to have her back in his arms that he couldn't help but smile.

"I'm such a terrible wife!"

"The worst in all of history," he whispered against her tangled hair.

"I argue with you and scheme against you, and . . . and sometimes you make me so angry I want to smack you. And just so you know, I get angry at the magic, too," she confessed on another sob. "Providence thinks it's so smart and benevolent and always doing what's best for mankind, when it's really arrogant and self-serving and . . . and just mean sometimes. The magic hates me because it knows I don't like it."

"It has no sense of humor," he added gruffly.

"I don't understand why you married me!" she wailed, her fingers kneading his chest as if she couldn't decide whether to push him away or crawl inside him. "You never should have saved me from that dog at the tournament. For the love of Zeus, you're a *theurgist*. You should have known I was mortal and that I'd be stubborn and opinionated and . . . and would never be a dutiful wife."

"Yes, I should have known, because no, you certainly haven't."

"You were a powerful and handsome young warrior who was supposed to be looking for a sweet, obedient maiden to marry. A royal *lady* who would give you dozens of children and . . . and who wouldn't sneak baby goats into the palace or knock a stupid emperor in the ocean on purpose or . . . or . . ." She leaned away to cover her face with her hands. "You could have married anyone you wanted!"

Titus barely stifled a shudder at the notion he might

have spent the last forty years married to a sweet, obedient, *boring* lady. Although Rana certainly had tried—only to fail miserably, thank the gods. "I married you, Stasia," he said softly, pulling her hands down so she'd see his smile, "because I wanted the most terrible wife in all of history. And I saved you from that dog to win a kiss from the stubborn, opinionated, irreverent, lusty woman I saw hiding inside the beautiful maiden giving me the fiercest scowl I had ever seen." He gently ran a finger over her flushed cheek. "You were the only anyone I wanted, Stasia," he continued thickly, "because the moment our gazes met, I saw a woman who would have the courage to love me *despite* who I was."

"But I'm not brave," she whispered, hiding her face in his chest again. "I can't even drive up a stupid mountain alone."

"Aye, but ye are brave, lass," he said, quickly losing his smile when she reared back in surprise.

"A-Aye?" she repeated. *"Lass?"*

"I've found myself admiring the Scots lately." He kissed her frowning forehead and pulled her against him again before she caught his amusement. "In fact, they gave me the idea for us to walk home. Except the MacKeages usually kidnap their women rather than fish them out of the sea, then carry them off to a cabin in the woods and make love to them until the lasses promise to love them forever." He felt her stop breathing, her tears apparently forgotten. "I've heard rumor ropes may be involved," he continued with barely stifled laughter, "though I don't suppose a lass would run very far if all her clothes had been burned."

She reared back again, her eyes huge as she darted a

worried glance at the rope holding up the sail, then at the fire, then back at him. "Um, you do know I already love you forever, don't you?"

"Aye," he said on a heavy sigh, "but I'm thinking ye may have forgotten, what with being such a terrible wife and all."

That got him the feminine little snort he was after, though it was cut short when her completely dry eyes suddenly narrowed. "I thought you were angry at me."

"I am," he said, rolling her onto her back and smoothing a lock of hair off her face. "Which is why I'm giving you the next few days to make up to me." He closed her slackened mouth with his finger then began unbuttoning her shirt. "Wives do still try to appease their husbands in this century, don't they?" He stopped when her hand covered his, his amusement vanishing at her uncertainty. "I need to hear you sigh my name as I'm entering you, Stasia, and feel your warmth and aliveness surrounding me again." He lowered his lips to just above hers. "I want to make love to the woman whose response has the power to make me forget who I am."

"Oh, Titus," she said on a sigh as she pulled his mouth down to hers.

In all their forty years of marriage, he never knew who he'd be making love to on any given night. Sometimes he would gather the shy maiden from their honeymoon into his arms, and other times the lusty woman who owned his heart would attack him with glorious abandon. And every so often, for reasons he couldn't—and probably never would—fathom, his stubborn, irreverent, terrible wife would empty the palace of staff once dinner had been served, then over dessert quietly ask if he happened to know of a handsome warrior she could spend all that night, the whole next day, and the following night completely alone with. After which she would get up and silently walk away, and he'd follow her clothes strewn like breadcrumbs to the throne room, where he'd find her sitting on his seat of power wearing nothing but his royal sash and a smile that always brought him to his knees. And for the next thirty-six hours they would stay locked away from the maddening world, making love everywhere but in their bedroom.

The first time Rana had staged her grand seduction, he'd thought it was because she had been feeling neglected. But by the fourth time in as many years, he'd begun suspecting it was more for his benefit than hers, as it appeared to happen whenever he wasn't feeling particularly benevolent toward mankind.

And she couldn't understand why he'd chosen her, when he wanted nothing in life *but* her.

He soon found out who was in his arms tonight when she began trailing kisses over his jaw to his ear, into which she whispered a very unladylike word before gently nipping his lobe. She shoved at his shoulder as she slipped from under him, and Titus found himself on his back with his lusty wife straddling his hips—the campfire reflecting a familiar sparkle in her passion-filled eyes as she slowly finished unbuttoning her shirt.

"Did you also happen to learn how lasses *make up* to their husbands when they've been terrible wives?" she asked, opening the shirt just enough to expose only a portion of her plump breasts.

"I . . ." He cleared his throat. "I'm sorry, but the

highlanders don't seem to discuss what happens *after* they steal their women."

He saw her glance toward the rope holding the sail, then arch an eyebrow as she looked down at him, apparently not realizing she was *caressing* her breasts while slowly moving her hips over him. "Then I guess I'll just have to . . . improvise," she whispered, the huskiness in her voice nudging a memory in the back of his mind—though he couldn't remember if he should be alarmed or excited.

He was having no trouble, however, focusing on the fact that her moist heat was pressing against him rather intimately, since they were both naked. Well, except that she'd kept the unbuttoned, oversize shirt on, which was providing him with a rather erotic display as she slowly began rolling up the overlong sleeves, thus giving him tantalizing glimpses of her decidedly more defined cleavage.

She captured his hands before they could reach their prize. "Oh, no, my love," she purred, tucking them behind his head, the action brushing her heavy, rose-tipped breasts over his chest as her moist heat slid over him again. "You've had a rather hard day, so just lie back and relax. I've got this."

Titus clenched his hands into fists behind his head, suddenly remembering that that sparkle in her eyes and husky voice were telltale signs he should be alarmed.

Now if he could only remember *why.*

Although he was fairly certain it had something to do with her delicious mouth.

And then he stopped trying to remember anything, even his name, when Rana leaned down and kissed his jaw, his neck, his shoulder, his chest—her lips blazing a fiery trail lower and lower and her roaming hands making him nearly forget to breathe.

Being intimately familiar with his body, she knew exactly where to touch him to get the response she was after. And she wasn't shy or the least bit hesitant about what she wanted, either, which was his complete cooperation or else . . . well, in truth, he'd never quite been brave enough to discover the consequences of denying her.

He was snapped out of his musing again when that delicious mouth whispered its intended destination as it moved even lower, and sweat broke out on his forehead when he realized the words had been in French—his wife's language of choice when she was feeling particularly adventurous.

He did wish she'd hurry up and get there before he died of anticipation, but knew she was prolonging the sweet torture because she had a rather diabolical penchant for turning her powerful warrior husband into a quivering ball of sweat—which he'd discovered not two months into their marriage when his shy maiden had suddenly turned into a lusty and daring vixen.

In fact, he was fairly certain that was the night Maximilian had been conceived.

Titus couldn't stifle a shout when she found her target, although he did manage to keep from reaching for her.

"I'm sorry, did I startle you, my love?" she asked in French, her sparkling eyes lifting to his as she kept her pouting mouth pressed intimately against him.

"I'm not even going to get inside you if you keep this up much longer," he said roughly in Greek—his language of *regression* when she was feeling adventurous.

Her big brown eyes remaining locked on his, she

slowly and provocatively *and provokingly* slid her mouth down over him with a loud hum of pleasure.

Titus flopped back with a loud groan of defeat, resigned to becoming a quivering ball of sweat. For having learned that night not two months into their marriage that resistance was futile, he grinned up at the colorful sail through gritted teeth and surrendered to her diabolical loving.

But being an intelligent woman, Rana stopped pushing him to the edge of his control the moment she felt him start to lose it. She scrambled up his body to once again straddle him, leaned down and gave him a lusty kiss as she kneaded her fingers into his chest, and finally sighed his name when he took hold of her hips and slowly and provocatively *and provokingly* guided her down over him.

And as always happened, his stubborn, opinionated, irreverent, lusty, terrible wife proceeded to show him exactly who the true magic-maker was in their marriage.

Chapter Fifteen

Titus couldn't stop grinning like the village idiot as he followed his beautifully disheveled wife strolling through the forest ahead of him, appearing not to have a care in the world as she dodged patches of snow while noisily humming and chewing her way through the bag of figs. He *felt* like an idiot for not immediately recognizing he'd lost control of this kidnapping when he had awakened this morning to find her sprawled on top of him with her chin resting on her hands, her big brown eyes sparkling in the rising sun and her wild hair framing the smuggest, proud-of-herself smile he'd ever seen on a troll.

She of course had insisted they make love again. And being a dutiful husband, he of course had obliged her. But becoming distracted by her passionate response, he apparently hadn't heard the six subtle percussions down on the shoreline and had suddenly found himself kissing empty air when Rana had caught a glimpse of movement in the woods and, with a shriek of horror, scrambled from under him to slip on her oversize shirt just as the six wolves had trotted into camp.

Which is why they'd come damned close to having orca for breakfast.

Finally realizing she didn't have a clue if she had been strolling in the right direction for the last hour, Rana suddenly stopped humming and chewing, glanced around the woods as she shoved the bag of figs in her pocket, and turned to him. "Would it not be easier if we simply followed the shoreline?"

Titus shrugged off the dry bag he'd been wearing like a backpack and unzipped the top. "According to the gazetteer, the forest on this side of Bottomless is riddled with abandoned old logging roads," he said, taking out the large soft-sided book of Maine topographical maps he'd purchased at Ezra's store. He studied the map on the back cover, opened the gazetteer to the proper page, and folded it back on itself. He then held it for her to see when she walked back to him, and tapped the spot where he estimated they were. "If we head uphill in a northeasterly direction, in about a mile we should come across a main artery that runs north and south along the ridge. It would be easier going, as the road would be completely bare," he said, nodding at snowdrifts more than a couple of feet deep where the still low-hanging April sun hadn't yet reached.

She studied the map of the southern half of Bottomless, then took the book away from him and turned to the page that showed the northern end of the inland sea. "But that old tote road," she said, running her finger along the dotted line, "veers to the back side of Duncan's mountain, and we'd have to take a series of crooked spurs to get to the fiord." She handed the book back to him. "It could add two full days to our trek."

"Are you in a hurry to get home?"

She studied him as she licked her sticky fingers, then smiled. "No, I don't suppose I am."

He stuffed the gazetteer back in the dry bag, plucked the figs out of her pocket, then grabbed a handful before stuffing them in the bag. He popped one of the figs in her mouth when she started to protest, slung the bag over his shoulder, and headed uphill. "Since you rounded the southernmost island ahead of me yesterday," he said past his own mouthful of fig, "I suppose we can declare you the victor of our wager."

He heard her stop humming and chewing behind him. "Every time we passed each other, I saw you *eating* the prize. Is there even half a bushel left?"

"Probably not. But," he continued when he heard her snort, "I believe there were two parts to our wager, which means the second prize is still yours to claim."

He didn't have to look back to know she'd stopped walking. "That's right," she said just as he heard twigs snapping as she ran to catch up. "You must grant me one favor."

"So, what is your wish? Take your time," he said when she didn't immediately respond. "And choose carefully. Remember that your any wish will be my command."

"Anything?" she clarified from right behind him.

"Anything."

He grinned when she fell silent for several minutes but

for her slight puffing as the terrain grew steeper. "Even something magical?" she finally asked.

"If the magic is needed to grant your wish, then yes."

She pulled him to a stop and looked him in the eyes. "*Absolutely anything*?"

Since he'd just popped another fig in his mouth, he merely nodded. He held a fig up to her mouth, stared as she slowly and provocatively wrapped her lips around it, then quickly started off again before she could see his scowl.

Fairly certain she already knew what favor she wanted from him, Titus suspected it would take her some time to work up the nerve to *ask* for it. "You needn't decide this instant," he assured her after he'd swallowed, "unless your wish is for a horse to ride instead of spending the next few days walking."

"No. No," she said absently, obviously still thinking. "I enjoy walking. It reminds me of some of the trips we used to take before . . . um, before we moved to Atlantis."

Not all of them pleasant, if he remembered correctly, as they'd often been fleeing his enemies. But with time apparently softening her sense of desperation, he could see how she might recall the forced marches fondly as he also remembered she hadn't ever seemed scared. The one time he'd asked her why not, she'd merely melted into him holding their infant son and stated that worrying was wasted energy, since she was married to a big and powerful and *very devious* warrior.

He'd made a vow to himself that day never to let her regret that boast.

It took them a little over an hour to reach the old tote road due to a couple of potty breaks, which had him worried Rana truly might be with child as he recalled her embarrassment at repeatedly bringing their small entourage to a halt on their final run to Atlantis, when she'd been pregnant with Carolina.

The tote road was indeed bare of snow, and they walked hand in hand for several miles, the conversation limited to an occasional comment on the view as their elevation rose, for it seemed his wife was still working up the courage to ask for her wish.

"Will you look at that," she suddenly whispered, pulling him to a stop. "Oh, she's so homely she's beautiful."

"*He*'s magnificent," Titus said softly as the moose standing in an old clear-cutting stopped ripping the tips off a young fir tree and looked at them.

"*She* doesn't have antlers."

"*He* sheds them every winter. See those two swollen buds over each eye?"

The beast under discussion stopped chewing to listen, then turned its elongated head to the road behind them and lifted its cavernous nose in the air, its huge nostrils billowing as it tried to discern the new scent on the breeze. The bull suddenly gave a deep guttural snort and clomped into the forest, mowing down young trees in its way and throwing up clods of earth in its wake.

"Surely we didn't scare him," Rana said. "We're not even— Kitty, no!" she shouted when the wolf bounded into the cutting, two of his pod-mates giving chase behind him. "Titus, make them stop."

"Kitalanta," he called out, which brought the wolves stumbling to a halt. "Come," he commanded when Kit gave a longing glance toward the path the moose had taken.

"Would it hurt you to *ask* instead of snapping the order at him?"

"You do not insult a warrior by asking him to do something, you *tell* him." He took her hand and started walking again as the three wolves fell into step around them. "If you're looking for a good chase, Kitalanta, go hunt us up a couple of rabbits for dinner," he instructed, only to stop when he realized the wolves had stopped.

"I don't think Kit knows what a rabbit is," Rana said with a laugh. "You better draw him a picture or we're liable to be eating skunk for dinner—assuming the stench coming from your *warrior* doesn't kill our appetites."

The three remaining wolves came tearing down the road from scouting ahead and moved to stand at attention behind Kitalanta. Having no idea how to explain to a killer whale what a rabbit was, Titus sighed in defeat and began walking again.

But after covering two more miles in silence, he finally reached the end of his patience. "For the love of Zeus, just *ask*."

Rana shrugged free and shoved her hands in her pockets as she moved ahead of him. "Very well," she said, her tone as brusque as her pace, "my wish is to continue living in Spellbound Falls and give birth to our child in this century."

"Then consider it done."

"I can't very well drag Maude back to Atlantis," she continued as if he hadn't spoken, "after just moving her and Mathew here."

"No, you can't."

"Olivia and Julia and Peg need her. And the town needs a birthing clinic."

"I agree."

"And I need Maude, so the only sensible solution is for *me* to stay here, too."

Titus stopped walking and sat down on a knoll at the edge of the road, five of the wolves stopping when he did and Kit continuing to pad alongside Rana.

"You said yourself," she continued, "that they know more about growing babies in this century, which very well could make the difference for me this—" Finally realizing he was no longer right behind her, she spun around and briskly strode back to him, her hands now balled into fists at her sides. "Though I realize you might be uncomfortable having a male attend me, you can't deny that to have a highly trained physician like Dr. Bentley standing in the wing won't be reassuring."

"I agree."

"He graduated with *honors*," she went on. "And if you had heard how he grilled Maude to ascertain her skill level and how particular he's being about the equipment, not only would you *insist* we stay in this century, you would also insist that Roger be right outside the birthing room if anything should go wrong."

She began pacing back and forth in front of him, apparently too busy presenting her argument to realize she'd won, and Titus reclined against a mound of dried grass, cupped his hands behind his head, and closed his eyes on a smile. Rana could be quite persuasive when she felt strongly about something, which he'd learned in their first year of marriage when she had burst into his throne room during one of his weekly court sessions gripping the wrist of a horrified fourteen-year-old girl covered in bruises.

But instead of demanding that he imperially confiscate the young slave as their own, his wife—at the time barely two years older than the girl—had quietly remarked to everyone present how courageous a man must be to brutalize a defenseless young girl, and how impressed she'd been to see people scurrying past the one-sided altercation that was clearly none of their business. And then she'd turned to him and suggested he never allow the girl's *former* master to own female slaves ever again.

The entire assembly had remained silent throughout her little lecture, and he'd known everyone had been waiting to see how much sway their king's new bride carried. Despite the risk of openly wearing his heart on his sleeve, Titus had shown exactly how much power his wife wielded by not only imperially claiming the girl as *Rana's* property—along with any other slaves the man owned—but also banishing the bastard from the kingdom.

And that was the day the lowly blacksmith's daughter had truly become his queen. And not only did no one ever question her authority from that point forward, *they* also began wearing their hearts on their sleeves for her.

It had been that very night he had found himself explaining to his still-outraged wife that as a self-proclaimed theurgist, his role was to protect free will rather than force mankind to blindly follow *his* will. He could, however, he'd assured her, nudge folks in the right direction, especially now that he had a queen who not only shared his vision, but who obviously had the courage to let him begin implementing his plan.

Titus snapped open his eyes when he realized Rana had suddenly stopped in mid-sentence, then bolted upright barely in time to catch her when she pounced.

"You blackguard!" she cried as she wrapped her arms around his neck and hugged his face to her bosom. "You let me go right on talking, even though you had already decided we're staying before I even asked."

"There was nothing to decide, as I had given my word." He lay back and settled her against his side, then held her head to his chest. "And now, wife," he said quietly, "in return for granting your wish, I would have you explain exactly why you left me, when you should have been running *to me* at such a precious time."

She became busy toying with the pocket flap on his jacket, and he could almost hear her brain working as she searched for an answer. He gave her a gentle squeeze to let her know he would settle for nothing less than the truth.

"Even after all these years," she finally said, "I still can't always predict how you'll react to . . . unfavorable news."

"And you felt our having a child was unfavorable news?"

"Well, no." She tilted her head back to look at him. "But I remember what you were like after Carolina was born," she whispered as she looked away and toyed with the pocket again. "Everyone on the island remembers, as many of them bore the brunt of your anger. But what I remember most is that it took you three months to finally hold your daughter in your arms."

Titus brushed a thumb over her cheek. "I almost lost you," he said roughly. "But that still doesn't explain your leaving me now," he added when she tried to speak.

He felt her hesitate and then take a deep breath. "When I realized I was with child, I panicked." She moved her head inside his hand to look at him again. "Believe me, I would have been less shocked to find out *you* were pregnant." She went back to staring at his chest. "I left you for two reasons: The first being that you know me too well and would have quickly realized my condition, and the second is that I needed time alone to figure out what to do."

"There is nothing 'to do' if a child has decided to be born."

She patted his jacket with a humorless laugh. "I needed to figure out what to do about *you*." She slipped free and sat up, then arched an eyebrow at him. "You made a pact with *your enemies* to keep Carolina safe until her thirty-first birthday, and you wiped out Henry's entire maternal family when they tried to kill Maximilian. I was afraid you'd make an even more outrageous deal with Providence itself," she said, waving toward the sky, "to keep me safe. You were taken by surprise when I nearly died having Carolina, but this time you would have had *months* to plan and scheme."

"Thank you for the vote of confidence," he drawled.

That raised her hackles. "Do you truly expect me to believe you wouldn't go crazy when you found out?"

He held his arms away from his sides, his gaze locked on her glare. "Am I crazy now? Or did I go crazy yesterday when you shouted it at me in the middle of a battle? Or after, once you were safe?"

She blinked at him for several heartbeats, clearly nonplussed, then pounced. "No!" she yelped, ignoring his grunt when she hit dangerously close to his groin and started planting kisses all over his face. "You've . . . been . . . very . . . civilized." But then she just as suddenly reared away, her gasp drowning out his second grunt. "Because you don't believe I'm pregnant!"

"Poseidon's teeth," he growled, plastering her against his side before she finally unmanned him. "I will remain civilized either way. Now settle down. I need a nap."

She held herself stiff in his arms, obviously trying to decide if she believed him or not, then finally relaxed against him with a heavy sigh. "It's going to take us a month to get home at this speed," she whispered, apparently also happy to drop the subject.

"Are you in much of a hurry?"

She shrugged. "I don't mind missing Carolina's wedding if you don't."

Titus blew out a sigh of his own. "I offered Alec a bottomless satchel of money a couple of weeks ago if he would persuade Carolina to elope."

She looked at him. "That's why you rode your motorcycle to Pine Creek?"

He pressed her head back down. "The idiot thanked me for the kind offer, but said he likes being a poor ski bum because he claims it makes Jane feel superior."

Rana snorted into his chest. "You men do love creating that illusion for us."

"Ah, wife," he said as he gave her a squeeze, "we create the illusion hoping you women won't realize you have us on our knees."

She let out a noisy yawn and patted his chest. "How devious you men are."

Titus stared up at the puffy clouds marching northward from the Gulf of Maine, bringing with them the promise of an even warmer day tomorrow, and listened to his wife's breathing slowly even out in sleep. Though he would have preferred a less drastic means, he was glad the storm had stranded them out here in the wilderness, as it was obvious they needed this time together. And since they were on the subject of trying to anticipate each other's reaction to her . . . what had she called it? *Unfavorable news.* Well, this was probably a good time for them to discuss *his* news. Although now that he knew her secret, Titus didn't think his would affect her too unfavorably.

Only sentimentally.

It would, however, affect everyone on Atlantis. He doubted Maximilian would be very thrilled, and Carolina would probably throw a royal fit on the scale of one of Ella's. As for Nicholas . . . actually, the warrior might in fact prove to be an ally.

Not that it mattered, since last he knew he wasn't running a democracy.

No, the only person whose opinion he valued when making his final decision was Rana. He would tell her as soon as they began the day's hike tomorrow, so they'd have plenty of time to discuss the consequences of what he was about to do before they shared their doubly exciting news with the rest of their magical world.

Chapter Sixteen

Mac stood on the very same rock he knew his father had stood on not eighteen hours ago, and dried his chest with his shirt before slipping it on and buttoning it up as he watched Niall MacKeage pull what remained of the modern catamaran deeper into the forest. He turned to see Duncan and Nicholas emerge from the woods, Duncan carrying the mainsail of the catamaran and Nicholas carrying the oiled canvas bag Mac knew his mother always kept on her sloop, which was now resting in four hundred feet of water on the floor of Bottomless.

"They appear to have set out for home on foot," Nicholas said with a grin, tossing the bag into the bow of Duncan's speedboat. "Accompanied by six wolves."

"Why would they do that?" Niall asked, his gaze darting between Nicholas and Mac. "They had to know you'd come looking for them."

Mac slipped on his jacket. "If I were to hazard a guess, I would say Dad is taking advantage of some quality time alone with his wife while she can't run away."

"But that's at least a four-day walk and it drops below freezing at night," Niall apparently felt compelled to point out. He gestured at the sail Duncan had just tossed in the boat. "And they have no shelter or supplies." The highlander hesitated in apparent thought, then grinned. "Unless Titus should happen to find a backpack full of food leaning against a tree, along with a tent."

Nicholas was already shaking his head. "He won't use the magic around Rana unless it's an emergency."

"Mother is a mortal," Mac explained at Niall's obvious confusion. "And the magic upsets her stomach." He looked at Nicholas. "You said Dante had no warning the new god would try manifesting again yesterday?"

"No one knew, not even their leader, Sebastian. And last night Dante told me they still don't know. Everyone saw the storm from the settlement, but it was too far away on the opposite shore for them to think it was anything more than an ordinary squall. Dante said they're actually planning another ceremony later this week."

"According to Leviathan, we now have demons to contend with as well," Mac said. "Dad set the great whites on them and quickly ended the fight, but I wasn't able to find out if the entity survived." Only just now realizing what Nicholas had said, Mac stiffened. "If the storm was along the eastern shore and the new god *did* survive, it could be here on the same side as Mom and Dad. And that means they could end up in the middle of another battle."

Nicholas shook his head again. "The demons are no

match for Titus. And don't forget he has the orcas, which is probably why he took them." Nicholas hopped into the boat. "Leave them be, Mac. Your father has been protecting Rana since before you were born, and from enemies far more dangerous than a fledgling god and a few cowardly demons."

"When he was in his *prime*," Mac snapped, also vaulting into the boat.

"You might want to refrain from saying that to his face," Nicholas said with a chuckle. "As I believe he can still whip your magical ass."

Mac grinned. "He'd have to catch me first." But he quickly sobered as he looked up at the mountains forming a solid wall along the eastern side of the inland sea, then glanced out over the water before eyeing Nicholas again.

The warrior straightened with a scowl. "No. Leave them alone."

Mac merely grinned again.

"What?" Niall asked, stepping into the boat and sitting down at the stern as he glanced at Mac. "What are ye thinking?"

"I'm thinking that I see no reason why the orcas have to be their only protection."

"No," Nicholas repeated.

Mac merely folded his arms over his chest and leaned back against the gunwale.

"Would you please tell me why you've been treating Titus like a doddering old man lately?" Nicholas asked.

Mac stared at his childhood friend, then leaned forward and scrubbed his face in his hands. "Because," he said, dropping his arms to his knees, "he's up to something. I don't know what," he rushed on when the warrior tried to speak. "But ever since Mom left him, Dad's been withdrawn and more secretive than usual. Why wouldn't he tell us why he went to Atlantis last week?"

"Exactly how would you be acting if Olivia suddenly left you after only four years of marriage," Nicholas asked, "much less after *forty*?"

Mac dropped his gaze to stare down at his clasped hands. "Point taken." He looked up. "But I still say he's up to something. Mother leaving him might be a big part of it, but I can feel in my bones that he's planning something . . . epic. And if you're honest, you have to admit you've also felt it."

Duncan gave the boat a push, then hopped onto the bow as it glided away from the shoreline. "Has anyone learned why Rana left him?"

"No," Mac said with a shrug. "She'd confided in no one, not even Carolina."

"Nor Mom," Nicholas added. "Although I saw hints last fall that Rana was unhappy."

"But she and Dad were acting like newlyweds all winter after you got back from your mission," Mac pointed out.

"So what's the plan, gentlemen?" Duncan asked, sitting down behind the wheel but not starting the engine. "Do we send out a search party for them?"

"No. Instead, I think we should look for signs that the new god managed to reach shore."

Duncan's jaw went slack as he glanced up the inland sea. "You're talking about searching over fifty miles of shoreline on just this side alone."

"Which should take less than a day for a small army of gulls," Mac drawled.

He then stood up and spread his arms—stifling a grin

when he saw Niall stiffen—and braced himself against the surge he knew was coming. Feeling his body slowly begin to expand as he called forth the energy surrounding Bottomless, Mac silently summoned his feathered allies until the sky above the boat was filled with noisy gulls. He instructed them to search every nook and cranny of shoreline, beginning on the eastern side of the sea, looking for even the smallest sign that something had dragged itself ashore. The darting and diving birds circled in raucous chaos before suddenly dispersing in three directions: one group going north, the other south, and the third racing out to the nearest islands.

"Jesus, Joseph, and Mary," Niall whispered, dropping his gaze from the sky and his eyes widening even more as Mac slowly returned to his normal height.

Mac lowered his arms and grinned. "Have you not seen de Gairn ever work the magic, MacKeage?"

"Matt . . ." Niall cleared his throat and shook his head. "Nay, not directly."

"You've felt the brunt of it a time or two, though," Duncan said with a chuckle.

Mac looked at where his parents had come ashore yesterday, then sat down again to disguise his shudder as he recalled Leviathan's account of his father's struggle to save his mother. Why hadn't Titus used the magic to whisk her to safety instead of swimming more than a mile through frigid water in the middle of a vicious battle? He could have had her on top of Whisper Mountain with no more than a blink of his eye, far away from storms and demons and freezing temperatures. If nearly drowning didn't constitute an emergency, then what in the name of Hades did?

"So now what?" Duncan asked as he started the motor and slowly idled north.

"Now we wait," Mac said, "to see if the world has a new god."

"And if it does?" Niall asked.

"Then we wait to see if we've gained an ally or an enemy."

"And your parents?" Duncan asked.

Mac rested against the gunwale and looked toward the mountains. "We wait to see if they walk out of the wilderness holding hands or throwing rocks at each other."

The latter, he was afraid, being a real possibility if the secret Titus was keeping had made him desperate enough to kidnap his wife.

Slowly working the tangles out of her hair while strolling down the old tote road, Rana smiled as she remembered feasting like royalty on spit-roasted partridge last night, thanks to the hunting prowess of their four-legged warrior—Kitalanta apparently assuming that anything with feathers was edible. Then again, maybe the orca had learned a little something about the human palate during the time he spent on land with Alec and Carolina each summer.

She was just thankful he hadn't brought them seagull.

"No," her husband said gruffly, taking the comb from her and slipping it in his pocket before clasping her hand in his. "I like seeing you beautifully disheveled."

Rana continued smiling at the road ahead, wondering how he'd liked her falling asleep on him last night after only a kiss. And how beautiful he thought she had been this morning when she'd bolted for the woods just as he was reaching for her, or how he'd enjoyed listening to her throwing up spit-roasted partridge and figs and what she suspected was leftover seawater from her near drowning.

The morning sickness had caught her by surprise, since she hadn't had any bouts of nausea up to this point. She'd been in a constant state of queasiness at the beginning of her other two pregnancies, but both the midwife she'd had for Maximilian and Maude had assured her that throwing up was a welcome sign the babe was settling in strongly. And that had made her worry about not feeling sick with this babe, although she had been taking many naps and gaining weight.

Titus squeezed her hand just as she heard him take a deep breath. "What if I were to tell you," he said quietly, "that you're not the only one who's been keeping a secret these last couple of weeks?"

She lifted her gaze to his and widened her eyes. "You're pregnant, too?"

Instead of returning her smile, he looked at the road ahead. "Have you found yourself feeling homesick for Atlantis this past winter?"

She looked up at him again, alarmed by the seriousness in his tone. "Well, I'll admit I have missed my friends and our staff." She gave a soft laugh. "And the warm, sunny weather." She stopped walking. "Why do you ask? Are *you* homesick? Is that why you went to the island last week?"

He gently tapped the tip of her nose and started them walking again. "I went home to get you some of Mathew's peaches and figs."

"And Michelin's goat cheese and bread. Did you bring them back hoping to make *me* homesick?"

He gave her hand another squeeze. "That was not my intent, and I'm sorry if they did." He hesitated, then said, "I went back to walk the length and breadth of the island and merely . . . look around."

"And what did you see?"

This time he was the one who brought them to a stop, his deep green eyes troubled. "I saw the accumulated knowledge of mankind in practice; people living in peace and harmony and joy as they stretch their imaginations to add to that knowledge." He looked past her into the distance and shrugged. "I saw a myth."

"Atlantis is as real as you are," she said, reaching up and clasping his face so he'd look at her. "You built it precisely to prove that living in peace and harmony and joy is *not* a myth; that mankind *does* have the knowledge and resources to create a better world."

He wrapped her up in his big strong arms. "They're not getting the message. But for a few shining examples, the world is no better off than it was three thousand years ago." She felt his chest deflate on another sigh. "If anything, modern technology is accelerating humanity *away* from the truth."

His embrace tightened at her gasp. "You do *not* believe that." She wiggled her arms free to clasp his face again. "Mankind's stubbornness isn't new," she said softly. "So why has it suddenly become an issue? And what does it have to do with my being homesick, which is where you started this conversation?"

"Atlantis is no longer serving its purpose." He pulled her hands down and held them in his. "And I believe it is time for it to stop being a myth and finally be discovered so the world will have indisputable proof that the magic is real."

"But to what gain?" she whispered, feeling a cold chill race up her spine. He was talking about destroying their home. "What do you expect modern man to do with the discovery of an ancient, advanced society?"

"I would hope they would study it and learn the lessons it has to offer."

"And our people," she asked softly. "What would you have happen to them?"

He released one of her hands, but kept the other firmly clasped in his as he started walking again. "The majority of the population is the original settlers I gathered together, and I would give them the choice of returning to their countries in their natural time or following their children, who have already migrated into the real world."

Rana was at a complete loss as to what to say, much less think. Well, other than *he* had obviously been thinking about this for some time. Sweet Athena, his secret certainly put hers into perspective, didn't it?

"Do your thinking out loud, wife."

"You . . . you don't believe destroying Atlantis is a bit drastic to prove your point?"

"It has outlived its purpose," he repeated. "The Trees of Life are safely scattered around the world and are thriving, as are two generations of Atlanteans. Some of our people have already followed their children, which was always my intent." She looked up to see him smiling. "It is they who subsequently gave the world many of its great artists and scholars and innovators; men such as Da Vinci, Newton, Galileo, Einstein, and Buckminster

Fuller, to name a few." He shot her a wink. "And your good friend Johann Strauss."

"But Atlantis is your seat of power."

He went back to staring at the road ahead and gestured at the mountains to the north with his free hand. "Maybe it's time that we, too, let our children get on with the business of inspiring mankind by bringing a more modern-thinking energy to the world."

Rana pulled him to a stop. "You want to hand over your power to Maximilian?"

"Not my power—my *authority*." He ran a finger down her cheek. "The transfer began four years ago, when Maximilian created the Bottomless Sea and made Whisper Mountain *his* seat of power."

"And at the time, you knew this? But you appeared pleased with what he had done," she added when he nodded.

He started them walking again. "I was immensely pleased that our son not only had the gonads to pull that kind of stunt," he said with a grin, "but that he did it for all the right reasons—including for the love of a good woman." He gave her another wink. "Are you not also proud of *how* he did it? Moving mountains and creating an inland sea in the middle of the wilderness let the world know Maximilian Oceanus is in full command of his power, and that he sure as hell isn't afraid to use it."

"But you have successfully kept Atlantis hidden for millennia by disguising its appearance, whereas Maximilian's seat of power is right in the middle of the modern world, which has airplanes and cameras and satellites."

"Hiding in plain sight is often the best disguise."

Rana shoved her free hand in her pocket and scowled at

the ground. Titus had known for the last four years that their son had been positioning himself to take over? She shrugged her hand from his and smacked him in the side. "Did it ever occur to you to tell *me* what was happening?"

He captured her hand with a chuckle. "I'm telling you now."

"Four years *late*," she snapped.

"I'm explaining that the transfer *began* that day. It won't be complete until I decide it is."

"And . . . and you've decided?"

"Almost."

She glared up at him. "What do you mean, almost?"

"I'm waiting to hear the opinion of my most valued advisor and confidant."

She went back to scowling at the ground. "Who?" she whispered.

He pulled her to a stop and gathered her in his arms again. "That would be my stubborn, opinionated, irreverent, lusty, terrible wife."

She wanted to smack him again—which he must have anticipated, since he'd nicely trapped her in his embrace—but instead rested her forehead on his chest. "Oh, Titus, can you not let Maximilian come into his power without destroying Atlantis?"

"The world doesn't need two reigning theurgists," he said, even as she felt his embrace tighten, "which is why I also intend to renounce the *divine* aspect of my title along with my crown."

It was a good thing he was holding her, because her knees buckled.

He pressed his lips to her hair. "Immortality is no blessing, Stasia, if it can't be shared with the one person who gives it meaning. When I say I love you more than life itself, I'm speaking literally."

"But what you want to do is . . . Titus, it's blasphemous."

"No, Stasia. For me to face eternity without you is." He swept her off her feet when her legs gave out completely, then walked to the edge of the road and sat down with her in his lap. "I know it wasn't your intention," he said, smoothing a hand over her hair, "but these last couple of weeks without you gave me a frightening glimpse of my future and exposed my cowardice." He ducked his head to look her in the eyes. "I'm afraid, wife, of seeing sunsets you won't be seeing, of lying in bed listening to rain you won't be hearing, and of breathing air you won't be breathing. It will not be life without you—it will be madness. Please, little one," he whispered against her cheek, "allow me to join you in life ever after."

"Do . . . do you even have that kind of power?"

"Yes. That is the very definition of free will."

She leaned away enough to look him in the eyes, and started trembling when she saw not only his love shining brightly, but his utterly calm conviction.

He pressed a finger to her lips when she tried to speak. "I'm not talking about deliberately ending my life, Stasia. I'm talking about renouncing my immortality. The moment I do, from that day forward we will simply grow old *together*."

She turned to lean back against him and stared out over Bottomless. "You know what I think you're really afraid of," she whispered so she wouldn't burst into tears at his ultimate gesture of love. "You're afraid I will come back and haunt you if you even smile at another woman after I'm gone." Feeling him still in surprise, she nodded curtly. "Because you know me well enough to realize I'm not one of those altruistic women who would want you to move on and be happy. Because what really scares you is knowing that if I ever caught wind of you trying to impress another woman with grand—or worse, *small*—gestures of your esteem, I would . . ." She turned to let him see her smile, making sure it was warm and sincere and very threatening. "Well, let's just say you're not the only devious one in this family." She set her finger under his chin and closed his mouth, then leaned back into him again. "I love you for loving me that much, Titus," she said, even as she wondered why she sounded hoarse, "but I'm going to need some time to think about everything you just . . . about your news."

He folded his arms over her chest and hugged her to him as he rested his chin on her shoulder. "You do know that I'll just wait until you die and *then* renounce my immortality."

"So long as you know I'm going to make you court me all over again on the other side."

He jostled her with his quiet laughter. "Then I will be sure to bring a heart-shaped pebble and *two* bushels of peaches."

Chapter Seventeen

For as much as he was enjoying his little kidnapping despite having lost control of it, and even though his wife was obviously enjoying herself, Titus realized his feet hurt to the point he was starting to limp.

So if wishes were horses, why in Hades were they walking like beggars?

His belly wasn't all that happy, either. The last of the figs had vanished down Rana's throat by the end of the first day, she'd licked every last morsel of goat cheese out of the container by noon yesterday, and he was tired of eating partridge for breakfast, lunch, and dinner.

So since he was already wishing . . .

Titus made sure not to grin when they rounded a curve in the road and Rana suddenly stopped. He also made sure to appear equally surprised as they both stared at the ink-black horse tied to a tree, the huge beast dressed in tournament finery and sporting two bulging leather satchels slung over its saddle.

"Now where do you suppose he came from?" Titus said, making a production of glancing around and even behind them.

Rana arched an eyebrow. "Yes, where indeed?"

"Well, since he *is* here, we can't very well leave the poor beast stranded in the middle of the wilderness."

"You're not supposed to use the magic. It could hurt the baby."

"Does your stomach feel upset?" he asked as he started them walking again.

"Well . . . no."

"Then I guess this must be an ordinary horse."

"It's the warhorse you owned when we met," she snapped, tugging against his hold on her hand, "which should be several thousand years *dead*."

"Then he must be a figment of our imagination. Or maybe even a mirage."

The figment of their imagination let out a loud whinny when it spotted them and began impatiently tossing its head and pawing the ground.

"By the looks of the bushes and ground around him," Titus continued as they drew near, "I would estimate he's been standing here nearly an hour. So if he is indeed magical, he must have arrived when we were a safe distance away." He finally let go of her hand when his trusted steed reared up on its haunches, knowing Rana's reluctance now had more to do with the fact that it was a warhorse than a magical manifestation. "Behave yourself, Salt," he commanded, shrugging off his dry bag and then untying the reins from the tree. "You're in the presence of a lady."

"Maybe he smells the wolves," Rana said from several paces away—even as her eyes took on a sparkle. "Or else the tournament dress makes him think you're taking him to the games, as I remember Salt being more of a show-off than *you*."

Titus stroked the horse's neck. "What I remember is that you only agreed to meet me in the meadow if I promised to let you ride him."

"Yet another one of your devious tactics to get me alone."

He shot her a wink. "Which worked pretty damn well."

His beautifully irreverent wife smiled smugly. "Until my father showed up."

"Quickly followed by your mother, thank the gods. Come, m'lady," he said with a deep bow as he swept an arm toward Salt. "Your noble steed awaits."

"I think you should take him for a gallop first, while I sit here with the . . . luggage."

Which she likely intended to paw through the moment he was out of sight. Titus pulled off the leather bags and set them beside the tree, vaulted up into the saddle, then gave a loud whistle to call Kitalanta as he controlled the prancing horse. "Kit will stay with you until I return. Are you comfortable being alone for ten or twenty minutes?"

She waved him away, already heading for the satchels. "Take all the time you want." She sat down beside the tree and patted one of the bags, smiling at him. "I promise to be right here when you get back."

"Will there be any food left when I get back?"

Her eyes widened in mock surprise as she looked at the satchels. "You believe they're full of food?" She looked at him in mock wonder. "How lucky we are to have stumbled upon a mirage carrying what surely must be a veritable feast."

"Just don't drink the wine," he said with a laugh, finally releasing the impatient warhorse and tearing up the road at a flat-out gallop.

Rana waited until Titus was out of sight, then threw herself onto the nearest satchel and gave it a fierce hug. "Oh, thank the gods," she sobbed in relief at the thought of having real food. "I swear if Kitty trotted up as proud as a peacock with another partridge in his mouth tonight, I was going to throw rocks at him."

She really remembered camping as being more fun—or at least less grueling. Sweet Athena, it was taking all her energy not to let Titus see she was *limping*. And she stank, and she itched, and she missed her soft bed tucked under the eave of her house. And if her maddening husband told her how beautifully disheveled she was one more time, she was going to throw rocks at *him*. And not pebbles, either, but fist-sized rocks that left *marks*.

Except the blackguard appeared to be enjoying himself so much, she simply didn't have the heart to tell him she was miserable. A bath might help. Heck, even a sponge bath would go a long way to making her feel human again. But she needed a pot in order to heat water.

She sat up and began unbuckling the clasp on the satchel, only to stop in mid-unbuckle when she spotted Kitty sitting in the middle of the road, his head cocked sideways, studying her. "Yes. Well. I'm going to have a baby," she explained, wiping her cheeks with the dirty sleeve of her jacket. "And pregnant women cry for absolutely no reason. So let's not mention this little episode to Titus, okay?"

His silver lupine eyes reflecting the warmth of the sun, the wolf cocked his head again, then let out a huge yawn and walked his feet forward to lie down.

Rana went back to unbuckling the satchel, not really sure how much Kitalanta understood, since she couldn't *magically* talk to him the way everyone else in her family could. Oh, she spoke and read most every language on the planet like all Atlanteans, but she'd had to learn them the good old-fashioned way by working with tutors until she'd thought her eyes and ears and lips would fall off. She could not, however, communicate with animals.

"Yes!" she cried, reaching inside the satchel. She pulled out the small cast-iron pot and held it toward Kitty when he raised his head. "I'm having a sponge bath tonight." She set down the pot and dug in the satchel again, this time pulling out *two* bottles of wine. She ran a thumb over one of the labels, then set them beside the pot with a sigh of regret. "If I find out he fabricated that story about wine being bad for unborn babies," she said to no one in particular, digging in the satchel, "a few fist-sized rocks will be the least of his worries."

Her eyes started leaking tears again as she pulled out ancient delicacies fit for a king and starving queen. But then her relief turned to alarm when she saw there was enough food to last them a whole friggin' *week*. She quickly opened the other satchel and went back to crying in relief when she found it filled with warm clothes, a beautiful quilt, soap and scented oils, and a gold and pearl barrette.

"What, no mirror?" she muttered, holding the cavernous

bag upside down and shaking it, then tossing it away with another sigh. "Well, maybe that's for the best, as I would probably scream if I saw myself right now. But at least I can have a sponge—"

She stilled when Kitalanta suddenly jumped to his feet, his hackles raised and his lips rolling back on a growl as he stared down the road to the south. It was then she heard the pounding of galloping hoofs coming from the north and quickly started stuffing everything back into the satchels.

"Rana, come," Titus said as he pulled Salt to a stop and held his hand down to her. "Now, wife!"

She immediately scrambled to her feet and ran over while stuffing whatever food she'd been holding into her pockets, then lifted her arms to him.

"No, behind me," he said as he took his foot out of his stirrup.

She clasped his wrist as he gripped hers, slipped her foot into the stirrup, and used the momentum of his pull to swing up behind him. Wrapping her arms securely around his waist as he spurred Salt into a gallop, Rana glanced over her shoulder to see Kitalanta disappear into the woods, then pressed her cheek to her husband's back and watched the trees zooming by. Despite not knowing what they were running from, her heart nevertheless raced with hope that it was the new god or goddess, as that would mean the entity *had* survived the demon attack three days ago.

"Hang on," Titus said roughly, one of his hands dropping to clasp her thigh as he turned off the road. The horse lunged over the ditch without breaking stride and began mowing down bushes as it struggled up through the narrow clear-cutting. "Protect your face," he added, his grip on her leg nearly bruising when they plunged into the forest and he expertly guided the horse weaving through the trees as they continued climbing the steep ridge.

Hiding her face in his jacket again as branches slapped against them, Rana found herself wondering how much her husband was enjoying their stroll home now. Because personally, she had thought they were centuries past having to flee for their lives. Or rather of Titus having to flee for *her* life—and the lives of his people—as he had done countless times before they'd moved to Atlantis. Tactical retreats, he'd called them, when she knew he would have preferred to stand and fight.

Well, that's what he got for championing *mortals*.

She didn't quite manage to stifle a scream when Salt skidded to a stop, the horse's sides expanding in billowing pants as Titus looked at her—one regal white eyebrow lifting over vivid green eyes shining with excitement. Rana rested her head against him again at the realization that contrary to the fact that they'd just ridden hell-bent for leather away from some unnamed threat, he definitely was enjoying himself.

"Are you okay?"

"Wonderful. Do you know what we are running from?"

"That."

She straightened to look at where he was looking and saw a towering tree racing up the road from the south, the dark, unmistakable silhouettes of no less than a dozen demons chasing it. The tree suddenly stopped, its massive, leafless branches slicing through the air with the force of cracking whips as it turned to face its attackers.

Titus swung his leg over Salt's neck and slid to the

ground, then helped her dismount as she continued watching the road below. "It's the new god or goddess," she said as he hugged her from behind. "It survived. Oh please, Titus, you must help it," she softly petitioned when the demons began circling the tree like snarling jackals.

"I'm sorry, I can't," he returned, his voice thick with an emotion she couldn't identify. "He must want to manifest badly enough to fight for the privilege. Don't worry. What doesn't kill him will make him stronger."

"And if it's a goddess?"

"I'm sorry," he repeated. "If she can't defeat a few paltry demons, then what good will she be to mankind?" He stopped her from turning to hide her face in his chest when the tree suddenly gave a blood-curdling roar. "No, don't look away," he softly commanded, dropping his head down beside hers. "Witness the birth of a god."

"Or its death," she rasped as she watched the entity repeatedly lash out at the snarling demons, the roars and screams of the vicious battle echoing up the ridge. "The odds are twelve to *one*."

"Then let us hope what he lacks in strength he makes up in cunning."

"What do you mean? Wait, you said *he*. You know it's a god?"

He straightened away with a chuckle. "Even a fledgling goddess would quickly figure out that demons don't have the brains of a slug, and would use their stupidity to her advantage." He snorted. "Gods being physically stronger, our *first* instinct is to fight rather than think our way out of situations."

Rana caught her breath. "Did you have to fight for your life?"

"I earned my place in your world." He ducked his head beside hers again. "With the help of a wandering mortal who thankfully had more muscle than good sense when he stumbled upon a scene not unlike the one below."

"A mortal came to your aid?" She leaned to the side to look at him. "Is he the reason you championed mankind?"

Her husband gave her a quick kiss then straightened. "Let's just say that was the day I learned I'd rather have a man guarding my back than most gods. There," he said gruffly, turning her to face the battle again. "It's about damned time."

"What? I don't see anything. Where did he go? Is . . . is he dead?"

"No. He finally realized he has the power to stop being a large, vulnerable tree and simply turned himself into a less obvious target."

"What did he turn into?" she asked, scanning up and down the road and seeing only the perplexed demons running in circles and now snarling at each other.

"Come," he said, leading her over to Salt. "We need to get out of here before they catch our scent."

"But what did he become?" she asked as he lifted her onto the saddle.

He swung up behind her, settled her onto his lap as he slid forward into place, then wrapped an arm around her waist and shrugged. "Since he appears to be an earth god, I imagine he turned into an innocuous twig or weed," he said, reining the horse uphill and urging it into a brisk walk.

Rana leaned around him to see the road. "Where are Kitty and the others?" She twisted to look at him. "They won't go after the demons, will they?"

He nudged her to face forward again. "They're covering our back trail. Kitalanta will stay out of sight and not give away our presence." He chuckled when his stomach suddenly gave a loud rumble, then dropped his hand from around her to pat the front of her jacket. "Did I see you stuffing food in your pockets when I came for you?"

She pressed back against him to reach inside both pockets at the same time, her right hand reemerging with a small waxed wheel of cheese and the left with a bunch of smashed grapes, which she held up for him to see.

"I do love a woman who thinks fast on her feet," he said, giving her a squeeze. "Will you be very disappointed if we cut our trip short and ride straight through the night to the MacKeages'?"

Rana lowered her hands with a loud, exaggerated, very disappointed sigh. "I suppose we must, since the wilderness has suddenly become so crowded," she said, lapping juice off her fingers and then sucking two grapes into her mouth.

He nudged her arm. "Feed me."

She reached up and pushed several of the smashed grapes into his mouth. "We can't just drop in unannounced on Duncan and Peg in the middle of the night." She shoved two more grapes in her own mouth. "I don't want to alarm the children."

"We won't be arriving unannounced," he said with another chuckle, gesturing at the sky, "thanks to your son's small army of feathered spies."

Rana looked up through the tree canopy to see several gulls circling overhead. She then looked at where Titus was now pointing and spotted the bald eagle perched at the top of a giant pine, its sharp golden eyes following their progress before it suddenly spread its wings and took flight—heading directly north, she noticed.

She pushed the remaining grapes into his mouth. "I can't imagine where *your* son could have picked up the habit of spying on people. Titus," she said as she stared down at the wheel of cheese. "What happened to the man who helped you the day you manifested?"

"I gave Lombard a hero's burial."

"You . . . your magic couldn't save him?"

"It can only save those who choose life over death," he said quietly, "and Lombard preferred to join his slaughtered wife and children. I believe he was wandering the countryside looking for a good fight to hurry his journey to them, which is why he charged into the swarm of demons to save my life with no concern for his own."

"If you learned that about him," Rana whispered, "that would mean he didn't die in battle."

"I kept him as comfortable as I could for eight days." He gave a humorless laugh. "During which time it became clear to both of us that I hadn't manifested to be anyone's nursemaid." He ducked his head beside hers again. "In return for my crude care, Lombard passed the hours by giving me a glimpse into the mortal mind, and I became enthralled to find myself having candid, philosophical discussions with a learned man who had strong opinions on religion, politics, and life in general."

"All these years and you never told me about him."

He straightened away with a shrug. "Not for want of hiding anything. When I met you, Lombard was nearly a thousand years dead."

"But you were a young man of twenty-two when we met."

Her back vibrated with what she suspected was a silent chuckle. "I couldn't very well present myself as a doddering old man to a beautiful young maiden who happened to have a well-muscled blacksmith for a father."

"How old were you, then?" she asked, twisting to look at him. Catching his grin before he could disguise it, she jabbed him with her elbow hard enough to make him grunt. "You were a lecherous old man!"

"Ah, Stasia," he said with an outright laugh, "have you not learned in the course of our magical marriage that like *time*, age is also a human contrivance? We are all of us as young or old as we feel." He pressed his cheek to hers. "And the moment I looked into your scowling eyes that day at the tournament, I felt like a young warrior in his prime who also was old enough to know the difference between lust and love. And," he whispered against her ear, "wise enough to follow you home."

"But you said you almost gave up on me."

"Zeus knows I tried," he said with a chuckle, reining Salt to a stop when they emerged onto another, much narrower tote road. "I even made it ten miles out of town before remembering something Lombard had said about women in general and stubborn young maidens in particular."

"What did he say?"

"He told me the harder a man must work to capture the heart of a beautiful maiden, the more of a prize she will be." Titus lifted her right leg over Salt's neck and turned her to sit sideways inside his embrace. "Because, Lombard said, a woman who knows her own worth will settle for nothing less than *all* a man has to give. And he assured me a stubborn, opinionated, irreverent wife will keep a man young, and that their marriage will never, ever be boring."

"I would like to have met Lombard," she said, twining her arms around his neck, "as he sounds very wise."

Her husband's deep rich eyes took on a twinkle. "I believe he would have approved of my choice."

Instead of being gathered closer to be kissed, Rana gasped when she felt herself falling, the blackguard's laughter accompanying her down as he threw a leg over Salt's neck and slid to the ground. He held her steady until she found her footing, then turned her toward the woods and gave her a pat on the backside to get her moving. "Go take a potty break," he said, plucking the cheese out of her hand, "before our final push to the MacKeages'."

Rana walked into the woods, scowling and rubbing her backside, and decided her big warrior husband was enjoying himself way too much. But then she broke into a smile at the realization she was only hours away from sinking into a blessedly hot bath before collapsing face-down onto one of Peg's blessedly soft guest beds.

And by the gods, the next time Titus wanted to go camping, he'd better show up in a fully equipped RV bus like Maximilian and Olivia's, or she would make sure the blackguard wished he *had* continued walking out of town forty years ago.

Chapter Eighteen

Worry was an insidious infliction, Titus decided as he lay staring up at the ceiling only a few feet above his head, in that it tended to consume all rational thought until a seemingly innocuous concern grew into an overwhelming problem. Like with Rana; her worry over what he might do upon learning she was with child had become such a huge, scary problem in her mind that she'd run away.

And like with him now, Titus thought as he toyed with the silky, rose-scented hair splayed across his chest; for the last three days he had been consumed with worry over what Rana's reaction would be when he told her they weren't having a baby.

She would be heartbroken. And considering he always turned into a blithering idiot whenever she cried, he was afraid he would start promising her the moon.

He frowned at the ceiling. Then again, there was

nothing to say *he* had to be the one to tell her. And anyway, wasn't that sort of news better received from a midwife, since only another woman could truly empathize with such a deep disappointment? Because no matter what century it was, having—or losing the ability to have—children would always be the business of women. Men paced outside the birthing rooms, waiting and insidiously worrying, then rushed in when it was over and kissed their wives and babes and told them they were beautiful.

Which had him wondering what sort of man—Roger Bentley in particular—would take on the work of doctoring women. He could understand being interested in the science of pregnancy, and he supposed men might be better able to deal with the gruesome details of modern operations. Although in truth, he could just as easily see Maude wielding a scalpel.

Nevertheless, he would be standing right outside the door to comfort his wife when she came out of her exam with Maude, which he would insist she have today. There was no sense drawing this out any longer; the sooner Rana knew she wasn't with child, the sooner they could get back to being a happily married *couple*. And, Titus decided with a sigh, if she preferred to live on the shore of Bottomless rather than looking down at it from the top of Whisper Mountain, he supposed he could move into this unpainted, crooked-roofed, overstuffed hovel with her. Although he didn't much care that the bed had obviously been built for a gnome, or that it was tucked under an eave that left him in danger of hitting his head if he sat up without thinking.

They'd reached the fiord two miles south of the MacKeage homestead shortly before midnight to find Duncan camped out waiting for them, thanks to Maximilian's spies. Titus had slid off Salt with his half-asleep wife in his arms, asked the highlander to take the warhorse, and persuaded Rana that he could have her home in less time than it would take them to ride to Peg's. She'd glanced out at the darkened fiord then gone boneless against him, mumbling something about not caring where he took her as long as it had a hot shower and soft bed. But then, it wouldn't be the first time she'd ridden above the waves on Leviathan's back across open water—although she usually hadn't had a choice because they had been fleeing for their lives.

After all these years and everything they had been through together, Rana still continued to amaze him with her practical mind, whatever-it-took resilience, and unwavering faith in him. There were also times her sense of humor left him speechless and utterly enchanted. But mostly he was humbled by her courage, emotional strength, and her innate wisdom that bordered on frightening.

Because she had been right; he would have promised anyone anything to make sure she wouldn't die in childbirth this time, either. Not that he could ever admit that, lest it encouraged her to continue scheming to keep him safe, as he now understood she'd run away to prevent him from selling his soul to save hers.

Although once she realized the full ramifications of his renouncing immortality, she'd have a new and unfamiliar worry to deal with. But, he decided as he kissed her head when he felt her stir, he was in no hurry to broach that subject, either.

"What time is it?" she asked, her voice heavy with sleep.

"Judging by the sun shining through your window, I

would say early afternoon. Why?" he asked, realizing his own voice also sounded thick. "Do you have a pressing engagement?"

"No, I don't suppose I do." She cuddled deeper against him like a kitten curling into a sunbeam. "Are you comfortable enough?"

That made him chuckle. "I really can't say, since I can no longer feel my body. Well, except for my feet sticking out through the ironwork on the footboard, as they are only half asleep. So based on the fact that I all but had to kneel in your shower to wash my face and hair, I take it Averill Latimer wasn't a very tall man?"

He felt more than heard her sigh brush over his chest. "I'm apparently bigger than Averill was, since I can't even button up his welding jacket." She began toying with his chest hair. "There's no reason I have to sell my house immediately, is there?" she whispered, this time her voice sounding heavy with regret. "I mean, we could use it as a retreat this summer."

"If you sell it," he returned just as softly, "then where would we live?"

Her head came up, her eyes widened with surprise. That is until they suddenly narrowed. "You would live in a crooked, unpainted hovel?"

He snorted. "Of course not. But I would live here temporarily while our new home is being built on the fiord."

Her eyes widened again. "Where on the fiord? Near Carolina and Alec?"

"Absolutely not," he said with a laugh, cradling her back to his chest. "They're building at the northern end, which leaves us plenty of shoreline to choose from."

"Which side?" She lifted her head again, this time her

eyes shining with excitement. "I think it should be on the Nova Mare shoreline. I don't know how Peg puts up with lugging her children back and forth across the fiord every day, as I swear she spends more time behind the wheel of her boat than she does her truck. And she's going to have *seven* children in a few months, and the older ones attend school events that often have them crossing in the dark. I have no idea how Duncan got her to agree to live over there."

"I told you, the MacKeages kidnap their women and don't let them leave until they promise to do whatever they say."

"You said it was until they promised to love them forever."

"Same thing," he said, pressing her head down again so she wouldn't see his grin. "Peg is obviously an obedient wife."

That got him a poke in the ribs.

He trapped her hand against his side and touched his lips to her hair. "Will you go see Maude today? I will accompany you and sit outside while you two . . . talk."

"I'll see her soon, but not today. I want to give her a couple of weeks to get used to working with a doctor. There's really no rush. I'm not the first woman in history to get pregnant at my age, and I've been taking very good care of myself." He felt her shudder. "I've even been drinking that nasty ginger tea under the guise of showing my support for Olivia and Peg and Julia."

Titus scowled at the ceiling, wondering at her reluctance. "But why not go see her today, *before* Dr. Bentley arrives?"

"He's arriving *today.* And besides, I want some time to myself before she gives me an endless list of what I can and can't do. Peg's right; Maude is a bully, only no one realizes it because of her disarming smile."

"Yet you felt compelled to bring her here to bully Olivia and Peg and Julia and Carolina?" he asked, knowing damn well that wasn't the reason she was stalling. Could she suspect she wasn't pregnant and simply didn't want to hear the undeniable truth that she was aging? He stroked her back. "Would you consider seeing her today for my peace of mind, then?"

Her head came up again, her eyes studying his. "Are you going to spend the next seven months worrying us *both* crazy?"

"No," he said truthfully, even as he wondered if he couldn't rile her out of her stubbornness. "Are you worried she might tell you we're having twins?"

All that accomplished was to make him bolt upright when she suddenly scrambled off the bed, and he slammed into the ceiling hard enough to leave a dent before falling back with a curse. "Poseidon's teeth, I was *joking,*" he growled, rubbing his forehead as he glared at her.

"I knew that," she said, her cheeks darkening as she brushed down the pajamas she'd put on when he'd been in the shower. "Are you hungry?"

That made him laugh as he carefully freed his feet from the iron footboard. Remembering he couldn't sit up, he rolled off the bed, only to sigh when his head brushed the ceiling as he stood in the *middle* of the room. "Have you stocked your cupboards since I was last here, or are we going to have to ride your electric cart to the Drunken

Moose?" he asked, looking for the towel he'd worn upstairs after his shower. Only he stopped looking when he saw her face redden even more.

"I can't remember if I plugged it in to recharge the—" Her eyes suddenly widened on a gasp, and she ran over and touched his arm. "You're hurt!"

He looked down as he twisted the skin on his arm and saw the bright red welt he knew came from preventing a large tree branch from slapping her on their flight up the ridge yesterday. He lowered his arm with a shrug. "It doesn't hurt."

"But you've never gotten as much as a mark on you before. Ever." Her hands lifted to her mouth. "Sweet Zeus, you've already become mortal."

He swiped the towel off the bureau, wrapped it around his waist and tucked it in on itself, then turned to her and silently nodded.

She slowly backed away, her face ashen. "I'm going to have to worry about you getting maimed riding your motorcycle. Or . . . or you can get sick and *die*."

Damn. He'd hoped it would take her a while to realize she now had a new and unfamiliar worry to . . . worry about. He pulled her into his arms in a fierce hug. "That was the only thing that made me hesitant to renounce my immortality," he said softly. "That I could very well die before you do."

She kept her nose buried in his chest, saying nothing.

"Do your thinking out loud, wife."

He felt her take a deep breath and finally lean away to look up at him—unable to believe his eyes when he saw a distinct sparkle in hers. "Would I be a widow for very long, do you think?" She batted those big brown eyes even as she tossed her head and ran her fingers through her hair. "I haven't exactly let myself go to seed, and one rarely sees handsome, wealthy widows sitting on a shelf growing cobwebs."

It took him a couple of heartbeats to remember what a stubborn, opinionated, irreverent, *terrible* wife she was before he draped her backward over his arm and dropped his nose to within an inch of hers. "I will do more than haunt you, *Mrs.* Oceanus," he said ever so softly. "I will set a pox on any suitor who comes calling."

"Such a possessive man you are," she whispered, pulling him down the rest of the way, her delicious mouth reminding him he'd left off *lusty.*

No, their marriage had never, ever been boring.

Rana sat up on the narrow table and pushed the hem of her blouse down over her elastic-waist pants with trembling hands. "But I've gained nearly ten pounds," she whispered so she wouldn't shout. "And my bosom has grown."

"It's your body adjusting to the change," Maude returned just as softly.

"But I haven't had my woman's flow for over two months now. It wouldn't just stop all of a sudden with no warning, would it? Maybe . . . is it possible you just can't feel the baby yet, or that I'm only a few weeks along instead of nine or ten?"

"You're not pregnant, Rana, and you never will be again."

"You're absolutely *certain*?"

The midwife started to give her a disarming smile, but

then dropped her gaze and merely nodded—only to flinch when Rana jumped off the table with a shout and ran out of the cubicle. She sprinted through the church's freshly painted basement full of shiny new equipment and, ignoring Maude calling to her, threw open the outside door and didn't even wait for her startled husband to finish turning before she hurled herself at him. "We're not having a baby!" she cried as he lifted her off her feet and buried his face in her neck. "Not now and not ever again!"

"Ah, Stasia, I'm sorry," he said gruffly, squeezing the breath right out of her as she felt him also start to tremble. "I'll give you one if you wish," he rushed on thickly. "Just don't cry. I don't want—"

"Are you insane?" she yelped, rearing back. "I'm too old to have a baby!"

He went as stiff as an oak, still holding her off the ground. "You don't . . . But you were so . . . Then why in Hades are you crying?"

She smacked his shoulder. "They're tears of relief, you idiot." She laughed and hugged him again. "We're both too old," she whispered against his hair, "for nightly feedings and changing diapers and chasing toddlers." She squeezed him tighter. "We just got our children grown and settled, and now all I want is for us to be Granddad and Gram as we grow old *together*." She leaned away to clasp his face and searched his eyes. "Are you very disappointed we can never have more children?"

This time he did the laughing. "Sweet Zeus, no! I barely survived the two we have!"

Rana gave him a big noisy kiss on his mouth, wiggled for him to put her down, then turned to Maude standing in the doorway gaping at them. "Yes. Well," she said, tugging down the hem of her blouse and then wiping her cheeks on her sleeve. "Thank you for the news, Maude. Oh, and the clinic is beautiful. I can't wait—"

A compact car covered in road dust—the front and back seats loaded to the roof with what appeared to be trash bags and mounds of clothes—came rattling down the driveway beside the church and braked to a stop when the driver spotted them. He shut off the engine, which rattled even louder before finally dying, then opened his door and slowly contorted himself out of the tiny car. Rana watched with amazement as the blond-haired, red-bearded, thirtyish-year-old man stood with one hand on the door and the other on the roof, and slowly finished unfolding his lanky body until he reached his full height of somewhere just over six feet tall.

"Please tell me one of you speaks English and that I'm not two hundred miles into Canada," he rasped, sounding as tired as he looked.

"Dr. Bentley," Maude said, rushing to him with her hand extended. "I recognize you from your picture," she added when he looked startled. "I'm Maude White-Cloud, your midwife."

Roger Bentley grabbed her hand as if it were a lifeline. "Oh, thank God. I really thought I'd overshot Spellbound Falls and was about to drive off the edge of the world."

Maude gave a laugh. "Yes, I imagine it might feel like that to a man from the city." She led him over to Rana. "Dr. Bentley, this is Rana Oceanus, our clinic's benefactress, and her husband, Titus."

Roger Bentley shook Rana's hand with a polite smile, shook Titus's hand, then frowned at Maude. "I'm sorry, but I thought Olivia was underwriting the clinic. Or that's what I assumed when she and Mac came down to Boston and interviewed me."

"Our daughter-in-law's support," Rana said, drawing his attention again, "is more in the way of administrative help, as well as providing you with housing at Inglenook. Welcome to Spellbound Falls, Dr. Bentley." She gestured toward Bottomless and then at the cluster of buildings behind him. "This might truly be the end of the road, but I believe you'll be happy with your decision to practice medicine here once you meet the townspeople. In fact, the ladies of our local grange are planning to host a welcome reception for you next weekend."

Roger set his hands just above his hips and surreptitiously stretched the kinks out of his back as he turned to look at the waves gently lapping the shoreline not a hundred feet away. "It really is an inland sea," he murmured, shaking his head in disbelief, "with actual tides and the smell of salt in the air." He took a deep breath and looked over his shoulder at them. "Is it true it has whales and sharks?"

"And orcas," Titus added.

"*Friendly* orcas," Rana clarified. "They don't much care for the taste of humans."

"What about the sharks?" Roger asked, looking at the water again.

"In the four years since it formed," Titus said, "there have been no reports of any unpleasant encounters with any of the sea creatures."

"Would you like to see our clinic, Dr. Bentley?" Maude asked.

"Please, call me Roger," he said, turning back to them—his eyes widening when Maude gestured toward the small door in the granite foundation before he lifted his gaze to the building above it. "The clinic is in a church basement?"

"Temporarily," Rana said. "We're having difficulty finding a building right in town, which is where we want the clinic so it will be easily accessible to the women."

Roger sighed tiredly again and started toward the church, only to stop when a four-door pickup, its bed loaded with camping gear and towing a sleek-looking boat, came down the driveway.

"Oh, Carolina and Alec are here," Rana said excitedly. "Our daughter and her fiancé," she clarified for Roger.

"And the first one of our patients who will give birth," Maude added as they all watched Alec drive past with Carolina waving wildly at them. He turned the pickup in a large circle and backed it down the boat launch, stopping just at the water's edge.

"Mama!" Carolina cried as she threw open her door. "Oh, thank the gods," she said as she ran—or rather waddled—up to them and leaned over her bulging belly to hug Rana. "I called your cell phone for two days before finally calling Mackie, and he said you went camping with Daddy," she continued in a panting rush, her gaze darting to Titus then to Rana again. "Are you two back together?" she whispered.

"We were never really apart," Titus said before Rana could answer. "MacKeage," he went on, shaking Alec's hand. "Have you come to your senses yet about my offer?"

"What offer?" Carolina asked before Alec could answer.

Rana reached over and pinched her husband's arm, but to no avail.

"I offered to make him a wealthy man if he persuaded you to run off and get married *before* you became parents."

Carolina gasped so hard she took a step back—just before she stepped up to Alec and poked him in the belly. "You better not even be *thinking* about it."

"Of course not," he said, rubbing his belly with a grin. "I *like* being a kept man."

Carolina then rounded on her father. "We're getting married in two weeks, on the top of Whisper Mountain, in a beautiful ceremony with all my friends as witnesses." She then turned to Roger and held out her hand. "Jane Oceanus."

"Roger Bentley," the good doctor said, shaking her hand and then continuing to hold it as he frowned. "Is it Jane or Carolina?"

"That depends on who's doing the— Wait, you're *Doctor* Bentley?"

He nodded, finally letting go of her hand. "You're cutting it a bit close, aren't you?" he asked, nodding down at her belly.

"Yes, I am," she said smugly, shooting Rana a wink then giving Maude a frown before looking at Roger again. "So, Doctor, do you see any reason a perfectly healthy woman can't camp out in the wilderness the last two weeks of her pregnancy?"

"How deep into the wilderness?"

She waved toward Bottomless. "It's about four miles to the fiord, then another twelve miles to where we're going to spend the summer camping out while our home is being built."

"Am I expected to travel the sixteen miles for the

delivery?" He shook his head. "It's a moot point, anyway. So, Carolina-Jane, do you want to have your baby out here in the parking lot?" he asked—his smile even more disarming than Maude's, Rana realized. "Or would you like to go inside and see if we can't find you someplace more comfortable to ride out your labor?"

Carolina cupped her stomach with a gasp, her panicked gaze shooting to Maude. "I'm not in labor! My muscles are just tight because Alec hit *every* pothole between here and Pine Creek."

Apparently surprised that Roger Bentley—who looked more like a vagabond than a doctor—had read the subtle signs that *her* patient was in labor, Maude finally stopped gaping at her new boss and looked at Carolina. "Sorry, but you've had at least two contractions since you've been standing here."

Carolina smacked Alec's arm, further paling the highlander's complexion. "You made me go into labor!" She then clutched the arm she'd just smacked and looked at Rana. "Mama, I'm having my baby," she whispered, her complexion also paling as she looked at Maude again. "But it's too early."

"Exactly how early?" Roger asked.

"She's not due for another three weeks," Alec said roughly, sweeping Carolina off her feet. "For the love of Christ, would it kill you to listen to me just *once*?" he ground out, heading for the basement door. "I told ye we should stop at Aunt Libby's and let her check you out before we left."

"But I can't have the baby now!" Carolina cried over his shoulder. "Mama, I'm not married yet."

"Because you thought you were smarter than Mother

Nature," Titus called after her, even as he stopped Rana from following when Maude ran ahead to open the basement door. "We need to go find the minister of this church," he said, "and bring him here to marry them immediately."

Despite being aware Roger had halted on the way to his car and was looking at them, Rana glared up at her husband. "You can't possibly be serious. We have a huge wedding planned for Mayday up at Nova Mare. Everyone from the island is coming."

"Then they'll be attending a reception," he snapped, "because the ceremony is taking place *today*."

"Is this her first child?" Roger asked.

"Yes," Rana answered.

He glanced at his watch and shot them a grin. "Then you don't have to drag the minister away from his dinner, because this is probably going to take a while." He turned serious. "They are planning to get married, right? Because I think I should warn you that I don't allow *shotgun* weddings in my delivery room."

"I believe my wife paid for that delivery room, Bentley," Titus said tightly.

"She may have paid for it, but I've got a contract saying it's mine for the next five years." Roger calmly began rolling up his shirtsleeves as he nodded toward the church. "You walk through that door, you play by my rules."

Rana clutched her husband's arm when she saw him stiffen, so excited by Roger's response that it was all she could do not to jump up and down. "Behave," she whispered when Roger turned away and opened his car door. She stepped in front of Titus, then had to clasp his face to get him to look at her—his glower turning to surprise when he saw she was smiling. "You have to admire the man for not caring who signs his paychecks when it comes to his patients," she continued softly. "Oh, will you stop," she said with a laugh. "You can't have it both ways."

He went back to glowering, this time at *her.* "What are you talking about?"

"You can't hand over your authority to the next generation and then hold them to the standards of *your* generation. In this place and time, babies are commonly born out of wedlock. All you should care about is that Alec and Carolina are fully committed to each other, and will marry because they *want* to, *when* they want to. And if that means saying their vows while holding their infant, then so be it." She brushed her thumb over his tight lips. "Be happy for them, Titus," she said softly. "Our beautiful, stubborn, *intelligent* daughter searched all of time to find her match, and Alec loves her more than life itself." She gave his face a squeeze and broke into another smile. "Although he went against MacKeage tradition and *rescued* his woman from kidnappers."

"And then kept her for ten days," he said in a growl. He pulled down her hands and held them in his as they both watched Roger sprint to the church with a bulging red backpack thrown over one shoulder. "I dislike it when you turn my words back on me."

"Yes, dear, I know." She pulled free and threw her arms around him. "Oh, Titus, Caro's having her baby today! Come on," she said, slipping her arm through his and starting toward the church. "Come see what a beautiful job Maude did on the clinic while, instead of helping, I was strolling through the wilderness with the love of *my* life."

He pulled them to a stop. "I will see it some other time,

when it's not in use," he muttered, eyeing the basement door like it was going to explode. "Meanwhile, I'll wait out here and keep Alec company."

"Oh, Titus. Alec is going to stay with Carolina."

"In the birthing room?" he said in a strangled whisper.

She patted his chest. "Fathers don't pace the halls in this century, husband. They hold the mother's hand and mop her brow, and they even cut the umbilical cord."

He turned as pale as snow and took a step back. "Sweet Zeus, *why*?"

"To witness a miracle." She leaned into him and rested her cheek on his chest to hide her smile, even as she wondered how he was going to survive the twenty-first century. "You would have stayed with me had I been with child, would you not?"

There was an interminably long silence before his arms came around her with a heavy sigh. "Yes, of course," the blackguard blatantly lied, "if that had been your wish."

She wiggled free and slipped her arm through his again, then headed out the driveway.

"Are you not going to attend your daughter?" he asked.

"Roger is right; it will be hours yet. Meanwhile, I intend to order one of everything on Vanetta's menu and stuff my face until I can't walk." She stopped and glared up at him. "And the next time you feel like going camping, you better show up in an RV bus."

Chapter Nineteen

Now this was the proper way for men to conduct themselves during a birthing, Titus decided as he drained his mug of beer: men descending on the nearest bar—this one conveniently located a stone's throw away from the church—while their women gathered around the mother-to-be. Word had quickly spread by way of cell phones, and everyone had rushed to town, with Mac and Nicholas and Duncan dropping off their wives at the clinic before heading to the Bottoms Up. And not wanting to kick out five paying customers when closing time had rolled around, Vanetta had handed the keys to the new chief of police and told Niall to lock up when they left.

Well, all the men were here except for Alec MacKeage. Titus decided he needed to have a talk with the idiot about wearing the britches in his family—assuming the highlander ever *became* family. Thank the gods the good people of Atlantis couldn't see how badly their king had lost control of *his* family; what with his wife running off, his daughter getting married *after* having her babe, his son treating him like a doddering old man, and his grandchildren wrapping him around their magical little fingers.

Yes, he was quite happy to be mortal, Titus suddenly decided, not wanting to hang around to see what other outrageous traditions future generations came up with. What in the name of Hades had Providence been thinking, making Winter MacKeage the first female drùidh? Hell, next thing he knew, *goddesses* would be running the world.

Then again, there would probably be fewer wars—likely because all the gods would be too busy looking for their gonads.

"That old warhorse of yours is an ornery bastard," Duncan said from across the table, his eyes looking a bit bloodshot. "I had to chase him over a mile when he broke out of his stall, then turn the hose on him when he went after one of my mares."

"Who?" Nicholas asked. "Which warhorse?"

"Salt was before your time," Titus said. "I had him when I met Rana."

Nicholas's own bloodshot eyes narrowed. "And just how did he happen to show up in this century?"

"A *bird* must have dropped him off in the woods," Titus said, glaring at his son.

Mac leaned back in his chair with a smug and somewhat drunken grin. "Really? I heard a *limping* old wizard conjured up a ride and two bulging satchels of food."

"Which the new god is likely right now gorging himself on," Titus muttered.

"So did you finally find out why Rana left you?" Nicholas asked.

"It turned out to be nothing more than a misunderstanding. All that matters is we are back together." Titus lifted his empty mug toward Duncan in salute. "You MacKeages may be onto something when it comes to kidnapping contrary women."

Duncan snorted. "Now if we could just come up with a way to control the lasses *after* we've caught them."

"Speaking of birds," Niall said, walking over with five full mugs of beer in his fists. "Ye actually saw the new god? What did he look like?" He scattered the drinks around the table then sat down. "The markings we found where it dragged itself to shore left a trail wide enough for a blind man to follow. So as the police chief, I'd like to know what I might be dealing with."

"He was a medium-sized oak when I saw him," Titus said. "But he finally smartened up and turned himself into something inanimate to escape the demons." He shrugged again. "I imagine he'll eventually settle on a human form, once he has time to acclimate to being here."

"And until then?" Duncan asked. "Do we seek him out *before* he starts causing trouble?"

Titus looked at his son. "I guess that would be up to Maximilian, since his magic will soon be all that is protecting mankind."

Mac stilled with his beer halfway to his mouth. "Excuse me?"

"In three weeks," Titus said quietly, "my authority will be yours to command."

Stark, absolute silence fell over the table.

"Sweet Zeus, why?" Nicholas finally whispered.

"Because it's time." Titus stared directly into his son's eyes. "Atlantis no longer has any real purpose now that you've established your seat of power here in this place and time, which is why I've decided it would better serve humanity for the island to stop being a myth." He looked down and fingered the handle of his empty beer mug. "And I have also renounced my immortality."

An even deeper silence ensued, only broken when Maximilian pushed back his chair and stood up.

"It's done," Titus said quietly. "I am now mortal, and will finish aging naturally with my wife." He finally looked up. "The day will come that you, too, will have no desire to spend eternity without Olivia. Gentlemen," he went on, gazing around the table at their shocked expressions, "I assure you I'm not dying tomorrow. Contrary to what *some* people apparently think, Rana and I are still of sound mind and body, and have many years of grandparenting ahead of us." He grabbed the full glass Niall had set in front of him and lifted it toward Maximilian in salute. "To the new reigning theurgist, may he serve mankind with a stronger, more modern, and hopefully wiser magic. And," he added on a grin, "with the same patience and sense of humor as his predecessor."

Still nothing.

"Poseidon's teeth; I'm *retiring*, you idiots, so quit looking as if I just told you I'm dying."

Maximilian very slowly reached down and picked up his beer, but lifted it to his mouth instead of in salute, and drained the entire glass in one swallow.

Duncan and Nicholas did the same, but apparently Niall was too busy trying to decide if he liked this new turn of events. The highlander cleared his throat. "Ah, can I ask what ye mean by Atlantis no longer being a myth?"

"He means he's destroying it," Mac answered—still staring at Titus. "And the people?" he asked softly.

"Most will follow their offspring into the world. Those without children will choose where and in what century they wish to live out the rest of their natural lives."

"Does Mother know?"

"Yes—both about Atlantis and my mortality. It's the natural order of things, Maximilian, for new generations to continue building on the foundations of the previous." He grinned. "And for new gods to be born and old gods to quietly fade away."

"Did it ever occur to you to *ask* me if I wanted your job?"

Titus stifled a snort as he stood up and walked around the table. "You've been positioning yourself to *take* it for the last four years." He stared into the mirror image of his own sharp green eyes and clasped his son's shoulders. "I'm sorry I stole your thunder, but I was growing tired of waiting for you to make your move."

"You were supposed to live *forever*," Mac said roughly, his face darkening with his admission, "which always made me wonder why you even needed a son."

Titus chuckled and gave the boy's shoulder a vigorous pat. "I guess I've always been a mortal at heart. So exactly how were you intending to take me down?"

Maximilian didn't even try to stifle his snort. "Do I look that drunk?"

Titus pulled him forward and gave him an even more

vigorous hug. "I'm proud of you, son," he whispered thickly, wondering if *he* wasn't a bit drunk. "And I would have been sorely disappointed if you hadn't at least tried."

"It's a boy!" Alec MacKeage shouted as he slammed through the door. "Jane gave me a strapping, screaming son!" He ran over to the table, grabbed the first beer he came to and chugged it down, then collapsed into Titus's chair, set his elbows on his knees, and hung his head in his hands. "I swear by all that's holy I am never going through that again," he muttered to the floor. He looked up, found Duncan, and gave him a glare. "If you ever see me heading for a delivery room again, ye have my permission to break both my legs." He then turned his glare on Titus. "I thought the church was going to burst into flames when your daughter started cussing in every language on the planet."

"That's why men belong in the nearest bar getting drunk," Titus said, grabbing the remaining beer and handing it to him, "while their wives *or girlfriends* are cursing them for having had the fun of putting the babes in there with none of the work of getting them out."

Chapter Twenty

Titus stared up at the ceiling not three feet above his head as he listened to Rana moving around in the kitchen below, and found himself rethinking this whole mortal business. Poseidon's teeth, his head hurt; the problem being he'd never experienced a headache before, or anything even resembling a hangover, for that matter.

It wasn't that immortals didn't feel pain; battle was just as bloody and gruesome for gods and demons as it was for humans. And taking a bad fall off a horse sure as hell hurt, as did a poke in the eye or stubbing a toe. But the pain lasted only until he got his bearings again, unlike the incessant hammer pounding his skull hard enough to make his teeth ache. Granted, he would always have command of the magic, but he figured using it to cure a hangover sort of defeated the whole purpose of *being mortal.*

He closed his eyes with a muttered curse, guessing he was in for a long day.

And come to think of it, what in Hades was he supposed to *do* all day once he fully retired? He'd never fostered any hobbies, what with being so busy saving mankind from itself. And he didn't believe there were many positions he could apply for in this century when his only marketable skills were winning wars, ruling kingdoms, and nudging humans—sometimes with a hammer to the head—into smartening up. Although he had done a pretty good job of cultivating the Trees of Life, and he did happen to be living in the middle of a vast forest, so maybe he could become a logger. Then again, his talent lent itself to *growing* trees, not cutting them down, and Mother Nature already seemed to be doing a good job of that around here.

Titus lifted his hands to his throbbing head and carefully scrubbed his face with a groan. He then carefully rolled out of bed and slowly straightened—in the middle of the room—with a sigh. Maybe he could purchase an RV bus like Rana suggested and take her on a cross-country camping trip like Maximilian had taken Olivia on for their honeymoon four years ago.

But then he sighed again, figuring that would only use up six months or at best a year of their time before they ran out of wondrous sights to see. So then what? And anyway, he doubted Rana would leave her new grandbabies even for a month.

He swiped his pants off the chair and slipped them on, only to brighten when he remembered he had a house to build. And by *not* involving the magic and considering he sure as Hades wasn't building a tiny hovel, construction should take at least two years, with landscaping and building a barn and outbuildings taking another.

He eyed the bed built for a gnome as he shrugged on his shirt and buttoned it up, then studied the ceiling above it. He would never survive long enough to move into their new house if he had to sleep in that bed two more years, so maybe he should do a little remodeling here first—including straightening the roof.

Swiping his socks off the bureau, he rushed toward the stairs to tell Rana about his plan, only to stagger to a halt and grab his throbbing head. "Slowly," he muttered, holding the ironwork banister as he carefully descended.

He not so carefully stubbed his toe on the leg of a table at the end of the couch, then banged his throbbing head on a bookcase crowded against the opposite wall when he bent to rub his toe. He cursed again when he had to catch several falling books before they landed on his other bare foot, only to straighten to see his terrible wife standing in the kitchen doorway holding her hands to her mouth. Stifling her laughter, however, did nothing to disguise the amusement in her eyes.

"Yes. Well," she said, tugging down the front of her blouse, "now that I have a big strong man around to lift the heavy stuff, I guess I can start thinning this place out."

Titus turned to scan the crowded living area—noting with satisfaction the plant in full bloom—then turned back and smiled tightly. "Today?"

"Oh, no. I have too much to do today," she said, disappearing into the kitchen. "Are you hungry?"

He limped into the kitchen to find her standing at the

gnome-height counter as she wrote on a pad of paper. "What are you doing today?" he asked, going to the small table crammed between the door and fridge and sitting down to put on his socks—only to discover he was missing one. He leaned over to see it on the floor next to the toe-stubbing table and stood back up with a sigh. "Because I would like to go get some of my clothes and belongings first," he said as he headed after his wayward sock.

"Oh, sure," she called over her shoulder to him. "You can take my truck and I'll use the cart to do my errands in town first, and save my trip to Turtleback for after my lesson with Zack this afternoon. Or I can drive you to the marina to pick up whatever vehicle you drove there the day of our race."

He hobbled back into the kitchen and sat down again. "What time is Zack coming? Maybe we can get all our errands done before he arrives."

She stopped writing and slowly turned to him. "We?"

He stilled with one sock half on. "I thought I would accompany you on your errands, since I have nothing else to do today except get my clothes."

"Or," she said very softly, "you could visit with your new grandson, since Carolina and Alec will be staying in our cottage at Nova Mare for the next couple of weeks." She turned back to the counter. "By that time I'll be done with my errands and welding lesson and can meet you there. Then we can have dinner at Aeolus's Whisper and follow each other back down the mountain."

Titus finished putting on his socks. "I'll buy a change of clothes at the Trading Post and get my belongings tomorrow instead," he decided out loud. "If they're using our cottage, I imagine both Carolina and Alec would rather spend the day sleeping than visiting. So," he said, standing up and walking to the counter to read over her shoulder. "After Ezra's store, what's our first errand?"

She stopped writing again and stared down at the counter, saying nothing for several heartbeats before he heard her sigh. "I was going to a furniture store in Turtleback to get a small crib to have here for when Carolina comes to visit. I was also going to stock my cupboards, take some food items to Roger's cabin at Inglenook, run up and see Carolina, run back down for my lesson with Zack, then cook you dinner."

Okay, then; apparently being mortal meant he might be a little slower on the uptake, as it was just dawning on him that she had planned on doing her errands *alone*.

Then what in Hades was he supposed to do all day?

"Could you not postpone your trip to Turtleback until later in the week?" he asked, partly because he didn't want her going alone and partly because he had no idea where they were going to put a crib in this overcrowded . . . house. "Just until we have a better idea of what the new god is about. And also until Niall has had a chance to deal with the protestors," he added for good measure. "And if you're going to go see Carolina anyway, I could meet our new young highlander and grab a few of my clothes," he continued, mostly because he didn't want to do *his* errands alone.

She ripped the top sheet off the pad. "I'll meet you in the truck in ten minutes," she said, heading back toward the living room.

"Wait. Do you have any . . . aspirin? I believe that's what mortals use for headaches," he said when she stopped in the doorway. "If you don't, I can pick some up at Ezra's," he quickly added, not liking the smile she suddenly gave him.

"You men do a little too much celebrating last night?" she asked way too sweetly as she walked back into the kitchen. She turned on a burner under a kettle. "I have just the thing for a hangover," she continued, getting a cup from the cupboard. "Ginger tea."

"I thought you said it was nasty?"

"But very soothing to beer-soaked stomachs."

"It's my head that hurts."

"Ginger is good for just about any ailment," she said, dropping a spoonful of loose tea into a screened ball and setting it in the cup. She then walked into the bathroom and opened a closet door. "And a hot compress will loosen your— Oh, Titus? Can you unlock this panel for me?" she asked, stepping back to look at him. She waved at the closet. "Zack told me there's a small chamber under the stairs, but he doesn't know what's inside. Apparently his grandfather put a puzzle lock on the access panel several years ago when he replaced all the floor stringers with steel beams."

"Gene Latimer sold you his father's house without knowing if he was leaving anything valuable behind?" he said, walking in the bathroom and crouching onto his heels when Rana sat down on the toilet to watch.

"Gene, his wife, and their two children all went through the house and cleaned out Averill's personal belongings and took anything that was dear to them. But when Gene told me they couldn't get into one of the cupboards or the shed, I promised I would show him anything I found. But apparently Zack forgot all about the chamber and Gene obviously didn't know about it, or they probably would have cut it open."

"Which cupboard?" Titus asked, glancing back toward the kitchen.

"The end one on the peninsula," she said with a laugh. "Our little princess had it opened in under a minute."

He turned, still crouched. "You weren't worried her magic might harm your babe?"

She gave a dismissive wave. "Ella didn't need to use her magic, only her brilliant young mind."

Titus looked back at the panel. "Did she try opening this puzzle lock?"

"I didn't dare ask her to, because I wasn't sure what we'd find inside. Zack had told me the peninsula cupboard was where Pops kept his liquor."

"Pops?" he murmured, reaching in and slowly running his hand around the panel's perimeter.

"Everyone in town called Averill *Pops*, apparently. Um, Titus?" she asked softly, drawing his attention again. "Will you still be able to work the magic after you turn your energy over to Maximilian?"

"Yes," he said, feeling along the panel again, "as I'm only giving him my authority."

"Will you be just as powerful now that you're mortal?"

He stopped and looked at her, then nodded. "Once something is learned to the point it becomes inherent, it can't be unlearned. I was born out of the imaginations of men and spent the last several millennia *becoming* the magic. The same way it could be for you," he said gently, "as I have told you repeatedly these last forty years.

You're no less powerful than I am, Stasia." He turned to the closet to hide his grin. "You're merely lazy."

"What? You've never said *that* in the last forty years."

He began running his hand over the right edge of the panel. "You consider me old-fashioned and set in my ways, yet I can't help but notice you've remained content to let me do all the hard work. Like with this panel," he said, straightening to his feet and stepping back as he gestured at the closet. "Why don't *you* simply open it?"

"Because I'm a dumb mortal," she snapped, also standing up and pushing past him when the kettle started to whistle.

He caught her arm and turned her to face the closet. "I'll make the tea while you open the panel," he said, walking into the kitchen.

"I can't," she growled over the blaring whistle.

"*Try*," he growled back, shutting off the burner. He grinned again when she turned her glare on the closet, and lost whatever she softly muttered to the slowing whistle of the kettle. "What does it say about *my* intelligence," he asked as he poured water into the cup, "to have fallen in love with a dumb mortal?"

"It says you're dumber than I am," she quickly returned, despite her attention being on the panel more than on him.

"I would rest easier," he said, moving to the bathroom doorway, "knowing that if I should die first, you will at least be able to handle small matters like this one."

She shot him a grin and went back to staring inside the closet. "I believe that's what grandchildren are for."

"So it truly is your way of controlling us," he said quietly.

That got her full attention, her face paling but for two telltale flags of red. "What do you mean?"

He smiled warmly and pressed a finger to her lips. "What began as a young maiden's only defense against her powerful husband had become a habit by the time she'd learned to trust him."

"I trusted you enough to marry you," she whispered behind his finger.

"Not completely and definitely not in the beginning," he gently contradicted, moving her to kneel facing the closet as he crouched behind her. "I've been doing a lot of reminiscing since you left, especially since that day you asked me what I thought your life might have been like if you had taken a different path. But it wasn't until I looked back over our marriage that I realized you've been defending yourself against me for so long that you don't even realize you're doing it." He wrapped her up in his arms as he spread his knees, then pulled her back against him when he felt her begin to tremble. "You wouldn't have died in a crooked hovel giving birth to a toothless bastard's child," he continued softly, "partly because neither of your parents would have allowed it, but more importantly because you knew your own self-worth. Which, I believe, explains how you had the courage to marry a god." He chuckled. "You also had the intelligence to realize you needed to control me. You began by making me vow never to use my magic on you, and then proceeded to make exceptions whenever it suited your purpose."

He stopped her from trying to turn and touched his lips to her hair. "You're no longer that fifteen-year-old maiden, Stasia, and you no longer live in a time when women hold only the power their husbands give them." He dropped his arms from around her. "Open the panel, wife."

Silence settled over the house but for the ticking of a tired old clock he could hear in the living room and the thump of Rana's heartbeat as she hesitated and then slowly crawled forward on her hands and knees and touched the panel.

"Don't look for anything," he quietly instructed. "Close your eyes and let your fingers become Averill Latimer's fingers as they run over the panel until you feel them itch to trip the first hidden lock." He smiled when he heard her suck in a deep breath just as the first piece of the puzzle released with an unseen metallic click. "Where do Pops' fingers wish to go next?" he asked, watching her hand skim upward along the right edge of the panel then stop and press into the smooth wood.

Another lock tripped.

Her movements grew more certain as her searching fingers suddenly changed direction and pressed the lower left-hand corner of the panel, making another lock click open. But then she hesitated with her hand hovering over the final hidden release, and sat back on her heels.

"Do you know what's inside?" she asked.

"Yes."

"Is it something good?"

"I imagine Gene Latimer will be pleased. You said he has two children?"

"Zack, who's eighteen and starting college this fall, and a sixteen-year-old daughter named Sarah."

"Strong biblical names. Can I assume Gene sold this house to pay for his children's educations rather than keep it in the family?"

"Yes," she said, glancing over her shoulder when he chuckled.

"Well, that's one worry he'll no longer have." He nudged her forward again. "Because among other things, there are enough United States savings bonds in there to let both children attend any university of their choice through to their doctorates."

"Where would Averill have gotten that kind of money?" she said, reaching out and tripping the final lock without even thinking about it, then catching the panel with a gasp when it popped free. She tilted the heavy piece of wood to see it was framed in metal with four intricate clasps welded on the back, then slid it to the side and crawled inside the small chamber. "There are several boxes in here," she said, backing up as she pulled one of them with her, then ducking inside again as Titus set the first box behind him. "Oh, this one is heavy and seems to be full of old photo albums. And this one appears to be a jewelry box." But she backed out empty-handed and shook her head. "I don't think we should go through the Latimers' personal things. I'll show Zack the chamber this afternoon and let him bring the boxes home to his family."

Yes, mortality must be making him slow, because he didn't read her intent in time to do more than fall backward onto the kitchen floor with a grunt of surprise when she suddenly pounced. "You take back what you said," she growled, straddling him with her fingers digging into his chest. "I am *not* lazy, and I sure as Hades am not a controlling woman. I'm a *good* wife."

"The best in all of history," he quickly agreed, vigorously nodding.

"And the only reason I never tried to cultivate the magic was because I didn't want to upstage you."

More like she didn't want the responsibility that came with it, he thought as he nodded his throbbing head again. "Yes, two magic-makers in the house definitely would have complicated things."

"Oh, Titus," she sighed, dropping down to hide her face in his chest. "Sometimes you make me so mad I could just smack you."

And sometimes you actually do, he silently added, grinning up at the ceiling. "I'm a terrible husband," he said gruffly, tilting her head to look at him, "which often makes me wonder why you continue to love me."

"Because you continue to be handsome and charming and tender when no one is looking," she whispered, running a finger over his lips as she stared at his mouth. "And you never stop trying to impress me with grand gestures."

"You don't seem to mind some of those—"

He stilled at the realization she'd switched to French.

Okay then, he decided as he stood up with her in his arms and headed toward the stairs in the living room; he may have just discovered a rather interesting cure for hangovers.

Epilogue

Rana found her missing daughter—wearing a beautiful sapphire ball gown instead of the wedding dress that had been made to fit a very pregnant bride—sitting on the ground and leaning against a big old pine tree as she stared out over Bottomless. She was holding a bouquet of Atlantis-blue lilies in one hand and her soon-to-be-husband's wedding gift in the other—both, if Rana wasn't mistaken, looking a bit damp with tears.

"How did he know?" Carolina whispered when Rana silently sat down beside her. "Was it your suggestion?"

"No, baby. I was as surprised as you when he asked if I could have it made."

She heard her daughter draw in a shuddering breath. "You always told me getting married was the easy part, and that *being* married would require me to show up every day of every month of every year after that."

"Especially on the days you would rather not," Rana added softly.

"How did he know the perfect thing to give me?" she repeated.

"When a man truly loves a woman, he knows what tokens of his esteem will most touch her heart."

"But Alec doesn't even like the magic."

"He likes *your* magic. That's what he's telling you with this," Rana said, touching the heart-shaped gold locket and feeling the energy of Atlantis gently humming inside it. "Alec is saying he loves Carolina Oceanus and Jane Smith, because each of those women touches his own heart."

Her daughter looked over, her eyes swimming with uncertainty. "How am I supposed to live up to that kind of love?"

"By showing up every day, even when you don't want to." Rana leaned into her with a soft laugh. "Showing up for the wedding would be a good start."

Carolina rested her head against hers. "Sometimes he makes me so angry I could just scream."

"I can't tell you how glad I am to hear you say that, Caro." She straightened when Carolina leaned away in surprise, and gave her daughter a tender smile. "It's terribly difficult to live with a perfect man, not to mention terribly boring." She arched a brow. "Do you believe I've spent the last forty years married to a perfect husband?"

That got her a smile. "Will you tell me the real reason you left Daddy?"

"I thought I was pregnant," Rana whispered, only to laugh when her daughter gasped and looked down at her belly. She shrugged. "But I found out I was just old."

That got her another gasp. "You're not old!"

"I'm at least old enough to no longer worry about having babies," she drawled, standing up and holding out her hand, "and can now concentrate on spoiling my grand-babies instead. Come, daughter, let's go put your poor old father out of his misery and make the man who takes your breath away deliriously happy."

Instead of taking her hand, Carolina plopped the locket in it and stood up on her own. "Can you put it on me?"

Rana stepped behind her and clasped the fine gold chain around her neck.

"When is Daddy going to destroy Atlantis?"

"In another week. When everyone leaves here, they're going back to the island only long enough to gather whatever they wish to take with them."

"Are . . . Is everyone okay with what he's doing?"

Rana looked down at the inland sea. "Titus had to give a few of them a nudge—mostly the younger ones, believe it or not. He said it's like pushing fledglings out of the nest to convince them they can fly. Apparently living in peace and joy and harmony can foster complacency." She turned Carolina to face her and grasped her shoulders. "I want you to know that I couldn't have asked for a more wonderful daughter, and I can't be more proud of the woman you've become."

That got her a look of disbelief. "I was a brat."

"Which kept me from ever growing complacent," Rana said, twining their arms together as she headed up the path toward the summit. "And glad that I had no more children after you," she added with a wink. "Now, daughter, how much longer are you going to make *your* precious little brat go without a proper name?"

"You don't like *Satchel*?" Carolina asked in mock surprise. "Because Alec says he doesn't mind lugging more luggage up and down the mountain, even if that particular piece leaks a lot."

"Nor *Squirt*," Rana said dryly, "or *Little Gaisgeach*."

"That name came from Alec's father. Morgan claims the kid has the makings of a true champion." Carolina stopped walking when the large gathering of people came into view. "Oh, Mama, have you ever seen two more beautiful men?"

Despite knowing her daughter was referring to Alec and the child tucked against his chest inside his kilt, Rana only had eyes for one man standing tall and strong and powerful—and scowling—beside them on the gazebo. "No, I can't remember ever seeing anything more beautiful. So," she went on as she started them walking again, "shall we go show these beautiful men the power of feminine magic?"

LETTER FROM LAKEWATCH

July 2013

Dear Readers,

Every day I sit down at my computer with the best of intentions to tell the story my fictional characters are telling me. *We don't always see eye to eye, but then, I don't always agree with a lot of things* real *people do. If I were making some of their decisions, I might make different ones given my unique model of the world.*

I'm saying this because as a reader, you bring your *model of the world to my stories, which means that each one of you is in essence reading a different book. I imagine that living here in Maine and based on my upbringing, my viewpoints are probably different from those of a person living in Los Angeles or New York City—or Brazil, Germany, Thailand, or South Africa. What's not different, however, is the universal desire to find joy, contentment, love, peace, and happily ever after.*

I write imperfect stories because I am human. I could have used a different word there, not written that scene, given that character less or more of a role, added more action, or set the book someplace else entirely. But because perfection is really quite subjective, bad reviews don't bother me overly much. What one person thinks is silly or stupid or downright aggravating, another sees as funny or brilliant or endearing. So you're not alone if you don't like something one of my characters says or does, because sometimes neither do I. But more often than not I do agree with them, because . . . well, they're figments of my *imagination. These people are in my head because* their *views are usually quite similar to mine.*

I'm not trying to copy the world; I'm trying to exaggerate it—yeah, sometimes outrageously. And I don't know about you, but I'd rather laugh at some of the crazy things people do than cry my way through a story. (Forget reading that sort of book, I could never spend months writing *a tear-jerker.) Too often we must take things seriously in our every-day lives; so why, if I read to escape, would I take a book too seriously?*

Laugh at the antics of my characters. Shake your heads and wonder, What are they thinking? *Do what I do and talk back to them. Yell at them. Kick the book across the room. But then go pick it up and keep reading, because even though you might not agree with how they get there, applaud that these characters eventually do find happily ever after. That is, after all, the whole point of a romance novel and the one thing guaranteed to happen.*

Because everything that occurs before the last page is open to interpretation.

Until later from LakeWatch, you keep reading and I'll keep writing!

Janet

Read on for a look back at where it all began.

Spellbound Falls

by Janet Chapman

Now available from Jove Books.

Apparently Mark Briar wasn't used to anyone telling him no, be it the girlfriend who'd just sent him a Dear John letter or some lonely widow to whom he was magnanimously offering sexual favors. Not only did Mark keep trying to point out what Olivia would be missing if she didn't come to the bunkhouse tonight; it appeared that her repeatedly gentle but firm refusals were making him angry.

Well, that and the Dear John letter he'd crumpled into a ball and thrown at her feet after reading her the more interesting parts. Added to that, his driving had gone from reckless to downright scary. If she'd taken ten minutes to pull the rear seat out of her van, she'd be in only half the mess she was in now; she might still be dealing with an angry young man but at least the pine trees wouldn't be speeding by in a blur.

"Look, Mark," Olivia said calmly. "It's not that I'm not flattered by your offer, but I have a very firm rule about fraternizing with my employees."

"Employ*ee*. You only have one right now. So it's not like anyone can complain the boss is playing favorites or anything." His eyes narrowed menacingly. "What about the campers?" He snorted. "Or is that how you fill up your single father sessions?"

Olivia counted to ten to keep from smacking the belligerent snot. "Ohmigod!" she shouted, pointing out the windshield. "Quick, pull off the road!"

Mark hit the brakes then veered into a small gravel pit before bringing the truck to a stop and shutting off the engine. "What did you see?"

Olivia immediately undid her seatbelt and got out. "A moose just crossed the road in front of us," she said, pointing towards the trees when he also got out. "And hitting an animal that size would total your truck."

"I didn't see anything. You just made that up," he said, storming around the front of the truck. "What in hell is it with you women, anyway? You think you can just dump me like yesterday's trash to go after some rich guy just because he's got a career and drives a Porsche?"

"Hey, wait a minute." Olivia started walking backward. "I'm not your girlfriend; I'm your *boss*."

"Not anymore, you're not, because I quit."

Well, that took care of that little problem. Now she just had to deal with being in the middle of nowhere with this idiot. "Wait," she said, holding up her hand to stop him. "You have to give me time to consider your offer," she said, matching him step for step when he didn't stop. "It's just that you caught me off guard earlier."

He finally stopped and looked around the small gravel pit, his eyes growing suspicious again. "So what say we get a little practice in right now?"

Okay, maybe running would be wiser. Olivia bolted for the woods, figuring Mark would probably catch her in an open footrace down the road. Besides, maybe she could find a stick and beat some sense into the idiot. Only she shouted in surprise when he grabbed her shoulder, and yelped in pain when she stumbled to her knees and he landed on top of her.

For the love of God, this couldn't be happening. He was just a kid!

Olivia tried shoving him away; his fingers bit into her arms as he rolled her over, and she cried out again when his mouth slammed against hers. Okay, it was time to panic; they were in the middle of nowhere, she couldn't seem to get control of the situation, and the idiot was flat-out attacking her! Olivia kicked at his legs and squirmed to push him off as she twisted away from his punishing mouth. "Mark! Stop this!" she cried. "You need to stop!"

"What in hell kind of camp doesn't have girls?"

Olivia stopped struggling. Talking was good. If she could keep him talking then maybe he'd calm down. "Th-There will be girls your age in town once college lets out," she said, panting raggedly as his weight crushed her into the gravel.

"That's over two months away!"

Olivia shouted in outrage as she turned away from his descending mouth, and put all her strength into bucking him off even as she drove her fist into his ribs. He reared up, his own shout ending on a strangled yelp as his weight suddenly lifted off her. Olivia rolled away then stumbled to her feet, scrambling around Mark's truck—only to run straight into another vehicle. She stumbled back to her feet just as she heard Mark shout again, and started running toward him when she saw a stranger drive his fist into Mark's stomach. The boy hadn't even doubled over when the man's fist slammed into his jaw, tossing him into the air to land on the ground on his back, out cold.

"No!" Olivia cried, grabbing the stranger's arm to stop him from going after Mark again. "Don't hurt him any more!"

The man shrugged her off and turned toward her, the dangerous look in his sharp green eyes making her take a step back. "Forgive me," he said gutturally. "I was under the impression the bastard was attacking you." He gestured toward Mark even as he gave a slight bow. "I will leave you to your little game, then," he said, turning away and striding to his truck.

Olivia ran after him. "No, don't leave! He *was* attacking me."

He stopped so suddenly she bumped into him and would have fallen if he hadn't grabbed her shoulders. And that's when Olivia's knees buckled, the magnitude of what had nearly happened turning her into a quivering blob of jelly.

Her rescuer swept her off her feet before she reached the ground. He carried her to a small mound of dirt at the entrance to the gravel pit and set her down, then shrugged out of his jacket and settled it over her trembling shoulders. But when he crouched down in front of her and started to reach toward her throbbing cheek, Olivia buried her face in her hands and burst into sobs.

"It's okay. You're safe now."

"I can't believe he a-attacked me. He . . . he's just a kid." She straightened to pull his jacket tightly around her as she took gulping breaths. "Oh God, I can't breathe!"

He cupped her jaw in his broad hand, his penetrating gaze inspecting her face before coming to rest on her eyes. "You have my word; the bastard won't ever hurt you again. Henry, come here," her rescuer called over his shoulder.

The rear passenger door of the pearl white SUV opened and a young boy got out. Olivia immediately tried to stand up, not wanting the child to see her like this, but the gentleman set his large hand on her shoulder. "Come here, son. This lady has just had a fright, Henry, and she needs comforting," he said, gesturing at Olivia. "Sit here and hold Miss . . . what's your name?" he asked, giving her a gentle smile.

She didn't know if it was his smile that did it, or the fact that she needed to pull herself together for the sake of the child, but Olivia took a shuddering breath and released her death-grip on his jacket. "Olivia Baldwin," she told the boy—only to gasp. "You're Henry! And Mr. Oceanus," she cried, looking at the man. "You're arriving today!" She hid her face in her hands again, utterly humiliated. "Ohmigod, this is terrible. You shouldn't see me like this." But when a small arm settled over her shoulders, the young hand at the end of that arm gently patting her, Olivia quietly started sobbing again.

That is until she realized Mr. Oceanus was no longer crouched in front of her. Olivia shot out from under Henry's comforting arm. "No, you can't hurt him!" she shouted, rounding the vehicles in time to see Mr. Oceanus hauling Mark to his feet.

"He's just a dumb kid."

"Go sit in my truck, Olivia. I merely intend to have a little discussion with him."

"Not in front of your son, you're not," she said, grabbing his arm. "What are you teaching Henry by beating up a defenseless kid? He saw you rescuing me, but it's equally important that he also sees you acting civilized to my assailant."

"I would hope I'm teaching the boy that he has a duty to rescue a woman who's being attacked."

"But you did that already," she said, keeping her voice low so Henry wouldn't hear them. Good Lord, Trace Huntsman hadn't been kidding when he'd told Olivia that his friend didn't have a clue about how to deal with his newly discovered son. "Look, Mr. Oceanus, this—"

"I prefer you call me Mac. And if by acting civilized in front of my son you are suggesting I do nothing, then I suggest you and Henry go for a little walk. You have my word; I will wait until you're out of sight to have my little discussion."

He couldn't possibly be serious. "Please let him go, Mac," Olivia pleaded, her shoulders slumping as she pulled his jacket tightly around her. "I just want to meet my daughter's bus at the turnoff and go home before I fall down."

The sudden concern in his eyes disappeared the moment he looked back at Mark. "If I catch you within fifty miles of Spellbound Falls after sunset today, I will kill you. Understand?" he said ever so softly, his hand tightening around Mark's throat until the red-faced boy nodded. Mac released him so suddenly that Mark fell to the ground, and Olivia didn't even have time to gasp before her rescuer lifted her into his arms.

"Henry, open the front door of our truck," he said, striding to the SUV and setting her inside. He reached into his pants pocket and pulled out a handkerchief. "Your lip is bleeding," he said, handing it to her. "Where is the turnoff you spoke of? You said you wish to meet your daughter."

She took the handkerchief and shakily dabbed at her mouth. "It . . . it's another couple of miles up the road."

He nodded and closed the door, then opened the door behind her. "Get in and buckle up, son," he said, closing the door once Henry climbed in.

But instead of walking around to the driver's side, Mac strode back around Mark's truck. Olivia started to go after him, but the door wouldn't open even after she pushed all the buttons on the handle. She was just about to start pounding on the buttons when a small, unbelievably firm hand clasped her shoulder.

"Father will be civilized," Henry said, giving her a nod when she turned to him. "I believe he's just making sure the bastard understood his instructions."

"You *heard* what we were saying?"

"I have very good hearing." He patted her shoulder. "You can get over your fright now, Olivia; Father won't let that bastard hurt you again."

She twisted around in her seat. "Henry, you can't keep calling him a bastard; it's a very bad word."

His eyes—as deeply green as those of the man who'd sired him—hardened in an almost mirror image of his father's. "Is it not appropriate to use a bad word when referring to a bad person?"

Good Lord, he even talked like his father!

But Trace Huntsman, a military buddy of Olivia's late

husband who lived several hours away down on the coast, had told her that Henry had come to live with Mac only a few months ago, after the child's mother had died. And that up until then the two had never met, as Mac hadn't even known Henry existed.

"How come you call him *Father* instead of *Dad*?" Olivia asked.

Henry's tiny brows knitted into a frown. "Because that's what he is. He calls me Son and I call him Father." His frown deepened even as his face reddened. "And please forgive me, for I believe I'm supposed to call you Madam, not Olivia. My mama would be quite upset with me if she knew I was calling a lady by her Christian name."

Olivia smiled warmly. "And what's your mama's name?"

"Cordelia. But when father speaks of her, he calls her Delia. My last name used to be Penhope, but now it's Oceanus." He went back to frowning again. "Only Father is also thinking of changing my first name. I suggested we might change it to Jack or even Jake, only he said those names aren't noble enough."

"But what's wrong with Henry?"

The boy shrugged. "Father says Henry is too English."

"It's too—" Olivia turned at the sound of a truck door slamming, and saw Mark push down the locks before blindly fumbling with the ignition as he watched Mac through the windshield—who was standing a few paces away, his arms folded over his chest, staring back at him. The pickup started and the tires spun on the loose gravel as Mark sped onto the road without even checking for oncoming traffic.

"See; I told you Father would be civilized," Henry said, giving her shoulder one last pat before he hopped in his seat and fastened his seatbelt. "He didn't kill the bastard even if he did deserve to die."

Despite only meeting Mac and Henry less than thirty minutes ago, Olivia had a feeling they were going to be a tad more of a bother than merely setting two more places at the table. For as precocious and direct as Henry was, his father was even scarier. Maximilian Oceanus was an undeniably large, imposing figure; the sort of man who not only would stand out in a crowd but would likely command it. He had to be at least six foot four, his shoulders filled a good deal of the front seat of his full-sized SUV, and he had picked her up—twice—as effortlessly as if he'd been handling a child. But it was when he looked directly at her with those intense green eyes of his that Olivia felt her world tilt off center. Kind of like when a person stood in a receding wave on a flat sandy beach, and had the illusion of being sucked out to sea even while standing perfectly still.

She should have never let Eileen talk her into breaking her rule of no private parenting sessions. She should have at least recognized what she was getting herself into when Mac had summarily dismissed her repeatedly gentle but firm refusals to let him come to Inglenook three weeks early—much the same way Mark had dismissed them this afternoon. Only where Mark had attacked her, Mac had gotten his way using good old-fashioned bribery.

She was still shaking uncontrollably and fighting back tears, which is why she'd jumped out of the truck the moment they reached the turnoff, before she humiliated herself again. Only Henry had shot out of the truck right behind her. At first it was obvious he'd felt duty-bound to continue comforting her, but once Olivia had assured him she was feeling much better, the boy had taken off to explore the nearby woods instead.

That is, after he'd dutifully run back and asked his father's permission.

Mac had also gotten out of the truck but had merely leaned against the front fender, his feet crossed at the ankles and his arms folded on his chest, apparently content to let his son deal with the welling tears he'd seen in her eyes. She was still wearing his leather jacket, and should probably give it back since he was standing in the cool March breeze in only his shirt, but the warm security of its weight surrounding her simply felt too wonderful to relinquish.

She buried her hands in its roomy pockets with a heavy sigh. Now what was she supposed to do? Without Mark, there was no way she could get Inglenook fully functional in three weeks. Olivia started slowly walking back toward the main road, but picked up her pace when she realized she couldn't see Henry anywhere. "Henry?" she called out, scanning the woods on both sides of the road. "Henry, where did you go?"

"He's fine, Olivia," Mac said, straightening away from the fender. "He climbed down to the brook and is throwing rocks."

"There are some deep pools in that brook," she said, trying to pierce the dense woods. "And there's still snow in places. He could slip and fall in, or wander off and get lost. Little boys have a tendency to follow anything that catches their interest without realizing how far they're going."

"He may get wet but he won't drown," Mac said. He

pointed downstream of the bridge that sat a hundred yards up from the entrance of the turnoff. "And I will call him back if he wanders too far. Is it not my son's job to explore the world around him, and my job merely to keep him safe while he does?" He frowned. "At least that's what I've surmised from the books I've been reading."

Olivia couldn't help but smile. "You've been reading books on parenting?"

Instead of returning her smile, his frown deepened. "At least a dozen; only I've discovered a good many of them contradict each other, and one or two had some rather disturbing notions about discipline."

"Parenting is more of a hands-on, trial-by-fire sort of thing, Mr. Oceanus. And though several people have tried, no one's been able to write a definitive book on child-rearing because humans are not one-size-fits-all."

Good Lord; there she went sounding like Eileen again.

He finally found a smile. "So I have your permission to ignore everything those books said, Mrs. Baldwin?"

Oh yeah, his eyes definitely turned a deep vivid green when he was amused. "Actually, you have my permission to throw them away. And please, call me Olivia."

Up went one of his brows. "Forgive me; you led me to believe we were no longer on a first name basis."

"My mistake . . . Mac." She arched a brow right back at him. "Do you know where your son is right now?"

"Just downstream, crossing the brook on a fallen log."

Olivia turned, trying to locate Henry. "Where? I don't see him."

"Then I guess it's a good thing I have very good eyesight as well as exceptional hearing. He's just reached the end of his courage and is heading back toward us."

"Speaking of good hearing, apparently your son has inherited yours. You're going to have to watch what you say around him, Mac. He kept calling Mark a bastard."

"Is that not the appropriate term?"

"Not for a six-year-old boy, it's not." When she saw the sparkle leave his eyes, Olivia wondered if she'd ever learn to read this man. "I don't think you understand what Henry's doing. When Trace first called me, he said that in the course of only a few months your son's mother died and he came to live with you, even though the two of you had never met. Is that correct?"

Mac silently nodded.

"Well, coming to live with a complete stranger after suffering such a loss has been far more traumatic for Henry than for you," she said softly. "And from what I've seen in the last half hour, your son is trying very hard to be what he thinks you want him to be. Henry's like a sponge, soaking you up; emulating your mannerisms, your language, and how you treat people." She smiled, gesturing at the road she'd been pacing. "Heck, he even walks like you."

"Excuse me?"

Still unable to read his expression, Olivia widened her smile. "You have a rather direct stride, Mac. You want to see what it looks like sometime, just watch Henry."

"Are you saying I should discourage him from emulating me?"

"No. That's a good thing. It means Henry is looking to you as a role model." She shoved her hands in the jacket pockets again. "You really should be talking to my mother-in-law about this; Eileen's the expert. I'm just trying to point out that when you call someone a bastard, even if he is one, Henry's going to call him one, too. And if you beat up that bastard, even if he deserves it, Henry's going to beat up any kid his young mind believes might deserve it. So I'm only suggesting that you be aware of what you say and do in front of him. All children are highly impressionable, but Henry's even more so, because not only is he trying to figure out exactly where he fits in your life, he's desperately trying to find his place in your heart."

Mac unfolded his arms to shove his hands in his pants pockets, and turned to face the woods. "I have no business being anyone's role model, especially not an impressionable young child's." He glanced over his shoulder at her, then back toward the brook. "I am the worst son a man could have, and there's a very good chance I will be an even worse father."

"You already are a wonderful father, Mac."

"How can you possibly say that?" he asked without looking at her. "You know nothing about me."

"I know how completely focused you are on Henry. And your insisting on coming to Inglenook early and then staying through the entire summer certainly proves how determined you are." She started walking toward the main road when she heard the school bus approaching, but stopped and turned with a smile. "Parenting's not about you versus Henry, Mac; it's about you and Henry versus the world."

For the first time in nearly three months—since a mysterious, overly intelligent, pint-sized person had come to live with him—Mac felt a glimmer of hope that he might actually survive this. He hadn't even made it to Inglenook yet and already he was seeing his son in a whole new light; the most surprising revelation being that Henry was soaking up everything he said and did like a sponge. Which, now that he thought about it, was frighteningly true; within days of their tumultuous meeting, Henry had started mimicking him to the point that Mac realized he could be looking in a thirty-year-old mirror from when *he* was six. But maybe the most insightful—and reassuring—thing Olivia had said was that he and Henry were on this journey together.

And that simple notion intrigued him as much as the woman who'd said it.

Which could be a problem. He was here to learn how to become a good father, and he really didn't need the distraction of finding himself attracted to the teacher; no matter how beautiful she might be, or how warm and inviting her smile was, or how compassionate she was—to a fault. Damnation, he'd hadn't known which had angered him more: that she would have been raped if he hadn't happened along, or that she had in turn protected the bastard.

"It's a good thing we were driving by when the lady was being attacked, wasn't it, Father?" Henry said. "It's too bad she wouldn't allow you to kill the bastard, though, because I think he deserved it. Your letting him go might lead him to believe he can attack another woman and get away with it again."

Mac looked down to find his son standing beside him, the child's arms crossed over his chest and his feet planted to relax back on his hips as he watched Olivia walk across the main road in front of the stopped school bus. Sweet Prometheus, how could the boy possibly know his very thoughts?

Mac unfolded his arms and shoved his hands in his pockets. "Apparently 'bastard' is an inappropriate term for a six-year-old to use, Son. So maybe you should cease saying it until you're older."

"How much older?" Henry asked, also shoving his hands in his trouser pockets as he frowned up at Mac. "Can I say it when I'm ten? Or fifteen? Or do I have to wait until I'm your age?"

The boy always took everything so literally! "Maybe that's a question you should ask Olivia."

"And do I call her Olivia when I ask, or Madam?"

Mac dropped his head in defeat. "You might wish to ask her that, too. And, Henry, don't mention to her daughter what happened today," he said when he saw Olivia walking back across the road holding the hand of a girl who appeared to be a year or two older than Henry. "Olivia might not want her to know for fear of worrying her. Now go put your things behind your seat to make a place for her to sit," he instructed, looking toward the main road as Henry ran to the truck.

The two women could have been twins but for their ages; the younger Baldwin had wavy brown hair that fell over her shoulders to frame an angelic face, an effortless smile, and an energized beauty that seemed to swirl around her like liquid sunshine—exactly like her mother. The young girl even took on Olivia's same expression of concern when she spotted her mother's swollen lip and puffy eyes. She then tugged on the unfamiliar jacket her mother was wearing over her own. Mac watched Olivia glance guiltily toward him as she started unzipping it, but her daughter stopped her by grabbing her hand and pushing up the sleeve, exposing a bruise on Olivia's wrist that had darkened enough for Mac to see from where he was standing.

"Sophie looks just like her mother," Henry said, having come back from his chore to once again stand with his hands in his trouser pockets.

"Sophie?" Mac repeated.

"Didn't you hear Olivia tell me her daughter's name is Sophie, and that she's eight years old and in the second grade?" Henry glanced up at him then looked back at the women. "I don't think I would have let the bast—that man drive away if I had caught him hurting Sophie." He suddenly grinned menacingly. "I would have at least sent him home carrying his stones in his pocket."

Mac broke out in a sweat. Henry wasn't merely walking and talking like him; his son even *thought* like he did!

How could he have forgotten that people became who they lived with?

Especially impressionable young children.

There were a lot of things he'd forgotten, apparently, about the inherent nature of man; which, considering his line of work, could be hazardous. But indulging in the more pleasurable aspects of human desires for the greater part of his adult life, Mac realized he had obviously dismissed as unimportant many of the more mundane laws governing the universe.

Nothing like having a son to put everything into perspective.

Yes, for as much as he hadn't wanted to travel even this short a distance from the ocean, bringing Henry to Inglenook just might prove to be one of the wisest decisions he'd made in several centuries.

It's hard to resist a man who keeps coming to your rescue...

From *New York Times* Bestselling Author

JANET CHAPMAN

The Heart of a Hero

A Spellbound Falls Romance

Originally from the ancient mythical island of Atlantis, Nicholas has spent the last year deep in the mountains of Maine, serving as director of security for the Nova Mare and Inglenook resorts. Fully embracing his life in the twenty-first century, he finds himself irresistibly drawn to a trouble-prone employee, and is determined to keep her safe.

The last thing Julia Campbell needs is a man with a hero complex, especially one as handsome and imposing as Nicholas. All she has to do is keep it together until her younger sister turns eighteen, and then she can focus on her own life. But strange things have been happening at the resort—and it's Nicholas who keeps coming to her rescue. When Nicholas is suddenly the one in trouble, Julia realizes he's not quite what he seems—and that she'll do anything to help the man who's stolen her heart...

janetchapman.com
facebook.com/LoveAlwaysBooks
penguin.com

M1295T0413